KU-054-082

DANGER
UNDER THE MOON

by Maurice Walsh

DANGER UNDER THE MOON

Maurice Walsh

CHAMBERS

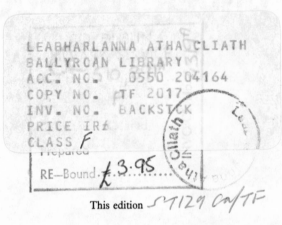

LEABHARLANNA ATHA CLIATH
BALLYROAN LIBRARY
ACC. NO. 0550 204164
COPY NO. TF 2017
INV. NO. BACKSTOCK
PRICE IR£
CLASS *F*

RE—Bound £3·95

This edition ST129 Co/TF

© Maurice Walsh, Ian Walsh and Neil Walsh 1980

All rights reserved. No part of this publication may be
reproduced, stored in a retrieval system, or transmitted, in any
form or by any means, electronic, mechanical, photocopying,
recording or otherwise, without prior permission of
W & R Chambers Ltd

Printed in Great Britain
by T & A Constable Ltd, Edinburgh

ISBN 0 550 20416 4

CONTENTS

DANGER UNDER THE MOON

CHAPTER I

CAT AND MOUSE

I

I WAS hurrying, and I did not like that, for it showed that I still had a taut nerve somewhere.

"Take it easy, you dam' fool!" I told myself. "Take it easy now! For this one evening, at least, you are the forgotten man in your own home-town."

So I took it easy. I stopped in the station yard to light a cigarette, and watched the smoke curl and drift in the still evening air. Feet moved by me and did not pause, people glanced at me and glanced away. I was only another stranger coming off the evening train at Kantwell-under-the-Hill.

Hands in the pockets of a flannel pants that was nine years old—or ten—I moved, straight foot over straight foot, down the station road, and into the town that I had not seen for —yes, nine years! Always nine years!

I knew this town of Kantwell-under-the-Hill, every street in it, every house in it, but the town would have forgotten me—for the time, only for the time. Nine years is a long time, as time sometimes creeps, but a spurred memory can take it in a stride; and to-morrow memory would stir again and tongues wag in recollection and speculation; and eyes, too, might brighten in malice.

Steady, lad, steady! Bitterness is the destroyer of life, and bitterness you have left behind you in the place where you were hidden. Life you have to face, and it might be a long life, too, in spite of the lure of Death. You are only thirty-two years old. Only thirty-two years! That would make that other one twenty-nine. Steady again! You are on forbidden ground now.

This Main Street, straight as a rush, had changed scarcely at all. There were a few more plate-glass windows, but the flat facades were still distempered in colours that did not tone too well: blues, greens, yellows, pinks, ochres; and the purple-slated roof lines were as crazy as ever. Behind and above them stood up the narrow spire of the Protestant Church, and beyond that lifted the more shapely one of the Catholic Chapel—Pugin the Younger had designed that one. And behind the town, and a mile away, the long easy sweep of Grianaan Hill made a background of softly-hazed greens and browns.

I was born and bred under that hill of Grianaan, and three hundred acres, that might still be mine, spread into the folds of it. Three hundred sound acres of tillage and pasture, and by the lord! I would claim them in face of all the world. Fair enough!

Some, not many, names were new on the facia boards above the shops; the long-pedigreed ones still flaunted their red and gold lettering; the old, uneven cobbled carriage-way had been replaced by tarred macadam, and the uneven pavement of Caithness flags by smooth concrete. And that was about all.

There were not many people about on the street, and scarcely any through traffic. A few cars were parked here and there, and their long bonnets and tails were strange to me. But fashions change, and I had not seen a motor car for nine years. Always nine years! Most of the shops were closed for it was after seven o'clock. Seven o'clock of an early-harvest evening with two hours of sunlight still ahead, and, then, long hours of gloaming declining slowly into the half-light.

The young people would be on the tennis courts behind the College, or in the playing fields across the Doorn River.

Folks with motor cars would be down at the sea, ten miles away, at the Bar o' Bel, for golf or a swim. It was a good time to slip through and out of town, and escape recognition. And no one recognised this tall lean man striding slowly, his face too pallid and his black hair too short. I wished I had my old tweed hat to pull down on my brow.

I paused to light another cigarette. Last week a cigarette had made three smokes. Now I had burned one away in half the length of a street. Flinching nerves again! I moved on slowly, schooling myself to calmness.

A slip of a girl came up the pavement, swinging herself, and swinging a racket in a free right hand. She was in thin yellow silk—or what looked like silk—and the evening sun over the roofs outlined her lissomeness through the flimsy material, and made a nimbus of her wheaten hair. It was then I noticed the character of the sunlight. It was the light of wide and free spaces, the light I had long forgotten. And this girl swinging along was light and free and careless. My blood moved a little. She was a girl, and I had not seen a girl for those nine desperate years.

She glanced at me as she went by, almost touching my shoulder. And then I heard her feet hesitate, and I knew that she had turned head to look back at me. I turned head, too, and lifted a finger; and she twirled her racket, and tossed her hair, and went swinging on her way. I went on, too, wondering if there was anything in me to make a girl turn her head. Damn the thing! But if that girl knew who I was she would surely turn to look at me, but she would not toss her head coquettishly.

I was moving more easily now, for no one looked at me with any interest. But, then, I was not expected. No! I was wrong there. There was one certain place where I was definitely expected, and on this very evening too. To that place I was now going. To that place I had to go willy-nilly, and keep going for three years. Three on top of nine makes twelve, and after that I would be a free man—or dead.

The long street curved at last, was joined by a tributary

street, curved again, and debouched on Daunt Square. There was a public house at the corner; there was a public house at every corner in Kantwell, and I might need a drink later on. My great-great-great—and a couple of greats more —grandfather gave his name to that square. His name was David Daunt, and my name was David Daunt, but I had come far and far-down from that David of old.

The Protestant Church squatted gloomily in an acre of tar macadam at mid-square; at one corner the delicate lines of the Pugin chapel flowed upwards; at another a broad white arch led into the yard of the Kantwell Arms, now a modern hotel, but not so long ago a coaching inn; on that far side between Chapel and Hotel were the two Banks that served the town. This old square had not changed at all in nine years, and had changed very little in ninety. Against that changeless background I felt purposeless and small, and that was good for me, inclined as I was to dree my ain weird.

I turned left—left is said to be the unlucky turn—and in twenty, thirty, forty slow paces I had arrived. I was there. A flat facade of roughly-cut limestone inside an iron railing, oblong windows that were cleaner than any windows in town, but without curtains or window boxes; the bottom windows, back of the railing, were small and they were strongly barred. I was acquaint of one small room inside one of these barred windows.

Six smooth limestone steps led up to the front door that was painted an even brown and was wide open. The bare hall inside looked cool out of the sunlight. No, not cool—aloof and chill and waiting. On the wall above the fanlight there was a round plaque, displaying a harp in a border of Gaelic lettering, and the lettering would translate into "Police Station". This was my destination. This was the place that would have a string on me for three years.

II

I looked up and down the pavement, and had an urge to hurry up those six stone steps. Instead I went up slow-footed, and into the hall. The hall was wainscoted in brown; and the scrubbed bare boards of the floor sounded under my feet. There was no one about. I had not seen a policeman all down the main street. There was one at the railway station, but he had not looked my way.

On my left was a brown door marked, DAY ROOM, in white paint, and behind it silence. Facing me down the hall was a brown door marked, PRIVATE. A murmur of voice came through, and someone's fist slapped on wood. Some of the boys would be in there, playing solo, or spoil-five, or twenty-fives, or forty-ones, for in this county one scored eleven for the best trump. On my right was an open door, and inside that was silence too. I walked in there.

A right-angled counter made a small square on the outside, and inside was a wide, high room, with a big table at the centre, and a high, sloping desk running along under three naked windows. The walls were distempered in light brown; and counter, table, desk, mantelpiece, every darn thing were in varnished brown; and the papers scattered on table and desk were brown too—or buff; and buff was the paper I carried in my breast pocket. But, then, brown is the colour of Justice, only, usually, it is not varnished.

There was one policeman in that big room: a man with heavy shoulders under blue serge. His back was half-turned to me. He sat on a high stool at the desk, his chin on his chest, his big, veined, brown paws on a closed ledger in front of him, and he was sound asleep, beautifully asleep, without snore or snort or drawn sigh or sawing of wood—sleep that I had never known or long forgotten.

"Why don't he tumble off?" I wondered. "He might at that!" And I brought my fist down on the counter with a resounding wallop.

He did not quite tumble. He checked on an indrawn

breath, lifted six inches, pawed with his feet, swayed and found his balance. Already he was buttoning his tunic.

"What did you break, you bastar'?" he wanted to know angrily.

"Your snoring," I told him.

"Blast your crooked eyes! I never snored in all me life." Then he woke and took a step towards me. "Sorry mister! are you wanting anything?"

"I am," I said, "and you have it for me."

"What is it, when did you lose it?"

"Sleep! Nine years ago. Sleep, oceans of sleep, full fathoms five!"

"I was up half the night with me wife's toothache," he said, and grinned at me. He was at the counter now, and had his blue tunic silver-buttoned. He was an oldish man for a police-man, his grizzled hair receding, wrinkles under his chin, and a grey film on his jowl. And he looked extraordinarily mild for a man who had named me so opprobriously. My black-blue eyes, though set too close to a nose one size too big, are not crooked, not quite, and there is no staff-sinister on my escutcheon—as far as I know.

"What is it anyway, young fellow?" Wrong again! I was not a young fellow. I was a million years old, for, as has been said, one is as old as one feels.

He looked at my hands, lifted his eyes to my face, and his eyes narrowed speculatively. My hands were on the counter. The last time they had rested there they were brown and lean and virile—mighty useful hands, though I say it myself. Now they were soft and white, an ugly white, a fish-belly white. And my pallid face—to hell with my hangdog face!

"You have it," I said bleakly. "No summer sun that ever shone will tan a hide in a thousand acres, where the walls are high, and freedom at the other side of the moon. Yes, I am a jail-bird sure enough."

"But for the mercy o' God what else is any of us?" said that ageing man remembering a certain saint. His eyes narrowed again. "You'll be——?"

"I am. There's my parole paper—Ticket-o'-Leave you call it."

I had taken a wallet from breast pocket: an imitation-leather wallet, but good enough to hold, for three years, the buff sheet, foolscap size. I smoothed it out on the counter.

The policeman did not need glasses, but he bent close to read.

"Ay-Ay! Ticket-o'-Leave!" he murmured. "To be sure! David Daunt." He lifted head and looked at me; and then he smiled, and there was nothing but kindness in his broad Irish face. "You are welcome home, Mr. Daunt."

"Like hell I am!" I said. "But thank you all the same. What do I do next?"

He drew the buff parole paper away as my hand reached for it, and straightened up to look at me, to consider me, to wonder at me. I was tall, and lean, and dark, and aquiline, and, yes, secretive looking. No doubt he was thinking how dangerous I could be, how deadly I had been. No doubt he was glad that he could wash his hands of me right now.

"I'll report any time, anywhere I have to," I said agreeably.

"I'm not the man you have to see," he said hurriedly.

"But dammit——"!

"Stand where you are wan minute."

Yet he hesitated. Probably he did not want to lose sight of me until he could pass me along. Then he picked up the parole sheet, lumbered quickly round the big table to a brown door in the far wall, tapped softly, almost diffidently, and slipped through. He left the door ajar and I heard the murmur of his voice. And then a clear, quiet, extraordinarily soft voice said:

"Put him through, Murty, you son of a gun."

Murty, the ageing guard, came out promptly, beckoned head at me, and pointed a thumb at a lifting-flap at the end of the counter. I lifted it and went through, and round the table. He was holding the door knob, and the door was not quite closed. He shoved the parole into my hand, and lifted his mouth close to my ear.

"Go on in now, and you'll be ate alive," he whispered pityingly.

"I died long ago, Murty," I said.

He opened the door, patted my shoulder forward, and pulled the door shut with a temerarious clap.

"Blast your eyes, Murty!" said the quiet voice mildly.

This was not a brown room. Brown has a certain warmth in its sameness, and this was a cool room, distempered a pale greeny-blue with a matt surface. And that was all I noticed about that room at that time, for the man sitting in the wide-armed chair behind a black-topped table at mid-room drew all my attention.

The first thing I noticed about him was his grossness. He was in civilian clothes, and the brown tweed of his jacket fitted his great shoulders as closely and unwrinkled as a hide. On his feet he could not be a tall man, but he was massive— just plain massive. His chest started close up under the quarter-circle of his chin, and curved hugely; that is, his belly did not hang or protrude, but chest and abdomen made one flowing line. His dark, close helmet of hair came to a point low on his forehead; he had no eyebrows worth notic-ing; his eyes, greenish-brown, well away from a flat wedge of nose, had no expression other than sheer laziness; and his mouth and chin were queerly porcine, which is hardly fair to the porker, whose mouth is by no means unshapely. His skin was sallow, but not pasty or greasy, and his hands were un-usually small. And, gross though he was, there was nothing revolting or repellent about him. He was just one formidable human being, and I felt his formidability, and wanted to press against it.

I walked forward on a brown coir matting. He gave me a single lazy glance, and went on turning the leaves of a fat file well out from the curve of his stomach. There was nothing keen or discerning or enquiring in that glance; it was just lazy and indifferent. The leaves rustled dryly under his fingers.

Without looking up he reached forward a thick right arm and his fingers groped. I knew he was feeling for my parole, but, instead, I gave him a firm handgrip. And I noticed the dryness of his skin. He had what is known as "cutlery fingers", fingers so dry that they will not film a blade.

He did not return my grip, nor did he jerk his hand away. He withdrew it quietly, and smoothed it across the file, and his skin made a dry rustle like a lizard's. He lifted his eyes slowly and looked at me dispassionately.

"Blast your nerve! I don't shake hands with an undischarged convict."

The words were insulting, but the voice was soft and equable; and, yet, it had the strange effect of doubling the insult. There was nothing I could do about it; there was nothing I wanted to do about it; my code of conduct had been established over many bitter days, and no police-bully could ruffle it—or so I foolishly hoped. Now I only slid the folded parole paper across the table between the file and an inkstand that was without ink or pens.

"To whom it may concern greeting!" I said. "David Daunt, his Ticket-of-Leave!"

He didn't look at it. He tapped the file with a short middle finger, and his cool voice went on.

"I was expecting you. I knew you would turn up like a bad halfpenny." He tapped the file again. "I was looking you up. Why the blazes they didn't hang you I don't know!"

"I don't know either," I said mildly.

He flapped the file shut and shoved it away. "Ah well! it was before my time or"—he flicked a finger and thumb—"you wouldn't be here to-day."

"I wouldn't be anywhere," I said. "Quicklime has a quick digestion."

"So you're going to be hardboiled about it," he said softly. "We'll see about that." There was no threat in his voice, but the threat was somewhere, and it was ominous.

He pulled the parole paper towards him, smoothed it open, and again there was the dry rustle of his palm. He moved a thumb.

"There's a chair there. You can smoke if you want to."

There was a plain windsor chair at the end of the table. I pulled it round to the corner, where I sat half-facing him, and instinctively felt for the butt of a cigarette in waistcoat pocket. There wasn't any, and then I remembered that cigarettes were no longer precious currency. I reached forward a packet of Sweet Afton where his eyes might see it, but he took no notice. Near his elbow was a brass tray half-full of spent matches and tobacco shreds, but there were no fag ends. I lit a cigarette, inhaled slowly, leant back in the windsor chair, and waited. In the sidewall was a big window, open at the top, and beyond it a wide concrete yard, and beyond that the tall end-wall of a ball-alley, with wire-netting on top. The evening sun, low down, glinted on the meshes of the net.

I heard him tapping the buff sheet, and turned head back to him. His soft voice was just above a whisper.

"Full remission—twenty-five per cent! Yes-yes! All the bloody ones know enough for that. It is the innocent slobs that break."

"Break, your grandmother!" I said rudely. "I broke three times, but a wise man soldered me again in Southland Jail."

"A wise man, or a foolish one!" he said musingly. "Did you persuade him that you were taking the rap for another— perhaps a woman?"

That is what he said without raising his eyes, and my heart turned over. This big man had got inside my guard already, and I must show where I stood once and for all.

"Your pardon!" I said equably. "I don't know who you are—Sergeant—detective officer——?"

"You'll come to know me well. My name is Jerome Farley—Superintendent Farley to you."

"You were never called Jerry, I'll bet a hat."

"You'd be surprised."

"I would, indeed. I crave your attention Superintendent Farley. I want you to get this clear. A long time ago I was accused of murder, and pleaded not guilty—as usual. I got a fair trial, and the verdict was manslaughter, but it was such a near thing that a Christian Judge, forgetting Christ, gave me as near a life sentence as he could: twelve years. Well! I took my medicine, and I took no rap for anyone; and I am now in the position that I can proclaim to you and the world that I killed my cousin, Robin Daunt. That is what I am proclaiming Superintendent, and what can you do about it? Dam' the thing! and excuse that long speech, please."

He said nothing to that—not yet. He slid the parole paper across the table, and I refolded it into its wallet, and returned it to breast pocket.

"Stay put!" he ordered as I moved my feet to rise. "I have not started on you yet."

"Sorry! I forgot that I am under your thumb. Carry on, O Tyrant of our little fields!"

His big chair squeaked as he pushed it well back from the table. His eyes were on mine and never left mine as he pulled open the middle drawer and fumbled for a pipe and tobacco pouch. He rapped the pipe, hit or miss, on the ash tray, and inserted it in his porcine mouth. It was a good-sized briar, but it looked ridiculously small in that expanse of face. And then he crossed his legs. I didn't think he could. He did what no corpulent man should be able to do: he laid, without any effort, his left ankle across his right thigh, so that the right-angle of his leg made a horizontal plane. That called for something like a universal joint somewhere.

I saw a neat brown shoe unusually small, and a neat ankle smoothly hosed. He kept those green-brown eyes on me as he teased black cut-plug, and filled his pipe, and lit it, and puffed smoke delicately; but his eyes were not speculative in any way, and did not signal his intention to vivisect me.

"Very well Mr. David Daunt!" he said agreeably. "Stick to your hard-boiled line, and I can't do a dam' thing about it. Can't I? There are many things I can do in this district of mine. I can keep the peace in it—my peace—and *My* is the operative word."

"And roughshod to qualify it?"

"Smooth like milk, brother."

"And bitter like gall, brother."

I was a fool to bandy words with this formidable man in his own bailiwick. He was trying to rouse me for some purpose of his own, and I must not be roused.

He stroked another match, relit his pipe, and looked at me lazily through the smoke. He went on half ruminatively.

"You are a danger to the peace, Mr. Daunt; and wherever you go, wherever you stay, you will be under watch and ward —for three years, maybe longer." He pointed a short forefinger at the fat file. "That's your case. I went into it. I added to it. It is all there. You pleaded not guilty, Mr. Daunt. A very interesting plea, and a very interesting family, the Daunts—and the women they married. I followed them up many a strange road, and there may be another killing at the end of one of them; and if there is a killing there will be a hanging this time, and you may be sure of that, Mr. David Daunt."

"You took the wrong road," I said. "There will be no killing, and there will be no hanging," and I could not keep the harshness out of my voice.

"Do you tell me that now?" he said softly, and I knew then that I had told him too much.

"The case is dead, and to hell with your probing Mr. Farley!" I said, and I moved to rise.

His moving finger stopped me. "I'm not done."

"If you have no instructions——"

"Your instructions are in your pocket—your address and for how long——"

"My address is Grianaan House under Grianaan Hill and I intend to stay three years—or till I go out feet first. Anything more?"

I waited. He lit his pipe again, aimed the match at the

ash tray and missed. The end of the match was still red, and the many small scars on the leather showed that many a match had died there. He put an elbow on the arm of his chair, and held his pipe between thumb and forefinger, and he was no longer looking at me. He was looking at the file before him, and there was some heavy quality in the quietness of his voice. He was not baiting me now.

"Grianaan House under Grianaan Hill—that place of sun and sorrow! Will you be welcome there?"

I did not answer that. I said, "It is my home. I own it."

"That is so. Prison does not break an entail. Ellen Furlong, your mother, lives there still."

"It is her home too." He had called her Ellen Furlong. Ellen Daunt was her married name, but everyone knew her by her maiden name: Ellen Furlong, the Rose of Irmond— but faded now.

He went on speaking in that quiet and heavy voice:

"I know you received no letter in Southland Jail—you refused to—and I know you sent none out. But, as every warden knows, news filters in and out. You will know that your mother has married again?"

It was on the tip of my tongue to call him a liar. My very own mother married again! I could not believe it. But there was no need for this man to lie. I had heard no word of a marriage, but, then, I had had no word at all of the outside world in Southland Jail. Of my own will I had cut nine years out of my life. But life went on all the same, and now I was reaping some of the crop. A bitter crop! And a more bitter one was ripe and waiting. But I must show no sign of the bitterness to this man. My voice was calm enough.

"Why not? She was a young woman nine years ago, and she will be lovely forever."

"Lovely forever—yes! And she is married six of your nine years. There is no need for me to tell you this, but I want to warn you that you will have to watch how you walk." His voice grew heavier. "She married your uncle, and her deceased husband's brother. Yes, William Daunt! And two

minutes ago you proclaimed that you killed his son, Robin."
He looked at me and looked down again. "Will you proclaim
that in your house of Grianaan?"

I did not answer him. I had no answer to give. My
widowed mother marrying my father's brother! And I did
not like a blonde hair in his pink hide. I looked down at my
ugly pallid hands, and clenched them slowly. I remembered
the long schooling I had given myself, and tried to pull my
forces close about me. *Don't run away from yourself, you poor
fool!* I warned myself. *The past is dead; you killed it over nine
hard years. You are beginning life again this very day, this very hour.
This thing you have been told is only a wind to blow you astray, and
it will keep on blowing. Let it blow!*

His voice was no longer heavy. "Do you think you will be
welcome. at Grianaan?"

"It is my house," I said steadily.

"You would not like to change your address?" he asked
softly.

I looked up and met his eyes. I was in control of myself
again. "Grianaan will be my address—for three years."

He moved his head heavily. "Yes! I was told you had a
tough streak in you. Well you know where you stand now,
and it was my duty to inform you—and to warn you. I cannot
stop you going to Grianaan, but I warn you to keep the
peace there."

"Your peace?"

"My peace." He slapped his pipe on the table, and his
voice had no silk in it now. "I have a job to do and I will do
it. I shall keep you under observation, Mr. Daunt, and there
are others I shall not neglect either. If justice has to be done
I will do it; if a wrong has to be righted I will right it; and
I'll show no mercy—not one scrap of mercy, as God is my
judge."

"Peace a desolation, and justice vengeance!" I rose to my
feet. "There I leave you, Mr. Farley."

"Had enough of it this time?" He gestured doorwards.
"Go then! but you'll not get rid of me that easy."

"You like to ride on a barbed bit," I said. "I'll get used
to it."

He was on his feet. I thought he would have to prise himself
out of that chair to the emission of grunts, but he was upright in one easy motion, and kicked his chair back actively:
a vigorous monster, with something in his mind that I refused
to consider.

III

In the room outside the ageing Station-Sergeant called
Murty hurried to lift the desk-flap. But I paused for a
moment. There were now at least half-a-dozen guards
suspiciously busy at desk or table: big, active-looking young
men without a trace of Nordic bovineness, and never meant
for desk work. They looked at me casually and without expression, looked away, and looked back again. I lifted a
finger.

"Take a good look at me, boys! I'm the Ishmael you must
not forget." Some of them smiled at me but not unfriendlily,
some looked down and did not look at me again.

Superintendent Farley brushed by me to where a tall
slender man was bent industriously over the desk. There was
a coaxing softness in the big man's voice.

"You'll have something for me, Joseph?"

The tall man, the whole six feet of his lean wiriness,
quivered and turned. His lantern-jawed, high-nosed face
was anguished in its appeal, and his hands were busy making
excusing motions. His Superintendent held out a cupped
hand, and his voice was gently persuasive.

"Put it there, Joseph! Ten shillings! and nine and eleven-
pence half-penny will not do."

The guard, Joseph, had the richest Southern brogue I had
ever heard. "Holy God, sir! I didn't hold a card, and any
time I had, Tade Murphy, the scut, drew from the bottom of
the pack and plastered it. But I saved half-a-dollar anyway."

The Lord ha' mercy on poor Joseph! I said to myself.

But his chief merely put a finger softly on the point of Joseph's nose. "Very well so, Yoseph! I have a job for you and you'll like it as you like fat bacon. Are you there, Tade Murphy?"

"I am sir." A big young man stepped forward. He had the wide cheekbones, the black hair, and the blue daredevil eyes of the West.

"I've a job for you too, sonny, and you'll like it less," Farley said. "Stay in! I'll be back in ten minutes—maybe an hour."

I nodded to Murty, and went out into the hall, where the boards sounded again under my feet. I stood at the top of the six stone steps and looked across the square. I was in the shade, but the Protestant church out there was in the orange glow of the slowly setting sun, and the shadow of its spire was elongated on the macadam, so that the top lay in the opening of the road to the hills. That was my road, the road to Grianaan, and a queer welcome at the end of it!

I went down the six stone steps, and a voice spoke softly at my shoulder.

"Let me see you out of town, young fellow!" I had not heard his feet on the boards of the hall, or on the stone steps.

"Fair enough!" I said. "I might make a night of it."

I lit a cigarette, and moved leisurely along the pavement. I would not hurry though I wanted to get away. He came up on the inside and went half-a-pace ahead—to show me where I belonged possibly. He did not shamble like most heavy men, but went with a short elastic stride that had a touch of jauntiness in it. His hatless head, that should have looked small above those massive shoulders, was big and round and solid, his black hair was like a close helmet on that solid ball, and he had shaved the back of a neck as thick as a pillar. He was not as tall as I was, but would outweigh me by stones.

A car or two went by under the shadow of the church, but there was only a single pedestrian on the pavement: a youngish man in waders, with a set-up fishing-rod swaying lance-like above his head. He passed us at the angle of the square. I knew his face, but could not recall his name, and he gave me only a casual glance as he went by.

"Evenin' Jerry!" he saluted cheerfully.

"Evenin' Mike! any luck?"

"Dam' all!" the man said over his shoulder. "Water like clear soup, and your bloody bailiff had his eye on me."

I turned round then and watched the fisherman shuffle along.

"That's only Michael Paddian," Farley told me mildly, "and he'd poach the eye out of your head."

"I'm waiting for him to drop dead," I said. "He called you Jerry."

That did not draw a smile or a frown. He moved his head and spoke as if to himself. "By all accounts he was a gay and fleering lad in the days of his youth, and he has a bit of steel in him yet."

"Are you for breaking it?"

"I'm trying the temper of it and if it breaks—The Lord ha' mercy!"

In the days of my youth I was, indeed, a gay enough hellion; but was I fleering? Was I only fleering now; when gaiety turns to fleering life has lost its savour.

He went on in his easy, jaunty stride, and I went up to his shoulder. At the corner of the debouching road, he stopped and beckoned me forward with his head.

"This is your road. Take it, and behave yourself! You'll be seeing me."

It was my road. How many thousand times had I trod it? It sloped gently down towards the river, a high demesne wall on one side, and a few scattered villas on the other; a country road curving out of sight to the Doorn River that it crossed on three stone arches. And beyond the river lifted the gently flowing slopes that folded in my own Grianaan—where I might not be welcome.

The policeman was waiting for me to move off, but another thought—probably fleering—came into my mind.

Just behind us was the open door of a public house, and the old name that I remembered, John Scanlan, was flamboyant on the sign across the front.

"Care for a drink Mr. Farley?" I said, cheerfully polite.

I expected a bland but contemptuous refusal. His voice was bland, indeed, but there was a trace of surprise in it.

"Are you offering me a drink?"

"Why not? I have some State money to spend, and we'll be seeing a lot of each other—for three years."

"That is so, indeed." He turned his head as if listening, and then, "Yes, I'll have a drink with you."

It was as easy as that. He lifted lightly on the single step to the door and I followed. This bar had not changed at all; it was older than fashion. No select lounge, no chromium, no cork carpet; sawdust on a scratched floor, a long, zinc-topped-counter, a partition jutting out half-way down, varnished oaken casks back of the bar, and shelves upon shelves upon shelves of shining bottles of all the "alcohol-aceous beverages" there are, cheerful, many-coloured, and splendid.

A murmur of quiet voices came from the inner bar, the other side of the partition. Irishmen, as a rule, take their drink gloomily, and a voice is seldom lifted. I tapped the zinc, and a young barman came along in the flat-footed way of his kind. He did not know me, of course, but lifted a diffident finger to the chief of police, and I thought he looked surprised.

"What will it be, Superintendent?" I said. "A double-one on sweated money?"

He took his time to decide. He had the build and thrapple to down quarts and then more quarts, and I expected him to order a couple. Finally he said:

"Yes! that will be it. A nice, mellow brown sherry—a small one."

"A small one would be just about right," I agreed. "And a draft-beer for me."

The barman went down along the counter, and I felt for a cigarette.

"You forgot your pipe," I said.

"So I did. No, I don't smoke these. Matches I smoke mostly."

"So I saw. You are a hard drinker too. A brown sherry on a warm evening! That's pure hell."

"Not a small one." He was too agreeably complacent. "Do you know this is the first bar I have been into—unofficially—in years. But I have a reason."

"I know. You want to see how your guinea pig behaves in public. You wield a nice scalpel, Superintendent."

"You might see in a minute," he said gently.

The barman brought us our drinks, and went away to make change.

"*Slainthe, agus bas in Erin!*" toasted the big man, and sipped his minute sherry delicately.

"To die in Ireland—fair enough!" I said, and lifted the filmed beer glass.

Only now I knew I needed liquid. I had been subjected to an ordeal, and I was dried out. My throat felt parched. I emptied half the glass, and paused for breath.

"Down with it, and try another?" he invited.

"Another time," I said.

My back was half-turned to the partition, and I had heard nothing. I was about to drink again, but the glass stopped half-way to my lips. A high-pitched, ugly voice made speech behind me.

"Christ God! The killer is back."

I turned slowly. He was standing by the edge of the partition, and two or three heads looked over his shoulders. A shortish, thick block of a man, with a heavy jaw and a loose mouth. His eyes were pale, almost white, and so was his tousled mass of hair.

I knew him. I knew him well. He was two or three years my senior, and, as a boy, had used his strength on me in rude horseplay. I never did lick him, though I had tried; and, no doubt, he could lick me still. But that did not matter. The important thing was that he had been drinking companion to my drunken cousin Robin Daunt; and, when I was tried for Robin's murder, this man was the principal witness against me. But his evidence had not been false. Let me say that for him. He was always a forthright, dirty-mouthed, base thug, but his loyalty to the murdered man was beyond question.

I knew by his eyes and the planting of his feet that he had drink taken. But he was innured to drink. He came forward on steady feet, halted within a yard of me, swayed, and planted himself. He thrust his loose mouth at me.

"Yes, begod! You are Dave Daunt."

"And you Bill Sheedy."

"That's my name and you have cause to remember it." he lifted an arm, and his voice lifted too. "And if God spares me I'll give you cause to remember it the longest day you live."

I was not going to wear any gloves with this man.

"You don't count any more, you drunken lout," I said contemptuously.

"Lout!" he reared up. "Lout is it? And who murdered my best friend—the finest man in ten parishes? Call me a lout!"

This was bad. This would be a brawl in a minute. Why did not the policeman interfere in the cause of the peace he boasted about? Then I got it. He was waiting to see how his guinea pig would react. Very well! I would show him. I must show him. I did not raise my voice.

"Look Sheedy! Robin Daunt was evil to the marrow of his bones, and you were only his base hanger-on. Go back where you belong, you albino thug!"

He poised, hands clenched, and then checked himself. He stepped backwards, and threw his arms wide. His high voice jeered at me.

"Ah-ha! I forgot. 'Tis easy for you to be bold, and you under the wing of the headman himself. Good evenin' to you, Mr. Superintendent!"

"And good evening to you, Bill!" returned the Super-intendent genially. He had put his half-full glass on the zinc, and rested his backside against the counter, his finger-tips meeting on the round of his paunch. He chuckled softly. "Albino thug! That's a new name for you, Bill. But you are making a mistake. I am not here at all—officially. Carry on and don't mind me; I'm not here at all."

Sheedy got the import of that, but was not sure that it gave him full license. He knew himself as the better man, and wanted to clout me one. But——? But he might provoke me to action, and then——

"Good man yourself, Super!" he cried. "I'll give Daveen a piece of my tongue, anyway, and if he wants more——"

And forthwith I dashed my half-tumbler of beer straight into his open and grinning mouth. And with the swing of my arm I lobbed the glass to the barman who caught it, and dropped it in his surprise.

Sheedy gaggled, and his head came down as he spluttered beer. At once I had him by the back of the neck, jerked him forward, and gave him hand and knee through the open door. He sprawled and rolled. I turned to Farley.

"You'd better come back, Mr. Policeman, your peace is broken," I said. "What next, blast you?"

"Out of my way, and I'll show you!" he said, briskly for once, and briskly he strode forward, brushing me aside as if I had no weight.

Sheedy had already scrambled to his feet, and came charg-ing in belligerently. He checked backwards, and tried to dodge aside, but he was too slow. The policeman's hands came down on his shoulders and gripped. And good night, Mr. Sheedy!

I did not see any great force being applied, yet the albino's knees buckled and jerked and buckled again.

"I'm back, Sheedy boy—by special permission—and you've got your lesson," Farley said, his voice effortless. "Do you need another? No—no—no!" He shook his dangling victim, and the victim's mouth fell open, and his eyes turned up in his head. "You were told to go back where you belong. Go! and keep going! Away!"

He gave the man a final, terrific, shattering shake—a shake that would winnow the life out of him if persisted in—whirled him doorward, and let him go. And Sheedy fell forwards on his hands and knees.

"Up with you!" urged Farley. "Up and run—and keep running! And here's to help you!" A foot moved and heaved, and Sheedy went out the door in a frog's leap, clawed at the pavement, and was running riverwards before he was upright.

Farley turned round, and beckoned finger to the three youths who were about to shrink behind the partition.

"Come lads! come on out!" That was more a request than a command. They came, and there was no hanging back. Three lads, country-brown, and no vice in them—yet.

The Superintendent moved his massive head sadly. "Ye had better go home now," he mildly suggested. "Bill Sheedy is bad medicine, but I'm worse, and ye can find out if ye try. Away ye go!"

They went shamefacedly. They had been subjected to tyranny, illegality, anything but fair play, but they hurried out, not even glancing at me.

And the tyrant was not done yet. He leant his great torso over the counter, and the young barman started back in alarm from the stabbing finger.

"Listen son! Sheedy is out. Serve him, when he has drink taken, and I'll raid you after hours, and for a month of Sundays. Tell Johnny Scanlan that, and he'll know."

"Yes sir, why not sir, I will sir!" said the barman hurriedly.

Farley turned to me and shook a reprimanding head. "A waste of good beer—and you after paying for it! Do you want another? No. And to hell with sherry! Come outside."

I followed him. He stood on the edge of the pavement, and dammit! he was almost preening himself.

"My turn next, sir!" I said in mock humility.

"You had it. I knew that would happen in there."

"Dam' your smugness! You couldn't. Damn'd if you could!"

"I have good hearing," he said mildly. "I can hear the grass grow. When you offered me a drink a while back, I heard Sheedy talking down the bar. I know all about Sheedy, I know all about you, I know all about everyone——"

"You know too much," I stopped him.

"Not enough yet," he said, and went on. "I wanted to kill two birds with one stone. I wanted to see how you behaved yourself—and badly enough it was, with a glass in your hand and the top of his head turned to you. And I wanted to give you an example of the way I keep the peace in this town."

"I don't believe it," I told him bluntly. "You went in there for only one purpose. Do you know what you were?"

"Maybe I do."

"Maybe you do! You were the king tiger warning the laughing hyena off your prey."

"Wait now!" he said reasonably, and lifted a finger. "Your zoology is away off. The laughing or spotted hyena is native to Africa south of the Zambesi, and the tiger is not. But have it—have it! I'll use tiger-stroke when the time is ripe, and you'll know all about it. Go home now! And your steel may not avail you."

He pivoted round lightly, and lightly went round the corner. And I turned towards the green hill of Grianaan. I was wondering about this Superintendent Jerome Farley. From the beginning I had thought he was a bully and a brute. A bully he was, but he was not brutal, and he had a strange and engaging vanity. He had played on me. He had roused me, he had prostrated me, but he had given me a vital bit of news, and he had roused me again to carry on. And surely he had his own way of keeping his Peace.

Chapter II

WELCOME HOME!

I

I leant over the parapet above the high middle arch of the bridge. Down below the Doorn water, faintly amber, ran wide and shallow over clean gravel. Fifty yards downstream it narrowed into the throat of a fine long pool, a pool I knew, a pool I had once taken four salmon out of in the afternoon of a brisk March day.

A fisherman in waders was ten yards out above the neck of the pool. He was not using a minnow or a prawn, which only call for a flick and a reel-in; he was casting a fly off a sixteen-foot rod, and he was casting it leisurely and expertly. The long line made a lovely, slow, flat loop backwards, paused, unlooped itself swiftly forward, and laid the fly down straight and light where the water began to curl. I watched half-a-dozen casts, and looked beyond to where the river began the immense loop that enclosed "The Island", which was not quite an island.

Over there was the Racecourse, and above the scattered hazels and alders that lined the bank I could see the red roof and white cement of the Grand Stand. In two months' time would be the famous three-day Autumn meeting, and I would be there, God willing.

On my left the low, round green hills dwindled away southward, patched to the summits with small hedged fields; and the white walls and brown and gray roofs of farmhouses stood out of the dark green of little orchards. And in the south, twenty miles away, along the skyline from east to west, loomed the blue and purple of the strung, strong mountains.

Westwards, ten-twelve miles away, a thin gold bar was laid down on the horizon: that was the sea under the setting sun. And beyond the sea, some three thousand miles away, was said to be a famous land thirled to liberty and some licence.

Girded by these hills and mountains and sea, this was the verdant Vale of Irmond, that has songs written about it; and it, too, had not changed in nine years, or ninety. It was my native vale, and it reclaimed me as if I had left it only yesterday. The change was in me, my spirit worn to a string, my gaiety only a flicker, and my heart hollow. But what did it matter?

Get a humble perspective on yourself, Davy. And to hell with Jerome Farley!

I straightened up and turned to face the hill that sloped gently from the river banks: a low, long hill of green pastures and sun-brown fields of wheat. It folded into a wide notch, and in the notch nestled a long white house of two storeys under a roof of purple old slates, and backed by a grove of deciduous trees; and the low evening sun was shining on the windows in a yellow flame.

That was the house of Grianaan: my very own house, the house I was born in, the house where my father, Eamon Daunt—God rest him—had died fifteen years ago, the house, alas! where my lovely mother, Ellen Furlong, had brought in as husband my uncle William Daunt. And was I only a Prince of Denmark?

But wait! Would my mother be living at Grianaan or with her husband at his farm of Beananaar round the hill? And then I remembered that Jerome Farley had told me that she still lived at Grianaan. Then William Daunt would live there too. And I did not like William Daunt, nor a blonde hair in the pink hide of him. I had never liked any of the Daunts. With the exception of my quiet and gentle father there was bad blood in every one of them. But I was a Daunt too, and I had served nine years for killing a man. No, I would not have it! My name was Daunt, but in my roots I was a black and fighting Furlong.

Already complications were intruding on the new life I had so painfully planned. How could I face Grianaan——? But steady again! The house and lands were mine, and I must face things as they arose. And I must face them now. I flexed my shoulders and walked forward off the bridge, that one purpose in my mind.

Here now was the fork of the road. One prong—the main one—turned south towards the mountains; the other, narrower, went slantwise, at an easy gradient, along the flank of the slope. That latter one I took. It curved over into the fold, and there, on my right, were the white gate-posts, and the white gate wide-open—the gate that was always open to Grianaan House.

There I paused and turned to look across the Vale of Irmond. I had always done that and I did it now. Below me was the swinging, shining reach of the Doorn and the foreshortened three arches of the bridge; and up the slope beyond were the huddled roofs of Kantwell, with its two tall spires and the crenellated walls of the old Norman keep on its bluff above the river. And, beyond, spread the great vale, green with pasture, dark with woods, softly hazed in the dying day. The gilded cross on the spire of the Catholic chapel gleamed golden in the last of the sun.

I was at the gates of home. I should be happy, I should be joyful, but I was only desperately resolute to follow desperately the brief road I saw in front of me. I returned as I had left, destitute and desolate. No, I was not quite destitute. In the hip pocket of the flannel pants that I had not worn for nine years were a few pounds of prison dole. But I was desolate almost to despair. There was only one thin, tough streak of resolution to carry me so far—and so far again.

II

I walked through the gate. I did not hurry and I did not loiter, but just moved steady-footed up the short curve of drive. It was clean of weeds, and well raked, and not more than a hundred yards long, curving across a cropped green lawn that had no flower-beds or clumps of shrubbery.

Here now was the front of the house facing me. A long, white house, two storeyed, the roof-eaves projecting far out over the walls. The windows were almost square, uniform in size, and each of them had twelve panes. And the hall door was not on the ground floor but on the first floor. Fourteen —well I knew the number—low, wide, balustraded, lime-stone steps led easily upwards from the raked gravel. They were so low and wide that a child falling at the top would not tumble all the way down. And, over a couple of centuries, many a child had run up and down—and tumbled too. Not in my time. I was an only child. Never in any time of mine, for I would give my name to no child of mine. I was Furlong at the base, but there was bad blood in me.

There was no one about, no one to hurry out and greet the prodigal. And there was no sound from withindoors. This house of mine was silent against me. I stood at the foot of the steps and looked up. The house was silent, but it was not obdurate against me, for the white door was wide open. It was a generously wide doorway, but not high, with leaded lights at each side, and an ornate fanlight above. The last of the sun was pouring through, and I could see the shining top-half of the brass face of the grandfather clock at the back of the hall, and I could see the turn of the carpeted stairs leading to the attic, where I used to play under the skylights. And still there was no sound.

The window to the left, at the top of the steps, was lowered and lifted as far as it would go, and a lace curtain moved as in a draft of air. But the evening was very still, and there was no stir of air to move a curtain. That was the sitting-room in there, and someone was taking a peep at me.

Why not? I was a man to be peeped at slyly. Fair enough! I would give whoever it was a closer look at me. I put a foot on the bottom step.

A door banged firmly down the hall, and footsteps clacked loudly on the parquetry of the floor. There was the pink top of a big round head, and the ruddy moon of a round face, and wide white shoulders, and a thick abdomen, and thick, short legs; and a man stepped out on the wide flag at the head of the steps.

He stood, short legs wide-planted, hands on hips, and head lowered to look down at me and on me. Though short-legged he was a big man, stout but not corpulent, and immaculate in a white linen suit. He was not quite bald. His fringe of blonde hair worn rather long, his dome of brow, his round, pink, smooth face, and his serene eyes gave him a look of wise benignity. But he never smiled. He was a hale man in his early fifties, and he was William Daunt, my blood uncle, and my step-father.

I looked up at him, and he looked down at me. Planted above me on his own doorstep, as it were, he had me at an advantage. I let him use it.

"We heard you were back." That is what he said, not adding "David" or "boy" or any word of intimacy, and at once I took that omission for a clue. He enunciated very clearly, and in a cultured voice that was not native.

"We sent Bill Sheedy running to tell you," I said easily. "Thanks for the welcome, Uncle Will——"

"Have I much cause to welcome you?" he asked coldly.

"You may have less," I said. "How is my mother?"

"How should she be? This sudden——" He moved a hand, and was definite. "You should not have come back at all—not like this."

"There is something in what you say," I agreed mildly. And indeed there was. In the circumstances there was no room for me in Grianaan—unless—unless what?

I had been wondering how this man would take my home-coming. Now I knew. He might be aloofly neutral, he might be effusively welcoming, he might be virtuously protesting as he was now; but underneath he would be the same William Daunt, out for his own ends. Maybe I was unfair to him, but I didn't care a curse. I was merely glad he took this attitude, for it decided mine. It made things easier for me.

I think he thought he had me going. Again he moved that protesting hand and his voice was condescendingly, virtuously reasonable.

"There was every reason why you should not have come back here—every reason, every consideration, every scruple of decency. You could have made a new life anywhere except in Grianaan, and your mother and I could have provided you with all the material help you needed." That sounded well even if pompous.

"Where and how I live can wait," I said. "I am here to see my mother."

"I shall not prevent that," he said permissively, and drove his point home. "But please understand that it is impossible for you to live here, anywhere near here, anywhere in this island. I must insist on that."

He had decided for me. The Mede had spoken. Nothing on earth would lure him back to cancel half a line. And I murmured a line from an old convict song:

"And when I wake my heart will break in far Van Dieman's Land."

I walked slowly up the steps, my eyes on the stone treads that were hollowed and smooth from all the feet that had used them. As a child I used to take a small pace and a hop and a whoop to each tread; now I went up in long slow strides, my head down, and silent.

I saw his white-strapped shoes move aside to make room for me, took the last step to the wide door-flag, and turned to face him.

We looked at each other eye to eye, two tall men, but where he was fleshy I was lean wire. I looked at him with curiosity, and wondered. As mild a looking man as ever cut a throat, and women fell for him! The round, smooth face, the healthily pink skin, the softly-rounded chin, the moulded mouth, all bespoke the civilised man. His eyes were lighter than hazel, darker than yellow, and, close up, they were no longer serene. They were surface-gleaming optics to look out of, to hide what went on in that centred and lusty mind. And I don't like a moulded mouth anyway.

"So you will permit me to see my mother?" I said tonelessly.

I was staring him down, and he did not like it. He looked aside towards the door, and gestured that hand again.

"You are welcome—she is in the sitting-room—but please don't distress her."

I left it at that. The parquetry clacked under my feet. I paused inside the door. This square old hall had not changed at all. The grandfather ticked out the seconds as it had ticked them time out of mind; the red carpet going up the curve of stair was the old carpet that I knew; the prints on the walls between the doors were still the "Cries of London"; the black skin rug before the clock was still there. Nine years had made no change. The change was in me. But, somehow, the time looked longer now than nine years. The old hall was static, it was everlasting, it was indifferent. And I was only drifting through for my brief space of time. Suddenly I felt lonely and alone and sorry for myself.

Don't be sentimental, you blame fool! I chided, and turned to the polished panels of fine old mahogany on my left. I glanced towards the front. William Daunt was going slowly down the steps, dignity and forbearance in the very carriage of his head and shoulders. He was condescendingly leaving me to my mother, whom, no doubt, he held in the hollow of his hands. And, no doubt, he felt that he held me there too. Had he not pointed out the road I should have taken, the road I must take, and had I not taken his directions meekly? Fair enough! And to-morrow was another day.

III

I did not tap on the panels, but turned the ebony knob quietly, quietly went through with the opening of the door, and quietly closed it behind me.

My mother was there, and she knew I was here, though she did not lift her head. I had no eyes for that graceful old room with its delicate furniture of one of the great periods. I saw only Ellen Furlong, my mother. She stood aside near a small table close to the nearer window, and the fingers of one hand rested on the board. The drooping, long line of her was all grace.

A tall woman, supple, slender but not lean, ageless, magnetic, one of those women who, at any age, can steal any man from any woman—if they want to, and most of them do. I could see the firm boss of a cheekbone, and the slightly hollow curve of a cheek, and the great waves of her hair that used to be shining jet, and was now shining silver, and lovelier than ever. But why was her hair white? Many a reason, and I was one of them: her only son, her only child, and I had shattered the splendid life we had lived together. She was waiting for me now, and waiting for me to make the first move. And I would have to make it.

I moved quietly across to her. She did not stir till I was at her side, and, then, with strange leisureliness, she turned to face me, her head up and her eyes searching mine. Yes, she would be lovely always, because her bones were shapely, and nothing could dim the depth of blueness in her eyes that were just one shade deepset. The wistful smile about her mouth told me all I wanted to know. I knew what to do now. I would be no chiding prince of Denmark.

For her face, wistfully smiling, was tender and anguished and afraid. Afraid! She that had never been afraid of anyone. Afraid of me? No, afraid *for* me. The searching of her eyes told me that. She was afraid that her son, David, would be broken and debased. And I was not debased. By the goodness of God and one man, His agent, I was not debased.

I crinkled my eyes at her as I used to do.

"Mother!" I said firmly, and reached my arms.

And she was no longer afraid. She came into my arms, and I held her gently. But she clung to me. That twisted my heart, for she was never the clinging kind. But now she was clinging to me as for protection, for aid, for solace, for the only solace that remained to her. Her face was pressed in against my neck, and I pressed my cropped black head into the mass of her white hair. And then she whispered:

"If I could die now! Oh, happy me! if only I could die now!"

What a desperate wish that was! What a desperate happiness! But it resolved everything for me. From the moment that I had been told, I had wondered why she had married William Daunt. I was wondering now. But it no longer mattered. Nothing mattered but this mother of mine. She was unhappy, and I had a job to do.

"Womaneen tidy!" I whispered back. That was my old playful name for her who was always generous and spendthrift, but never tidy. "Womaneen tidy! You and I will live a long time, and we are beginning now."

I heard the long intake of her breath. Her head remained on my shoulder, but she no longer clung desperately. Her breath fluttered a little, but no sobs shook her. She was just letting the tension slacken. Not for long. She fumbled gently for my handkerchief, used it, returned it to breast pocket, and patted the bulge. My throat tightened, for that is what she used to do in the days of my youth.

She straightened up and leant back from me, holding the lapels of my coat. There was wonder in the richness of her voice, rather deep for a woman.

"Why you are young as ever, Davy!" Maybe a touch of colour hid the prison pallor. And then there was sheer pride in her voice. "And you are brave and strong David!"

"Yes, ma'am!" I lied agreeably. "And tough like the Furlongs. A Furlong! That's me."

She stepped back out of my arms and held me by the

hands. She was very serious now. "No need to be tough, boy." Her eyes crinkled as of old. "I'll be looking after you. That will be my job now—all the time."

"To be sure! And I'll remind you any time you forget."

Her hand went to her breast. "Oh, David! can you still be gay?"

"I'll be whistling in a minute," I told her.

She chuckled then and touched a finger to my lips.

"But you've no tune. I'm the whistler."

That was so. Scarcely pursing her lips she could whistle like a mavis. And I remembered the old rhyme: "A whistling woman and a crowing hen! There's neither luck nor grace in the house they're in." But I did not quote it, for Ellen Furlong had not had much luck in the house of Grianaan.

I noted in my own mind that my mother did not seem to be aware of her husband's intentions towards me. She did not mention his name, and I could not, but I felt that her unhappiness lay at his door.

Suddenly she caught at my arm. "Oh, dear! Oh dear! And I'm forgetting already. You must be starving?"

"No ma'am! Only plain hungry. I had breakfast with Michael Ambrose, the warden."

"Michael Ambrose, yes," she said as if she knew about him.

"The warden himself, ma'am, the best man that ever wore shoe leather."

"You'll tell me about him, but not now, boy." She took my arm possessively. "The kitchen for you, or Julie Brady'll have a fit."

"Julie Brady—my own Julie! Is she with you still?"

"Where else would the creature be?" said my mother. "She's bawling her head off in there. Come along, boyeen!"

Still holding my arm she led me, as if I were still a toddler, round some pieces of bric-a-brac, to a side door that led into the back hall. Directly opposite was a green door, and my mother tapped smartly on it. A whimper came through.

"You'll know how to take her," my mother whispered, opened the door and pushed me in. She stayed in the doorway to watch.

This was a good-sized room. It used to be a bedroom in the old days, but when we gave up using the cavernous kitchen downstairs, we converted this room into a sort of kitchen-living-room. There was a polished linoleum of black and white checks on the floor; the walls were tiled half-way up; there was an oaken dresser of blue and brown delft, and a wall clevee of shining tins; but instead of the small, black-leaded range that I remembered there was now a big, white, patent cooker, with a hidden fire somewhere in its bowels. There was a white refrigerator too, and I noticed, for the first time, that electric light had been installed.

There was a wide, but not high, window along the back wall, with a porcelain sink below it; and through the panes, across a concrete yard I saw the apple trees in the kitchen garden. The apples were still green, except for the Irish peaches, and they were turning ruddy. I would sample one to-morrow.

Probably I did not take all that in this first minute, for my eyes sought at once the only person in the room. She was sitting in a kitchen chair at the side of the white-scrubbed deal table, and a blue-and-white check apron was thrown up over her head. She was swaying slowly back and forth, and her plump little hands were tapping softly together.

I did not creep up on her, as I was tempted to. I walked slowly across, and my feet sounded firmly on the lino. And as I came nearer her voice lifted in a woeful little *keen* that had an ancient rhythm in it. That woman, Julie Brady, had a remarkable voice, speaking or singing. There was a silver bell in her throat that sounded with every word, and when she was done talking, a pulsing overtone went on ringing. And now she was *keening* me, as if I were lying on my back and pennies on my eyes.

"My own little boy—my own boyseen—withered and worn—tattered and torn—and his white bones out through his skin! My sorrow and woe! One last look at him, and my eyes blind forever-and-ever-and-ever."

I put my arm lightly across her shoulders, and her shoulders quivered. I lifted the apron off her face, and got a hand round under her little plump chin. Her eyes were tight shut but from between the dark lashes tears were running down her cheeks.

"My baby!" I crooned to her. "Now baby! There now, baby! Let me wipe your eyes for you!" I bunched a fistful of apron, and patted the curve of her cheeks. "Blow your nose now—a good blow! Fine, oh fine!" I kissed her rounded chin. "And now you can take your one last look at me—open up!"

Her delicate mouth trembled, and her eyelids fluttered. Then one brown eye opened and looked up at me, blinked and looked again. The other eye was open now.

"Withered and worn, your grandmother!" I said.

She lifted to her feet under my hands, the whole five foot nothing of her. She pulled my head down, and examined my face feature by feature, and wonder opened wide her brown eyes.

"Holy mother in heaven, Daveen! You're not wan day older," she marvelled. "Out of a bandbox you are, and fun and divilmint in your eyes forever!"

She was one little darling, that spinster woman. She had a round and very lovely face, a round but shapely body, and small hands and feet. She was very little younger than my mother, but she had the skin and complexion of adolescence, and there was no grey in the mass of her dark-red hair. Brown eyes do not usually go with red hair, and there is supposed to be something sinister in their association. There was nothing sinister in Julie Brady. She did not age, and there was a cog missing in the gears of her mind. She belonged to my mother, and, through my mother, she belonged to me.

"Julie Brady!" My mother's voice sounded indignant. She was at the white sink below the window turning taps. "Do you want him to drop dead in your hands? He hasn't tasted a bite the livelong day."

That was not quite true, but one had to exaggerate a little with Julie.

"Mother o' Mercy!" she belled. "Have I no stem o' sense at all?" She swung me with surprising energy, and put me clump down on the kitchen chair. "Take the weight off your feet, you limb o' sin! You'll be fed, and after that you'll be fed again." She darted, light-footedly, to the white cooker, and doors slammed. She shuttled between cooker and refrigerator, and more doors slammed. "There'll be a rasher and two more of our own bacon, and a necklace o' sausages, and a turkey's egg and a bit o' green salad the woman-of-the-house is washin', and—and——" She stopped, and looked over her shoulder to listen. I listened too. My mother was busy at the sink, and she was softly whistling to herself an old and wistful little tune that I knew well.

"On the Banks of the Roses my love and I sat down."

Julie, her eyes glistening, tiptoed to my side, and put her mouth so close to my ear that it tickled.

"She's whistling! Do you hear me, she's whistling! The first time since you darkened the sky for her. She has you back now, and you're needed." Her whisper went tense. "You'll hear no complaint from her, but you are badly needed, my darlin' boy."

I was home now and I was needed. And there was need in myself too. There were many things I wanted to know, and many questions I would have to ask. And there was one question I longed to ask, but that question I would not ask at all.

I had supper—what a supper—and it was in the middle of supper that the phone rang. I did not know there was a phone in the house until it rang outside in the hall.

"I'll take it," my mother said. But as she opened the door the ringing stopped. She was about to close the door when the ringing started again. She stepped into the hall, but she hadn't taken a stride before the bell was again silent.

I did not like this. This might be some hound ringing of malice intent. I got quickly to my feet and went out. The phone was on a small table near the door to the sitting-room.

"I'll deal with this, Mother," I said.

My intention was to lift off the receiver, and let it dangle. But, as I reached forward a hand, the ringing restarted. I picked up the receiver, and a voice bellowed in my ear.

"Hell blast it! is anyone there? Is everyone deaf? Is the house dead? Where the hell is Dave Daunt? I want to speak to Dave."

"Shut up!" I blared into the mouthpiece. "Shut up, you great big oaf!"

"Ho-ho-ho!" That gale of laughter nearly burst an ear-drum. "That was Dave Daunt sure enough." He was shouting as from a mile off. "Are you listenin', Dave? Did you break out, Dave? Where are you, Dave?"

"I'm at home having my supper," I shouted, "and you go to hell!"

"But Dave—wait Dave! This is me, Charley, Charley Cashan."

"I know dam' well it's you, Charley, Charley Cashan."

"And who else! I want to see you, Dave?"

"Where are you?"

"At the post-office."

"You've drink taken?"

"Only two pints—maybe three."

"Take it easy Charley boy!" My voice quietened. "Will you please take it easy?"

"Yes, Dave!" he said subduedly. I could always subdue him.

"Listen Charley! I am at home with my mummy to-night and I am seeing no one."

"But all the news I have for you, a donkey's load of it— all about Jean Harrington and everything."

"That can wait," and my voice went harsh. "I'll see you to-morrow, and we'll talk the sun down the sky."

"But about Jean——?"

"Good night Charles!" I replaced the receiver for a
moment, and lifted it again to let it dangle. No doubt
Charley Cashan was still bellowing into the mouthpiece.

Yes, that was Charles Cashan, trusty as a setter dog, wise
as an owl, mad as a prophet, useless as a day-dreamer. I
shall have a good deal to say about Charley. He was one of
our old team, our team of three. Just the three of us; Charley,
Jean—yes, Jean Harrington—and Dave Daunt, and Charley
was the hewer of wood and the drawer of water. Well! the
team was broken. So broken that nothing under high heaven
could mend it again. Let that ride.

Chapter III

DANGER UNDER THE MOON

I

The question I wanted to ask I do not want to ask any longer. I will tell you why now.

I awoke shaken in the heart of the night, and there was a wan, ghostly light in the room. But there should be a small gleam of light about the edge of the peephole high up in the steel door, and a thin line of light along its foot. Why were the lights out? They hadn't been out for nine years of nights.

I had had too much supper, and I was just waking out of my bad dream: the old dream, the dream of claustrophobia, of desolation, of despair, of endless years, of eternity rolling in chaos and only one entity alive in it, lost in it, and that entity mine—the dream of the only hell there is.

I lifted on an elbow and whispered urgently, "Michael! Michael Ambrose! The lights are out. Where are you, Michael?"

I listened. There was no sound, and there should be some sounds: the groan of a troubled sleeper, the choked cry out of an evil dream, rubbered feet shuffling on the iron grating, the stern or quieting murmur of a warder's voice. But there was no sound at all, and no light but that wan suffusion.

"Michael! Where are you Michael?" I would be calling aloud in half-a-minute.

But Michael Ambrose would come to me, as he had come in that first month, nine years ago, when despair and confinement were driving me mad. I was, then, only a youth. I had lived in the open all my life, and I had twelve impossible years to face. I could not face them. I could not imagine myself facing them. I felt myself breaking. I could not sleep, I would not weep, I dare not tear a passion to rags. The warders could do nothing with me or for me. I paced my cell, I turned my face to the wall, I let myself drift sullenly towards madness. And then I broke. I will say nothing about that. And, then, Michael Ambrose, the head-warden, country-bred like myself, came to me, and, saying no word, took my arm and led me out along corridors and platforms, and down steel stairways in the great echoing shell of the Life House; and into his own room, and talked to me quietly of his own young days, of a salmon he had poached, and a coney that he had snared, and a pheasant that he had lured with raisins —and of the tragedy that was in his own life. And I cried. And Michael Ambrose cried too.

But wait! I am not writing of those nine years. Sometime I might, but not now. . . .

I kicked the covers aside, and sat up, my legs over the side of the bed. And then I came fully awake. It was the bed that first told me where I was. There was never a bed like this in Southland Jail. Of course! I was back in my own room at Grianaan, and I need call on no one to pull me out of the slough—not even Ellen Furlong, my mother. For I was a free man—within limits—and within these limits I could do what I liked. And I would too.

The wan light in the room was the light of a moon near the full, diffusing in through the unblinded window. I could see the ghostly blueness of the panes now, and outline the oaken wardrobe down the room, and that glimmer over there was from the mirror of the dressing-table. Yes, this was my own room in my own house, and no door was locked to keep me in.

I knew of old that, after my bad dream, I would be wakeful for hours. But that need not worry me any more, for I had the remedy outside the window. My toes felt for the floor, and the pale Indian rug was soft under my feet. I navigated round the chair that was piled with my clothes, and padded across to the window. It was pulled down from the top, and, making no sound, I eased it up from the bottom, and leant out into the night. The soft draw of air was balmy on my face, and cool on my chest where the pyjama jacket was open.

Let me see now! I used to have a good sense of time. Everything was still, space-deep still. No cat prowled to make love-music; no dog on the hill farms bayed the moon, no bird twittered. Yes, it was the deep-sleep hour of the night, about two hours before bird-song, before cockcrow, before the first streak of dawn. I would wager on that, and I had the whole world to myself.

The moon would be near the full, but I could not see it above the jutting eaves, and the stars in the pallid sky were faint and few. My room was on the first floor at the back of the house. The narrow, concreted yard below me was in shadow, but the kitchen-garden, beyond a low parapet, was in full moonlight, and the light was so strong that the spaced fruit trees cast solid, black shadows. I could almost distinguish colours and put a name to flowers. The roses would not be in their second bloom, but that white blob amongst dark foliage would be a white dahlia; and that was a red one, or purple— no I could not be certain at this distance. But I could go nearer if I wanted to. I was free to go out into the night, to go anywhere that I wanted to go. And where did I want to go? A small verse of Charley Cashan's came into my mind

> " If only courage I had,
> Any courage at all,
> Out of my house would I go
> After nightfall;
> And move, quiet as a leaf,
> Soft as a mouse,
> Under the trees in the garden
> Of your white house."

But, no longer had I that sort of courage, and I did not know where the white house was. Stop there! That is forbidden territory. But, outside it, the night and the world were mine. I could again taste freedom and breathe free air, and I could do it now. My old instincts were beginning to stir in me. I had always been a nighthawk, and untamed: something of a killer too, a hunter in the half-dark fields, a poacher in moonlit water. But, as God spared me, never again would I be a slayer.

I did not switch on the light, lest my mother, waking up down the passage, might see the gleam, and come to see why her son was sleepless. I fumbled for my clothes, and got them on anyhow, slipping the tweed jacket over the pyjama one, lacing my shoes roughly, and feeling for cigarettes and matches. And then I shuffled silently back to the window.

Grianaan House is built against the slight slope of the hill, so that the sill of my window was not more than seven or eight feet above the concrete yard. In the days, fifteen— seventeen years ago, when I first took to night-prowling, it was easy enough to drop down, but getting back again was something of a feat. I would not deign to use an old chair, or a block of wood, or a tenpenny nail, but would hang on and kick and heave and bust buttons until, finally I made it and grew expert. And my mother used wonder what I had been doing to the toes of my shoes.

Later had come the nights when I used slip off to country dances with—yes, Jean Harrington. I must get used to writing that name. I was twenty then, and I was in love. And, maybe, she was. I don't know. She was half Highland, with hair like new copper, and a flashing temper that would boil a kettle when roused. We had a row, and then a flaming row, and, possibly, in a pique, she had let an attractive blonde libertine court her, and fell for him, and married him. And that was the end of that. Or was it? Not by a long shot. The end was far off. That is why I am writing this. I've got it off my chest now, so let it be.

Leaning there on the sill, I recalled one morning long ago. Six o'clock on a June morning, and I swung myself in the window, handy as a monkey by this time. I had been at an American wake with Jean Harrington, our last time out. I slung off coat and vest, and would have a couple of hours' sleep at any rate. And then my mother came into the room.

"You are up early, boy!" she said. "Couldn't you sleep?"
"Sleep!" said I. "Acres of it! But someone has to work in this
place." And I reached for my jacket, and went out to the
byrne, my mother's chuckle behind me. She knew. She
always knew. But did she know that her son had blood on
his hands? It made no difference to her love, but a hell of a
lot to her happiness.

It sounds easy to slip under a lifted window-sash, and drop
seven or eight feet. It is not so easy unless you know how,
and then the proverbial log has nothing on it. I had not
forgotten how. I pivoted through, feet first, hung, toed the
wall and landed light as a cat. I listened. Did I imagine that
I heard a rustle amongst the fruit trees in the kitchen-garden?
There was no sound now, but I did not move for a minute.

Would I go up through the garden and the farmyard, and
so to the woods and pastures that were not new? No. The
farm bothy was that way, and probably a dog or two. Instead, I would move in the shade down to the front gate, and
stroll along the quiet hill road between my own fields. That
was the road that led to the other Daunt farm, Beananaar,
but I would not go that far. I dared not go that far.

Close to the wall, I moved round the house to the left.
Attached to the gable end was a one-roomed, flat-roofed
annex, that we called the Outside Room. I'll tell about
that later on. I rounded it, and slipped into the shade of the
hawthorn hedge that curved to the front gate. And at the
front gate I turned to look back at the sleeping house. The
front of it was shining white in the moonlight, and the
windows gleamed palely, but there was no glow of light
behind any of them. The moonlight was so bright that I could
count the panes.

II

I was about to turn away when something moved at the corner of the annex. It was as if someone or something moved from house to hedge. I stood behind the gatepost and watched and listened. No sound, no movement, and I gave plenty of time. Ah well! One of the farm lads might be a night hawk too, and it was a good time to get back to cover.

I stepped out into the open, and went across to the other side of the road where I could look down on the Doorn River unwinding its silver ribbon along the valley, and up at the grey-and-purple roofs of Kantwell, and across the diaphonous vale of Irmond to where the lighthouse was winking far out on the estuary.

I lit a cigarette, put hands in pockets, and strolled along at my ease. To-morrow I must look out one of my pipes. My mother would be sure to have stored them away for me. I would borrow a knitting needle, and, Julie Brady protesting, heat it red hot, and burn the old nicotine out of the bowl and stem, and I would go boldly into town and buy four ounces of cut-plug at Spillane's. I had been a pipe-smoker by choice, but I had no choice in Southland Jail.

The night was mine, and the land on either side of the road was mine too. I could breathe free air again. I threw away the cigarette, expanded my chest, and breathed deeply. The night air was like a caress on my face and open neck. The moon, barely gibbous, stood out serene and still against the pale blue of the sky, and all the stars were drowned except the planet, Jupiter. On my right, grey-green and dim, the fields sloped gently upwards; the brown road was firmly outlined between the black shadows and black bushes of hazel, blackthorn, hawthorn, and clumps of bramble briars. On my left the fields flowed gently down to the black and silver ribbon of the Doorn, and, beyond and above, a bank of trees was etched darkly against a saffron sky. And in the silence I heard the remote sough of water running over gravel, and, once, a motor purred distantly on the sea road.

Lazily, foot over foot, I drifted along outside the grass margin of the road. My mind a blank—if any mind ever is a blank. Thought or reverie did not occupy it. I was in the process of being attuned, of sloughing off a nine-year-old skin. Dimly I heard a chain clink in the field sloping to the river. Down there was our swimming pool. I paused between two bushes and looked over the low clay fence.

The wide spread of pasture below me—twenty acres of it —was scattered with the hulks of cattle lying down. This would be our herd of milch cows—shorthorns and dexters— chewing the cud. Cows are regular in their habits. Even on a thin pasture their grazing period never exceeds two hours at a time. These cows of mine would chew the cud until dawn, and graze again to milking time.

Only one beast was on its feet. That would be the bull. There was the old lady assured by an Irishman that it was safe to cross a field amongst cattle. "Safe enough, ma'am! They are all lying down. It's this way! If there are twenty cows lying down in a field, the one standing up is the bull." The bull was standing up now, and already he had seen me. He lumbered slowly up the slope, and the chain clinked as he came. Below the fence he lifted head and sniffed at me. He was not threatening, but curious. So was I, for the tall shape of him was new to me.

"Good night to you, stranger!" I said. He shook his head, and the chain again clanked.

This was no shorthorn. Not even an Ayrshire. Surely this was a Friesian or Holstein, grey-and-white or black-and-white. Friesian cows give an abundance of milk that is rather deficient in butter fats: I would have to enquire into this. And a Friesian bull can be wicked, and fast on his feet. That is why this fellow had a three-foot chain trailing from his nose ring. The chain would not incommode him while grazing, but if he charged head-down it would trip him, and give a biped time to make the fence.

"Back to your bed, brother!" I flicked finger and thumb, and turned away from the temptation to tease him a little.

It was as I turned away that, in the stillness, I heard a rustle fifty yards back the road. But there was nothing to see. An early rabbit might make that rustle, or a hedgehog, or a magpie in its bush. I moved on leisurely, and the bull paralleled me in the field until it came to the boundary fence. There it snorted, as much as to say *"I put the fear o' God in you. Keep going!"*

I kept going, and, in less than a mile from Grianaan gates, came to another fork in the road. The left fork went on above the river; the right one curved round the breast of the slope, and went on to the other Daunt farm, Beananaar, where it ended. A furlong along that road to Beananaar, and on the left, was a roomy five-room cottage that was a sort of dower-house to the farm. It was simply called, The Cottage. I must explain now.

When my cousin, Robin Daunt, married, he took possession of Beananaar, and his father—my Uncle William—went to live at The Cottage, with his step-son, Charles Cashan. Is that clear? Well, Robin Daunt was dead and God have mercy on his soul—I wouldn't; no doubt his widow was still living at Beananaar; William Daunt was lording it at Grianaan; and Charles Cashan would probably be at The Cottage. Fair enough!

Listen now! The girl that Robin Daunt married was Jean Harrington. Yes, Jean Harrington, who was half-Highland. I loved her, and I spent nine years in jail for killing her husband. That is all. I had to come to that statement some time.

Charley Cashan was a complete woolgatherer, and my Man-Friday or, rather, Man-Friday to Jean Harrington and me. He had bawled over the phone this evening, and he wanted to see me. He might see me now! Day or night meant nothing to Charley; darkness and light, hours and minutes, bedtime or morning, Charley ignored them all. He might be at home now, or on the prowl, or calling on a friend ten miles away. But I could slip along and look The Cottage over.

A short furlong, and there was the dark—probably green—gate in the polished escalonia hedge with pale—probably pink—blossoms abloom. The one-storeyed cottage was ten paces away across a green plot, flower-bordered, and I could make out the spears of gladioli. The moon was shining aslant on the front, and the limed walls seemed to shine with a white radiance of their own. There were two windows, rather highset, at each side of a white door. There was no light anywherè, but I noticed that the windows had lace curtains, and that surprised me, for Charley had no use for fripperies. One window, right of the door, was lowered and lifted top and bottom. The house had an occupied look, and I assumed that Charley was the tenant. My blood should have told me that I was wrong. It told me nothing.

I decided not to investigate. I would see more than enough of Charley Cashan later on. I would just light a cigarette, amble back home, and go to sleep before the dawn.

I lit a cigarette. I was facing the house, and the flame of the match, cupped in my hands, would light my face strongly. I threw the match over the garden gate, and turned away. And then a startled voice, that startled me astoundingly, cried out from the lifted window:

"Wait! Don't go! Who are you?" And the startle in the voice told me that there was no need to ask.

III

It was a woman's voice, and I knew every cadence of it: the small draw in it, the lift of it, the soft distinctness of it: a Highland voice, but of deeper timbre than I remembered.

I turned back, I put my hands on the gate—for support I think—but I had my voice under control. I could see a face dimly inside that window on the right.

"It is all right, Jean! It is only me, David."

"David—oh, David!" She no more than breathed the words.

"Sorry I disturbed you Jean—I didn't know. Good night!" And again I turned away.

What else could I do? For this woman was Jean Daunt née Harrington. And I had spent nine years in jail for killing her husband. It was worse than that, and I must say it now. She knew that I had not killed her husband, and she was the only one in all the world that knew. Having written that I will let it stand, and Jerome Farley will never see it.

There it is then! There was blood between this woman and me, whoever had spilled it, and it sundered us as if it were an ocean. I could only say, "Good night", and go.

But Jean Harrington—I will not call her Daunt—would not have it so. The window lifted higher with a jerk, and her voice was urgent.

"No David, no! You must not go—not yet!"

I paused, and again I turned. I could see her head and shoulders now, for she was leaning out, a hand holding something white at her neck.

"Come over here, boy! I want to talk to you." There was the old definite note that I knew.

Very well! Let her talk. What had happened was beyond repair. Not even a million words could mend it. But let her talk, and I would listen. But what you really want, brother, is a closer look at this woman! I threw my cigarette into the hedge, opened the gate, stepped across a flower border, and walked ten slow paces.

"Just a'e minute!" she said, and disappeared into the darkness behind her.

I waited, standing straight a yard from the open window. I heard a chair move, and the rustle of silk, and again she was at the window. She had thrown on a dressing gown of some light colour, not white, and was whipping a band round her waist. She leant out, grasping the sill, and I was looking directly into her face, for, as I said, the window was high-set. One stride forward, and I could have kissed her on the mouth. One stride! A million strides to kissing! I just stood where I was, and looked into her face, and I know that my heart was beating.

Alas! My sorrow and my woe! This was my style of woman. Ten years ago she had been only a slip of a girl, nineteen years young, laughing gay, debonair, sometimes fiery, never vindictive. In a temper she had accepted Robin Daunt, and loyally kept her bargain. And then, a year of unhappiness sobered her gaiety, but could not break her spirit.

The last time—no, the second-last time I had seen Jean Harrington she had a black eye and a bleeding mouth, and was crying with temper and humiliation. And if Robin Daunt had not been already dead when I found him I would have killed him with my bare hands.

That was more than nine years ago. She was twenty-nine years old now, a mature woman on the far edge of youth, and what the years had done to her I did not know. But I might find out.

The moon was shining aslant on her face, and I could see the gleam of her golden-grey eyes, and the sheen of her new-copper hair. She was of the broad-faced Celtic type that is almost Slavic, with moulded cheekbones, a down-tilted tip to her nose, and a mouth almost sensuous in its sensitiveness. Fair enough! But that says nothing. Not very tall, active but not exactly lissome, her shoulders wide for a woman, her neck, maybe, too columnar, but finely moulded, a breast to suckle sons. Fair enough still? But not enough. It was the emanation, the atmosphere, the aura, some force in tune with me that wrapped me round and possessed me. In brief, she was the mate for me. But I would never possess her. The blood—no! it was not the blood. She knew that I had not killed her husband, and she was the only one that knew. What then? Let it bide.

She was leaning forward, her forearms on the sill, and she was looking at me very closely. I was leaner than I used to be, and possibly the moonlight accented my prison pallor. I could see the startle in her eyes. She reached a hand out without touching me, and there was fear in the urgency of her half-whisper.

"David, you are not running away? Are you in hiding?"

I thrust my chin at her. "Would you hide me, Jean?"

"Of course I will," she said almost hotly, as if there was no need to ask. "You are coming right in."

She lifted from the sill. But I put a restraining finger on her wrist, and felt only the coolness of it. A small glow warmed me, but I would ware sentiment. I laughed.

"No, Jean! All is well! I was a good boy, and got remission after nine years." And then a thought struck me. Dammit! this was Charley Cashan's cottage, and where was Charley? And why was Jean Harrington here? Could it be——? Nonsense! I said: "Didn't Charley tell you I was home?"

"He's at Beananaar. I heard him passing up earlier on—singing."

Why had not Charley told her—he used tell her every-thing? And why was she here in The Cottage, and Charley at Beananaar? I would find out presently. But why had Charley not told her?

Jean would insist on plucking one string, and a string that hurt. There was a grievous note in her voice and her head drooped. "Nine years! Oh David! Nine terrible years!"

I thought I knew what was in her mind. Nine years out of my life—and why? There was nothing she or I could do about it now. But there was one thing I could do. I spoke lightly.

"Nine terrible years! Not on your life, Jean! Why, bless my soul! I was an ignorant hick, and got next door to an university education. The head-warden took me under his wing. I worked in his garden—a whole acre of it—and darn the thing he knew about gardening till I taught him. I played hard ball with him. I read his books—cubic yards of them. He taught me to play chess. A right bonnie player, Michael Ambrose!"

That last note, a little smug, got her. She nearly sniggered, and came back at me, "And, of course, the pupil beat the master at the end of the day. Yes—no?"

This was in our old style. From the very beginning we had a habit of taking each other down a peg when necessary and when not.

"To tell you the truth," I said, still smugly, "I had some difficulty in letting him beat me."

She chuckled then, and I chuckled too, and things were easier after that.

"The same old David!" she said.

"And the same old Jeanathan!" I said.

It was my mother who had christened us David and Jeanathan early in our inseparable years. There was an unbreakable tie between us then. Unbreakable? How do I know! But I could find out if we could still communicate across the chasm that held us apart. I said: "I would like to talk to you Jean."

"Why not, David?" Her voice was a little throaty. "Would you care to come in? No, not to-night! Do you really want to talk, David?"

"Surely. Have you a chair handy for yourself?"

"Oh dear!" said Jean Harrington softly, and there was a feeling in her voice that might be a wistful happiness. She was Jeanathan still.

Her shoulders moved, and I heard a chair scrape as she foot-hooked it forward. She sat in the window-corner, so that the moon outlined her cheek and the delicately strong contour of jaw and chin. There was a shadow under the cheekbone. She was thinner than that time when I used call her "butterball". Strangely she took the words out of my mouth.

"You are thinner too, David, but you are fit——"

"And tough. A good man but thin! Cigarette?"

She took one, and I held the match for her. Her dark lashes hid her eyes from me, but I noted that there was no thread of silver in the copper of her hair; and the down-tilt to the tip of her nose was as intriguing as ever. There were two spots of colour on the excited pallor of her face. I felt the excitement. I felt more. She was a mature and lovely woman, and—and—desirable, that's the word.

I leant shoulder at the other end of the high sill, and considered my opening gambit. She sat higher than I did and leant forwards towards me.

"Have you lost your tongue, good fellow?" she said lightly.

"There's the weather always," I said. "Isn't it a grand night ma'am and a romantic moon. Wouldn't it remind you of a balcony somewhere and—what was his name?"

"No, no, David!" She moved her head slowly, and her Highland voice was softly grave. "All that is bye." She reached a hand towards me. "But there is a good deal still alive, David, and I'll cherish it. I think there is something you want to know. Well?"

"And no more beating about a bush. Fair enough! For a start, then, how is it that you are here in The Cottage?"

"Your mother——? No, you would not ask, and your mother would let you find out for yourself. This is my cottage, Dave——"

"Of course! It belongs to Beananaar."

"It does not belong to Beananaar. It belongs to me."

"But——"

"I left Beananaar eight years ago," she said quietly.

"Blazes alive!" I exploded. "Did William Daunt trick you too?"

"William Daunt could not keep me in Beananaar," she said, still quietly.

"Was that the way of it?" I said consideringly. And then I struck the sill with the heel of my fist. "Yes, by the Powers! Someone will have to look into William Daunt's affairs."

"And into yours too," she said meaningly.

"I know—I know!" I was feeling hot under the collar. "You and my mother, two women to play on! Blast him! Did he think he could make his cheating stick?"

"Leave me out of it, Dave! He did not cheat me."

"He did too. You brought a good dowry to Beananaar, and it was needed at the time. One-third at least——"

"Listen David!" She stopped me. "I would not, could not go on living at Beananaar. But do you think a Scottie would let herself be cheated?" Her voice lightened. "You ought to know, you often tried!"

"And failed—and then you used to make up excuses, and slip a pound in my pocket—and I only wanted ten bob. Softie was your middle name."

"Oh dear, oh dear! But that was David Daunt. William Daunt could not cheat me. He tried, too. But I got back my tocher; I got this cottage and all in it, a garden patch, a run for poultry, and a shed to hold a light car. I'll give you a run some time."

"Chickenfeed!" I said. "Did you go back to teaching?"

"No—heavens no!" She ran a hand along the window-frame in some embarrassment. "You remember I used to do a bit of scribbling?"

"Losh yes! A hell of a vice till I belted it out of you. Don't tell me——?"

"I'm telling you." She chuckled—and hurried on. "I write for the Irish Press and Radio. I could land a job if I wanted it."

"All right! I'll forgive you so long as you don't start a novel! Murder! You haven't written a novel, have you?"

"Not under my own name. Anything else troubling you?"

"Let me see where we've got to!" I was only leading up to the question at the back of my mind. "You are here; Uncle-bloody-William is at Grianaan; where is Charley Cashan—Beananaar?"

"That's right! All by his lonesome as he wants it. He is supposed to look after the store cattle. It's good fattening land and all in grazing, with Charley for an indifferent herds-man. He says the cattle know better than he does, so why chivvy them about."

Her voice softened and warmed. "Charley is a dear—a darling, a darling but no young chevalier. He has been a tower of strength to me, a rock in a thirsty land. You know he digs my garden, and you used say he would not sleep sound, and a spade under the same roof. He markets my eggs and chickens too, and runs—actually runs messages for me——"

"And gets the price of two pints off you?"

"Well yes! And I let him read his murderous melodramas to me. Gosh Dave! he nearly pulled it off once. The Abbey kept a play of his for eight months. A hell of a play too! but the Abbey is like that. Poor Charley! If he was the marrying kind I might take him to wife. Oh! I'm unkind now."

"You'd wear the breeks all right, Scottie," I said. There was a pause then, and I said, "Have you hedgehogs?"

"Have I what? Should I get that?" said the Scottie doubtfully.

"I thought I heard one at the butt of the hedge yonder. Never mind! They don't bite—hard." But I had heard hedge-rustling that night when there should be none, so I kept a weather eye lifting. The rustling had stopped—too suddenly I thought—and nothing moved that I could see.

This Scottie was wise, and she must have Lowland blood in her too. She liked directness and frankness—sometimes.

"Come to the point, David!" she said firmly.

IV

I straightened from the window sill, took two or three slow paces across the grass, looked at my toes, rubbed the crisp hair at the back of my neck, and came back to the window. I did not look at Jean Harrington.

"Something troubling you, Davy?" she said gently.

"The question in my mind. It troubles me and I can't let it be. I can't answer it, and, maybe, you can't, or, maybe, you won't. Let it be!"

She stirred and her voice was troubled and low. "I will answer any question if I can. Ask it if you must, David." Was she guessing at something else that was in my mind? I would not have her doing that.

"All right Jean! I'll ask it. It is a simple question." I tapped the sill for emphasis. "Why did my mother, Ellen Furlong, marry William Daunt?"

That question came as a relief to her. She sat forward, and moved a hand confidently. "That question is easy to answer. You know William Daunt——"

"I know he has some hellish power with women," I said harshly. "Is that your answer?"

"It is not," she almost barked. "He may have power with some women, but he had none with Ellen Furlong. Oh yes! he used his wiles all right, and failed, and then he tried his guile. Listen David! Your mother married him for your sake."

"I am hard of hearing, ma'am," I said softly. "Will you please say that again?"

"Need I? All right! Ellen Furlong married William Daunt for the sake of her son David."

I was astounded. I wanted to curse. I wanted to deny violently. What was the use? So I said with dangerous mildness:

"You will now prove that for me?"

"Of course I will. And you can just listen to me, Mister doubting Thomas!" This was the forthright Jean I remembered. She leant over the sill, and I could see her eyes clearly and the flash of them. "I know William Daunt, and I know your mother—better than you do, because I am a woman. There were two things that William Daunt wanted with all the greed that men have. He wanted Grianaan, the whole three hundred fat acres of it, and the gracious old house; and, a good long way after that, he wanted your mother. He wanted her before and after your father won her. Do you accept that?"

"I accept it," I said tonelessly.

"Maybe you do. And when the time was ripe William Daunt set out to win the place and the woman. He succeeded, and the proof of the pudding is in the eating, David. Am I hurting you?"

"I can stand it."

"You'll have to stand more. Your mother is a darling, David. It is she that has the appeal and not you dam' men. William Daunt has turned sour, because he never really possessed her. But she was not much of a farmer, David. Was she?"

"She didn't need to be——"

"Yes she did," she came back smartly. "And she was not much of a housekeeper either. Your idolator, Julie Brady, was and is the housekeeper. But where would Grianaan be without your mother: her generosity, her warmth, her impulsiveness, her whole character—her womanliness? She is the great chatelaine needing a stewardess or two under her —and to blazes with housekeeping anyway!

"But a farm can go to blazes too David. You know that, who learned farming the hard way. When—when you were gone Grianaan went to pieces. There was no one to hold it together. Your old steward, Bill Canty, died, and some of the young fellows went to English factories. The hay was badly saved or was not saved at all. The corn lodged and rotted in the rainy seasons, the milking of the cows was vamped. You know how things pile up?"

"Yes. They always pile up."

"And William Daunt saw his chance, and took it. He stepped in quietly—very quietly—to help your mother. He surely helped her, for he was the real farmer who could get things done, and plan to get more done—and not soil his own soft hands. But he did more than mere farming. He healed the old family feud between Grianaan and Beananaar, the feud that had culminated in—tragedy. He was very plausible. He still can be, and I warn you of that. Take heed of that David."

"I'm watching out."

"He changed the whole atmosphere of gloom at Grianaan. The past would be forgotten—not forgotten—ignored. Everything would be built up for the future. Everything would be done against your home-coming, for you would come home, and find a thriving farm to step into, with prices soaring and work to be done. You would settle down. You—yes, you would probably marry; William Daunt would go back to a lonely life at Beananaar; your mother could take over this cottage—or come to Beananaar. And—you know—in the circumstances, a union might not be a bad thing, a sort of marriage of convenience to stop the tongue of scandal. Well! Need I go on David?"

"She was attracted by him?" I said gnawingly, and moved my feet.

"Why not? She was a live woman. But she found him out. She would—she lived in the same house. I don't know if she ever cohabited with him—not for years at any rate. But he had dug himself in then. He had the reins firmly in his hands, and Grianaan was his for all practical purposes; he was accepted everywhere as the laird of Grianaan. He showed his hand. He was no longer working for you. His tune changed. After all, on second thoughts, your homecoming might—would rouse what was moribund and better dead. The right and proper course would be for you to go away, and make a new life somewhere—anywhere—Far Cathay, under the Southern Cross, under any glimpses of the moon, but not in Grianaan. That is all, and excuse my longwindedness." She stopped abruptly.

She sat back, her head against the casement, and waited. I knew she was watching me closely, waiting for my reactions. But I said nothing for a long time. And then there was a trace of a taunt and a spur in her voice.

"My poor David Daunt, sent to lick his wounds in remote places!"

I leant forward and touched her wrist, and drew my hand away again.

"Thank you Jean! Thank you very much my dear. That was very clear. You had all that ready to say—yes you had." I kept my voice equable. "And you are right as rain. My good uncle gave me my marching orders this very evening."

She leant forward. "David, did he order you off?" Her voice was an eager whisper.

"He did, indeed! With true dignity and righteous indignation."

She sat back in her corner, threw up her head and clapped her hands. She chuckled and gurgled and almost crowed. The sombre mood that had weighed on us lightened strangely.

"Dammit, woman! 'Tis no laughing matter," I said indignantly, and she only choked. "All right then! Burst your boiler, and a happy good night to you!"

This was only pretence on my part, though I did not understand this suppressed merriment. As I half-turned away she caught my sleeve and pulled me back vigorously.

"You dumb bog-trotter!" she called me. "I was only thinking of William Daunt hoist with his own petard. You lean thug! Ride a high horse on me would you?" She shook my sleeve. "You never knew, but when I used to want you to do something down went my foot against it, and you fell over yourself in your hurry to do it."

I did not know that, and I did not believe it anyway. I said mildly:

"These be milder days Jean."

She was serious at once. She loosed my sleeve.

"So they are," she agreed. "Maybe you are leaving——"

"Not for a time." I stopped her, and added as an afterthought, "and I'll take my mother along." I said nothing about the string that would hold me for three years.

"That will be best, David," she said softly and sadly.

Another thought came to me. "I'll have to make some money first, though," I said.

"You've money to burn——"

"Like hell an' all! with William Daunt on the reins?"

"Not all the time. For years your mother banked every penny she could, and in your name, David."

"That is what Ellen Furlong would do," I said in my throat.

"And look, David!" She was diffident now. "I can give to pounds-shillings-and-pence what Mister Daunt took out of Grianaan."

"How could you?"

"Business methods, with Charley Cashan to supply particulars." She moved a hand with easy certainty. "But you needn't think you'll get anything back out of Uncle William —not in a thousand years!"

"Won't I begod? Steady on, you divil! Spurring me again?"

"But for the sake of peace at Grianaan——"

"There will be peace at Grianaan——"

"And the situation like gunpowder?"

"But nary a spark."

There was some regret in her tone. "Ah well! I suppose peace has its victories too. And, anyway, you're not smart enough to tangle with your uncle."

"And that's a sure thing," I agreed, and stepped back from the window. "Thanks for all your information, Jean girl. I wanted it, and I may want some more later on." And then I pointed a finger at her. "But say! how did you get to know? Not from no wee birdie—nor gluggerhead Charley either!"

"Your mother told me most of it," she said calmly.

My heart lifted. "My mother! You do see her, sometimes?"

She actually snorted. "Sometimes, your granny! I take tea with her every Wednesday—marketday in Kantwell, and the house to ourselves. And on fine Sundays I drive her across to the sea, and on other Sundays down to the mountains."

"It is what Jean Harrington would do," I said, and added softly, "and a good habit should never be broken."

She lifted to her feet, and put her hands on the bottom bar of the lifted sash. Looking up, I could see the lower part of her face, and her mouth was not steady. But her voice was steady enough, and very far away.

"No, David! You are home now, and you must take over. I did all I could, and I am not strong enough to do any more.

The strength is yours, and you will need it. Good night, my
dear! I am glad and glad that you are back, but you may not
see me again."

The sash came down slowly and without pause. I could
step forward and force it up again, and tell the woman I
would see her any time I wanted to. No, I could not! I could
take no action at all. I could only let the days drift by and
events shape themselves. And nature would take its course
too.

But I was no longer filled with rebellion and dourness. I
would be only resolute now, God willing; for there were fine
people in the world after all, and I had loyal friends.

Something is hellishly wrong in all this, I told myself, *something
that does not fit with Jean Harrington in spite of what I saw, in
spite of what she did. Something is going on, and I must be ready for
it. All I have now is one small bit of information that I got to-night,
one small straw blowing in the wind. Let the wind blow then.*

Chapter IV

WHY WATCH YE?

I

The window-sash had clicked into place. I could not see through the moonshine on the glass, but I lifted hand in salute, turned, and walked slowly towards the gate.

There was that rustle again, away up the hedge on the left. Well, hungry life would soon be on the stir, and this might be an early riser—or might it?

At the gate I turned and looked at the closed windows. Nothing moved inside it. But I lifted my hands high and opened them wide. That was our old signal, and it meant: "We are watching out, and to-morrow is another day." But would to-morrow be that other day? To-morrow and every morrow Jean Harrington and I might go our separate roads. She had implied that. And the window gave no sign now.

As I closed the gate I glanced sideways along the hedge. There was nothing to hear, and there was no single stir amongst the pale blossoms of the escalonia. If anyone were trailing me he knew his job. In that dry weather with the undergrowth beginning to sere an occasional rustle could not be avoided.

I was a nighthawk too, and knew a trick or two. I would try one now.

I turned for Grianaan, but I no longer strolled. I walked steadily but not too fast, and I kept well out from the margin of the road. My heels sounded firmly on the hard surface. At the junction of the roads, I took the acute angle to the right, without changing pace, and without a glance backwards. I stamped forward for twenty paces, halted, and went on marking time diminuendo, right-left, right-left, for a quarter-minute. And then, acrouch, I returned to the corner on tip-toe, and slipped into the flank of a hazel bush jutting from the hedge. I made only one faint rustle.

I waited. Something tickled my neck, something itched across cheek and brow. I twitched my hide and controlled my hands. I was being plagued by the minute, winged, green insects that thrive on the leafage of birch and hazel.

Luckily I had not long to wait, but it was almost too long, for I was on the point of stepping out on the road to brush myself off, when the very bush I was hiding behind rustled on the other side. I waited. Something moved forward, and through the frondage I saw the big, dim-grey, crouching figure of a man.

He inclined forward, and set his head for listening; inched again, and peeped round the belly of the hazel. I heard a disgusted whisper: "Blast his eyes! He's over the ditch." He came round a little more. He looked up the road I had taken; he looked down the road to Grianaan; and then he turned and looked suspiciously into the bush. He was looking right into my eyes, and I could have socked him if I wanted to.

"Go and teach your grandmother to suck eggs!" I told him, but not too rudely.

He was a superbly active man. He leaped backwards, six feet if not eight, and his right hand flashed towards his left oxter, and dropped away again—empty.

"Cripes, David Daunt!" he complained feelingly. "That was no way to frighten a man out of a year's growth."

"You are big enough as it is," I said. I stepped out on the road, and brushed hurriedly at my face and neck and chest.

The man was in grey mufti, buttoned up to the throat. Now he turned down the lapels of his jacket, and ran a finger round his collar.

"The midges are the divil right enough," he said. "They ate me alive."

I stepped closer to him, and he held his ground and grinned at me. In the bright light there was no mistaking the strong, broad face of him.

"You are Guard Tade Murphy?"

"To be sure sir! You got a good eye in your head."

"Look! Will you answer me one question?"

"I mightn't at that," said Guard Tade Murphy. "But you could try me!"

"Do you draw from the bottom of the deck playing forty-ones with Joseph?"

"Blazes no!" he said indignantly, and then added, "The boys would skin me, and, anyway, there's no need with Yoseph."

"Joseph what?"

"Yoseph, Joseph Yoseph, spelled with a Y. His grandfather was a Jew, and he's dam' proud of it. But he'll never learn to play forty-ones. The Super thinks he can teach him, but he can't. You've got to know the fall of the cards by native instinct."

"So you use Joseph Yoseph to milk your superior officer."

"Like hell we do!" He chuckled dismally. "Gives us what he calls a free, informal lecture once a month, and a small game of poker after it for relaxation. Free how are you!"

"A strange man, your Super!" I led him on.

"You don't know half yet." And then he laughed. "Begod, sir! this is a queer talk between you and me at the heel of a night. Don't let me be keeping you from your bed."

I would get no more out of him. "Bed it is," I said. "And now that we're introduced couldn't we walk along together?"

"Very good sir!" he agreed after a pause. "If you don't mind."

II

We walked at an easy pace down the road, but not quite together. The policeman's behaviour rather puzzled me. He would not take a cigarette because, he said, the smoke got in his eyes. His rubber soles padded softly, sometimes ahead, sometimes behind me, and his head moved continually from side to side as his unsmoked eyes scrutinized the black bulk of the bushes on either hand; and once or twice he turned to look behind; and all the time his left hand grasped jacket lapel, while his right swung free and ready. I knew he was carrying a shoulder gun.

"Your Super had a job for two of ye," I said. "Is Joseph or Yoseph on the prowl too?"

"Not yet—I mean——"

"You mean that your baby-elephant has a wholetime tail on me. Why? I don't intend to do any more killing."

"When did you begin, Mr. Daunt?" he asked quietly.

"Go to blazes!" I said, and changed the subject. "Is Joseph as good a tailer as you?"

"Better. I'm not good," he deplored. "I ought to have known you had me taped when you called me a hedgehog. By gorry! that name will stick if it ever comes out. And then I fell for your marking time, and I'd heard about that one."

I stopped and faced him. He gave a quick glance round and looked over my shoulder. I tapped a toe on the macadam and kept my hellish temper in check.

"So you heard me call you a hedgehog?" I said.

"I heard that——"

"Damn you! You heard a lot more?"

"Maybe I did," he half-admitted, and his voice firmed. "And if I did there is no need for you to be ashamed of anything I heard."

That was a good answer and a disarming one.

"Fair enough!" I said, and turned to walk on. "You'll tell your Super, of course."

"That's my job, Mr. Daunt."

"Don't tell him I untailed you. I won't."

"I will. You don't hide anything from Jerry Farley." And he added feelingly, "and won't I get merry hell!"

"Not so merry," I said.

I walked on head down, and let my memory drift backwards. What had been said in my talk with Jean Harrington that would be news to Jerome Farley? Damn him! he had his own way of finding out things. Let me see now.

He would learn that the old tie between Jean and me was not broken, but that the woman intended to break it. Why not? Had I not killed her husband? He would learn nothing new about that. He would learn how and why Jean had left Beananaar, what she was doing, how Charley Cashan was her standby, and of her friendship with my mother. And he would learn how William Daunt had got hold of my mother and Grianaan, and was determined to hold the latter, at least.

A man like Farley would know most of that already. The new thing that he would learn was that William Daunt had already given me my marching orders, and that I had taken them with extraordinary mildness. Why had I been so complacent? Because I would keep the peace at Grianaan, and because I felt that I was no match for my uncle. I smiled to myself, and glanced sideways at Guard Murphy.

"Got a good memory Guard?"

"Fair to hellish."

"Don't forget to tell your Superintendent that I am keeping the peace at Grianaan."

"I'll tell him—I heard you," he said, and was not very enthusiastic about my good intention.

"You see I admire the way he keeps his own peace, and I'm an apt pupil."

"God between us and all harm!" said Tade Murphy. "Well, sir! here you are at your own gate, and you'll have time for a sleep yet."

I lifted head. There was my white house up the slope, and the moonlight was still on it. But the moonlight was paler now, and the shadows longer, and the sky, north by west up the river valley was turning rose-pink. The house was still asleep.

"I would ask you up for a drink, but I'm not organized yet," I said.

"The will for the deed, sir! I'll see you to the corner of the house anyway."

We went across the grass together, and he, watchful as ever, kept to the hedge-side of me. At the corner of the Outside Room I touched his sleeve and spoke in a low voice.

"You made one other slip to-night. At the very beginning I saw you slip from here into the bushes there."

He stopped, and moved a hand. "Wait! You saw me—just here?"

"That's right."

"But——" he stopped. "You saw someone?"

"I tell you so, and you are now telling me that there was a third man on the prowl."

He hesitated, and then, in the shade of the wall I saw the nod of his head. "Yes, sir! as you say there was a third man on the prowl. I don't know who."

"I don't either."

"A smart devil! I could not get near enough to handle him. By God! if I could!" His voice grated, and then was troubled. "There's something going on, Mr. Daunt. I don't know what it is, and all I can do is to keep my eyes peeled. Come on now, and I'll give you a leg up. You'll never get in by your lonesome."

We found my window lifted as I had left it, and there was darkness behind it. I looked up at it. Seven-eight feet to the sill, and I wondered if there was still enough whalebone in me to make it. Tade Murphy whispered at my shoulder.

"I'm still on the job. Would you give me a leg up for one peep inside, and God love you?"

Why not? The man was doing his job as he saw it. I made a stirrup, and the rubber sole was warm to my fingers. He was an active lad, and my heave and his pull landed him

with his breast over the sill. The weight went off my hands.
I looked up at his dangling legs. No, he was not going all the
way in, but he was shining a torch into every corner. Twice
he did that, and then dropped lightly on the concrete.

"The wardrobe?" I suggested.

"Take a look."

"Under the bed?"

"You'll have time to kick his teeth in, and I'll be handy—
Up you go!" He offered me the stirrup of his hands.

I gestured him aside. "I'll try one shot at it. Don't let
me break my neck if I tumble."

"Dammit man! it can't be done," he protested.

"Maybe not, but here goes!"

One pace back, a thrust of foot, a heave, a pull, a vaulter's
hip-pivot, a gather and swing of my long legs, and I turned
over inside, my breast on the sill.

"Holy japers!" said Tade Murphy up into my face.

"Try it yourself, Tade?"

"No dam' fearo! not with my fourteen stone, and me
saving to get married." His whisper tightened. "Remember,
there's a third man playing tag with us, and I wasn't able to
touch him!"

"I'll touch him for you," I said.

"If he don't touch you first. Good night, sir! and pleasant
dreams!"

He went quiet-footed along the wall, and disappeared into
the shrubbery beyond the Outside Room. I knew he would
slip up into the kitchen garden beyond the parapet, and keep
my window under observation until the house waked.

I leant there on the sill and considered. Something was on
the move, or so Jerome Farley thought, but I was not at all
sure myself. But a third man had played tag with us. So he
had, but I knew who that man was, and I could put my
hand on him any time I liked. A mare's nest, Mr. Farley, I
fear!

And then down from the farmyard came the crow of the
first cock, and his clarion call was as lonely as the horns of

fairyland. The forlorn half-light of the dawn was already amongst the trees in the orchard, but it was dark inside the room when I turned round.

I switched on the light. I went across and opened the wardrobe door.

"Come out you hound!" I invited. But no feet protruded from behind the hanging suits.

I looked at the bed. An old-fashioned bed high off the floor, and the valance came down to the Indian rug. I went across and lifted it.

There was a man under the bed.

Chapter V

GOODMAN FRIDAY

I

The man under the bed was Charley Cashan. I knew him at once, though I had not seen him for those nine years.

His horselike face, unsmiling, looked out at me sheepishly from under the valance. Horse and sheep! Why not? Horse and sheep are not unlike in feature after all.

"You crawling behemoth!" I called him. "Come on out, or I'll kick your teeth in! I was told to."

"Dave, you divil!" he whispered anguishedly. "Keep your voice down, or Tade Murphy will be in on top of us."

"Let him. Out you come!"

"Draw the curtains first."

"I will not. I don't hide anything from Tade Murphy. Out you come, my little periwinkle!"

But it was like a turtle that he tried to withdraw his head. Too late. I had him by the collar, and hauled him out on his back. He was supine under my hands, but he had always been strangely helpless in handgrips, though he was as strong as a donkey.

I jerked him to his knees and to his feet, spun him round, and ran hands over him from armpits to flank. He wriggled and squeaked.

"What are you tickling me for?"

"Searching you for a gun, you murderin' hound!" I said fiercely.

"Holy murder! I'd run a mile from a gun, and you know that."

"So you would. Sit down then and explain yourself."

I put him sitting clump on the bed, and he looked at me dumbly, and swallowed twice.

I must introduce Charles Cashan.

William Daunt's first wife was a widow with one small son. This was he, Charles Cashan, and he was now as big as Buddha. He was three years older than I was, and we had grown up together at Grianaan and Beananaar. As a boy he was the most brilliant pupil in Kantwell College, and, showing signs of a religious vocation, was sent to a clerical seminary.

He stayed for two years, and then walked out. Just walked out without yes, aye or no, and disappeared—and could not be found. And, then, in another two years he wandered back to Beananaar, and told many strange tales, mostly fable. But he was no longer the brilliant Charles Cashan. He was Charley the Fool, but he was surely no fool, as Jean Harrington and I knew. I suppose he had had some form of brain storm. Some folk held that the dint of book-learning had softened his brain; others held plainly that he had a slate loose, as his father had before him; Jean and I knew that, a simpleton in some things, he had definitely chosen his own line of country and held it.

He was one of William Daunt's failures, for his step-father had tried, over the brink of barbarity, to make a toiler-and-moiler out of him, and failed. Not even in busy spring or harvest would Charley sweat except the spirit moved him, and it seldom did. Finally he had become a sort of herdsman at Beananaar, and that suited him. He left the cattle to drift from pasture to pasture, as they knew best, but sometimes he might insist, with his own type of obstinacy, that they drift the right way; and he would soothe them with doggerel verse.

Day or night or, indeed, distance, made no difference to Charley. He would walk four or fourteen miles across country to a wake—American or real—take three drinks of stout, and walk home again across country, ignoring all roads; he would lie out all night to hear a bird sing at dawn;

he would go with a tinkers' caravan through three counties without raising a fist, and that is one complete miracle. But though he was a night-rambler he was no bird of prey. He would go out with Jean Harrington and me, and be a capable sentinel, but he would not take bird or fish or coney. He would do little things off his own bat for Jean. I often wondered how he regarded Jean, but I think she was the Queen of his dream-heaven.

Strangely enough, though he had reverted to a primitive type, and generally used the crudest of dialects, he had not forgotten his education. He still read widely, and borrowed— some say lifted—books and journals everywhere, and never returned them—except to my mother who would not let Julie Brady give him a meal unless he returned two books at a time; and, indeed, sometimes the books were not hers. He dabbled in ballad verse, and Jean and I used spout it to each other. But his one great ambition was to write an acceptable play; to bring his dream-world alive, I suppose; but, invariably, he brought it alive in the bloodiest of melodrama, out-Hamleting Hamlet in its final scene.

II

That was the man who now sat on my bed, and looked dumbly at me. I pulled round the bedside chair and sat down, but I left a clear line between the window and Charley. Tade Murphy would be out there, probably on top of the parapet, wondering his head off. I lit a cigarette for his benefit. That would show him that I had the situation in hand. Charley did not smoke. I looked him over.

He had put on weight, but he had not aged at all; a massive, shapeless bulk of a man in patched tweeds, with a long, melancholy horse-face—or sheep-face—that seldom smiled. His eyes were a bleached grey and lazy, and without the telltale surface glisten. His sandy hair curled up at ears and neck, but had retreated from brow and temples so that

the carapace of his brain stood up, like a narrowing dome.
That is why I sometimes and reprehensibly called him a
"gluggerhead". Glugger is Gaelic for an egg gone bad—
addled.

He looked a completely harmless individual, and so he was,
but he liked to be treated as if he were a dangerous desperado.
And so I treated him:

"You've a lot of explaining to do, you thug," I said. "Did
you crawl in here to cut my throat?"

He had a slow method of speech, and, sometimes, one
could not tell whether he was sardonic or merely naïve.

"Give me another bleedin' chance and I'll show you," he
said. "Dambut! Dave Daunt, you were always a playboy, an'
durance vile hasn't sobered you."

"Shut up!" I said, and pointed. "You were under that
bed. For how long?"

"A bare minute. I got in ahead of ye."

"Ah-ha!" I pointed an accusing finger at him. "So you
were the third man on the prowl to-night."

"Of course I was," he admitted readily, "but how did
you know?"

"Tade Murphy knew, and he's out there watching you
through the window."

"Blast his eyes! Let me heave wan of your shoes at
him!"

That was the very last thing that Charley Cashan would
do. Mischief stirred in me.

"Careful!" I snapped. "He has a gun in his hand, and he'd
love to——"

Charley Cashan was as gun-shy as a red-setter gone wrong.
His hands came down on the bed, and, next instant, he might
be under it. I kicked him solidly in the shin, and that held
him.

"Sit still you dam' fool!" I warned him fiercely. "Put your
hands between your knees and relax. He won't shoot unless
you touch me."

I moved my chair to half-shield him, but his eyes would

keep lifting towards the window, and he kept his hands firmly between his knees: big, soft-looking hands, with soft-looking fingers that did not show a joint. I hadn't begun on him yet.

"Stop your playacting and attend to me," I ordered. "Why did you hide?"

"Because I had a power of things to tell you, and I wanted a quiet collogue."

"That's a dam' bad answer. You came over earlier to see me, didn't you? Against orders too."

"What are bloody orders to me? I kem over."

"When?"

"As soon as I could. Give me time and I'll tell you, you thunderin' tyrant. The ould fella consarn him! me saintly step-father, warned me against seeing you, or he'd put me out on the roadside for good an' all. As if I cared! Sure there is only wan thing now that holds me from the roads winding. And you know what that is?"

"I know. So you slipped away unbeknownst?"

"What else? across the fields. When I got to the top-end of the kitchen-garden out there, the moon was over the top of Slieve Mish—that's the time it was. And your window was lighted, a shame to the world, and you naked as a trout getting into your pyjamas. I was on the verge of coming down and getting you to haul me in when I heard a stir in the currant bushes. And it was no hedgehog. Eh?"

"I'll remember that. Go on!"

"It was the terriblest beast of all: the two-legged one. I moved in like a shadow, and it was Tade Murphy, hidin' and watchin' awkward as a rocherinous. I was for going home then, but had another thought coming. What was Tade after? Me duty to the team——"

"What team?"

"The ould team—the three of us. So I waited to see what Tade was after. Easy for me to wait. I'm used to waiting. I've waited all of a spring night to find out if the blackbird whistles before the dawn. He don't. The thrush does. I sat up against the wall atween two plums, and passed the time making up verses—about a virgin woman before——"

"Every poet has done that, you scandalous hound!"

"Maybe so. Everything to be said has been said, but a fella, here and there, might say it better. Very well so! After a time, long or short I dunno, right in the still time, there was a stir in the room, and your head out the window, and you listening, for you heard Tade move. You know what happened after that. You went round one corner, and Tade round the other, and I followed the way you went. Sometimes I was behind ye, and sometimes I took a circle in front, and Tade Murphy plodding away from bush to bush. Do you tell me he knew I was there?"

"He knew but not to name you."

"Did he notice anything else?" There was a sly note there.

"What? Out with it!"

He moved his hands, and thrust them back again between his knees. He leant to me and whispered,

"Dave, you said three men on the prowl. Listen! There was a fourth man as well."

"Who was he?"

"I don't know. He was too cute for me."

"That's a lie," I blazed. "No man could fool you at night. Who was he?"

"Damn'd if I know! But look! I know one man who could fool us all."

"Well?"

"Sheedy—Bill Sheedy. A poacher all his life, and he can see in any light or no light, being an albino."

I considered that, and lit another cigarette.

"Has Sheedy anything to do with William Daunt?" I asked then.

Charley nodded understandingly. "He has so. The ould fella has him under his thumb, and treats him like dirt. Sheedy don't like it, but don't want to lose a good job— with pickings."

"Leave that—it is not profitable." I lifted a finger at him.

"One or two more questions, Mr. Cashan, and you'll probably get your ears belted. How far did you trail me tonight?"

His eyes were on his hands, but he answered.

"I went as far as you went."

"And where were you when you went that far?"

"Holy angels!" he lamented. "Why didn't I go home? All right—all right! I was lying doggo behind the red-painted rain barrel at the corner of the house."

I changed the subject for a moment and put a quick question.

"Why didn't you let Jean know that I was home?"

He looked at me out of bleached eyes, and looked away again.

"I wanted her to find out for herself. She'd have more fun."

That was a patent lie. He had some other reason, but I left it at that.

"Doggo behind the rain barrel!" I said. "Listeners hear no good of themselves."

"Don't I know it, the way ye called me out of my name. But I'm used to that." And then his mood changed. His hands came up and forward appealingly, and there was appeal in his voice too. . . . "Look Dave, and God love you! Dave Daunt me sound man! Will you do wan last thing for me, and I'll never ask another?"

"I might not. What is it?"

"O God above! Don't let Jean Harrington marry me."

"The gallant Chairlie! She put it another way I think?"

"I know. Why didn't you tell her I was not the marrying kind?"

"How do I know?"

"Dam' well you know. I won't be spancelled. I'd—I'd lie down die dog and ate the hatchet. I would do anything at all for Jean, and I will. But don't let her marry me. She would listen to you, Dave, same as always. Wouldn't she?"

"I may not see her again. You heard her?"

He gestured contemptuously. "Och! that was only a woman's way of talking—hitting you and holding you. She'll be expecting to see you, if not to-morrow, the next day or the day after."

"My wise fool!" I said.

III

I did not like the turn the conversation was taking, so I headed it off.

"You came here for a collogue? How the blazes did a gob o' mud like you get in that window?"

"I fell off two times. Look! and a yard o' hide off me shin bone!" He lifted leg to display a tear across the knee. "There was wan or two things I wanted to tell you in private."

"Jean told me all I wanted to know."

"Maybe not. She did tell you the ould fellow is trying to rob you, and so he is."

"And I'm watching out."

"Mind you, he's cocksure of himself, as sure as night after day he'll send you packing." He leant to me. "Maybe you'll go too, Dave?"

"What would you do in my place, Charley?"

"Och! I'd take no notice, same as always. But you're another man entirely. You're the fighter. You'll fight the dirty dogs, and all the dirty dogs agin you. You'll never give in, but they'll wear the body and soul out of you."

"And what should I do?"

"What you'll not do, you tough! Strip Grianaan bare, and clear out with your mother. The world is wide, as I know, and a gallant life in it for a gallant man—a split new life, and no finger pointed at you." His voice lowered to a whisper. "And look, Dave! In a year—two at most—a bit of a letter to Jean Harrington!—you know what I mean?"

"I know what you mean, Charles," I said quietly, "but I'll have to stay put for some time yet."

"Under the one roof with William Daunt?"

"Not so easy?"

"No trouble at all, but they'll hang you for sure next time, and me with you, for I'll be holdin' the basin while you're cuttin' his throat."

"You bloodthirsty catiff! Anything else to tell me?"

His voice lowered again. "This is the important thing. Jerry Farley is horning in."

"Superintendent Farley?" He was on interesting ground now.

"And who else? A dangerous monster of a man, and obstinate as a hog! Let him get something into his head, and he'll hold it and worry at it till the sky falls and he catches larks. Listen Dave! he's not satisfied with your case. Why else is he going round stirring the whole thing up again? There can be only wan reason, that you didn't kill Robin Daunt, who is burnin' in hell this minute if hell is."

"But I killed Robin Daunt," I said equably.

He made a contemptuous gesture that angered and disquieted me, and his mouth twisted sardonically.

"So you say. But that won't fash Jerry Farley, as Jean would say. He's probing the daylights out of everyone concerned: Jean, your mother, the ould fellow, and Bill Sheedy; and he had a go at me as well. Damn the much he got out o' me!"

"Weren't you frightened?"

His bleached eyes looked aside at me. "Why would I be frightened?"

"I'll tell you," I hit him. "You were the man to probe. If I did not kill Robin Daunt you did."

But that did not fash Charley Cashan either. He seldom smiled but he sometimes laughed—or, rather, he made the sounds of laughter. He did that now.

"Ho—ho—ho! And you're damn near the mark there, Dave Daunt. I would have and I should have killed the skunk, and so should you. Stick-in-the-muds, that's all we were. Why didn't we take him apart before he got Jean on the rebound?" He rubbed his palms together, and his nostrils widened. "What you and me, working together, couldn't have done to him? Not a hair or hide left of him, and we'd grind his bones to make our bread. And look what happened?"

"What happened is by with," I said. "I killed Robin Daunt, and took my medicine, and no one else can be put in jeopardy."

He moved his head forlornly. "I suppose that's all there is to it," he half-agreed. He knew too much, this solitary man of the fields and woods. I did not tell him so. I only said:

"Anything else on your mind?"

"I might have. I don't know." He rubbed the back of his neck, and brought his hand wearily over the dome of his head and down over his long face. "I don't mind the length of the night, but the dawn always reduces me."

I turned and looked at the window. Already the dawn was paling the light in the room. I went over and switched off the lamp and at once the desolate dawn-light claimed its own. The trees in the garden were no longer black bulks. The sun had not yet risen, but the north-eastern sky, that I could not see, must be suffused with colour, for there was a faint pinkish glow among the branches.

And then I heard the birds singing. I had wanted to hear the birds singing, but I was no longer in tune, for the thing that this man had hinted was a trouble at the back of my mind. He was on his feet, and I spoke harshly to him.

"Get out, you hunk of cheese! And if you don't break your neck I hope Tade Murphy will."

"Japers, no Dave!" he besought, his hands fluttering. "Slip me out the front door and I'll run for it."

"Oh, very well!" I agreed. "Come on, and don't wake the house with your clodhoppers."

I moved to the door, and the door opened in my face. My mother came in. She had made no sound in the house. Her brushed hair was shining white, and her eyes were lustrous— just lustrous. She was wearing a creamy, flowing morning robe, and red satin mules peeped below it. She was carrying a small silver tray, whereon rested a tall glass foamy yellow. She took no least notice of Charley Cashan.

"You're up early this morning, son David," she said and crinkled her eyes at me.

"Come off it, old lady!" I said rudely. "Once was enough."

"I know, boy. You'll go to bed now."

I took the tray from her, and put it on the dressing table.

"Charley Cashan!" She spoke coldly behind my back. "You have no consideration whatsoever, bumbling away for hours."

"Lord, Ellen Furlong, ma'am! I never opened my gob," he protested. "Talked into the ground I was."

She walked directly at him, and he lifted his hands as if to ward a clout. But she only took his sleeve and led him door-wards. The door was ajar, and she drew it open.

"Away with you! Julie Brady will give you your breakfast." She saw his hesitation. "Your step-father will not be out of bed for hours yet. Run along!"

"Gallons of tea, ma'am!" he said, and shambled down the passage, and for all his bulk he made no sound.

She shut the door softly and turned round to find my arms around her. I muzzled into the fragrance of her neck, and rubbed my black head into her white pow, and she sighed deeply. Then she moved me back gently, and unloosed the top button of my jacket.

"You'll drink your egg-flip, and go to bed," she ordered. "I'll wake you in five hours for a late breakfast."

"But, mummy, I have a lot of work——"

"You'll have a lot of work many a day. Take your egg-flip!"

"It don't smell like egg-flip to me."

"There's a spark in it, and you need it. I heard you go out and I heard you come in."

"Do you mind, mother?"

"It is what you used to do, and I do not want you changed —not one bit Daveen."

"I'll tell you about it later on," I said.

"Maybe!" She smoothed down the side of my face, and went across to the window. I thought she was going to close it down, but, instead, she leant out propped on her hands. Her voice was low, but clear and carrying.

"Guard—guard! Are you there? Yes, you are—behind the Bramley! Come on down—down this way—Oh! it's you Tade Murphy? Good morning, Tade!"

"Morning, ma'am!" came Tade's voice.

"Over the parapet! that's right! Round to the front door, and you'll find something in the kitchen. Go on now like a good boy!"

Tade's fine brogue came up. "May that be your welcome in heaven, ma'am."

"Charley Cashan will choke himself," I said.

"Let him," said my mother carelessly. "You go to bed!"

She went out without saying another word, and closed the door behind her. She had taken the presence of the guard in the garden as if it were an ordinary happening, and I began to wonder why.

That egg-flip was laced with brandy, and brandy is a soporific at most hours. I poured it down and went to bed. I thought I would not sleep. I thought things would go shuttling back and forth in my brain. I was so busy pounding my ear that I didn't even dream.

Chapter VI

THE SMALL SHOWDOWN

I

I did not sleep all of five hours. I had, indeed, work to do
that day, and something in the unconscious jogged me wide
awake in three hours. The window was bright, with the
young sun shining aslant, and gleaming on the mirror of
the dressing table, and that gleam was reflected on to my
face.

An old instinct came alive. I rolled out of bed on to my
knees, and put my face in my hands. I said the Lord's
Prayer slowly, feeling for the meaning of each phrase. It is
the morning prayer, and might be the only one, but I said
the *Ave* too.

As in all old country houses, we used have a rather primitive bathroom in Grianaan. It was no longer primitive, thanks
to William Daunt and his delicate hide, I supposed. The
walls were tiled in pink; there was a big, low pedestal wash
basin, a roomy porcelain bath, and a shower in plastic
curtains; and the heated rails were draped in huckaback
and turkish towelling.

I felt the roughness of my blue chin, and wondered about
a razor. Ah! on the shelf of the bevelled shaving mirror was
an old leather case that I knew. I opened it. That was my
safety razor with a new blade in it, and a new tube of cream,
and a brush of badger bristles well worn but serviceable.

"Thank you, mum!" I said in a whisper.

I shaved and bathed and scrubbed and showered and
towelled, cleansing the last taint of prison out of my hide.
Then I used some coal-tar talcum out of a tin, and wiped the

film off the long mirror to see how I looked. I was one long, lean devil right enough, but my skin looked healthy, and long muscles flexed smoothly under it. And, already, I thought the prison pallor looked clearer.

Back in my room I opened the oaken wardrobe. That mother o' mine had been at work here too. But she could not have done all this last evening. Through the years she must have kept this wardrobe stocked and cared for, and scented with lavender, and guarded against moths. There were suits that I scarcely remembered, and the drawers were packed with underclothing and shirts and hosiery. I put my head amongst the tweeds and was inclined to tears.

"Softy!" I said. "All right! Softy it is. But I'll make that woman happy or break a bone."

Men's fashions change slowly, and in nine years they had changed hardly at all. Possibly, the jacket skirts had lengthened by an inch or so, and the trousers narrowed, and the vests might have a button less—or more. I changed from the skin out: thin, mesh underwear, grey flannel pants, a white silk—or was it this new nylon—shirt, a tussore tie with red and black stripes to match the checks in the plaid jacket I picked out. Yes, at the age of twenty-three I had carried more flesh, and the fit was now a shade easy, but it was comfortable, and, like all hand-made stuff it touched at the right places.

I went along the passage to Julie Brady's bright kitchen, and found her there alone.

"Mornin', Julie! Where's Mum?"

"Wouldn't Julie Brady do you?" She bridled, and relented. "It's her morning for tidying up the Outside Room." She turned from the white cooker, and her mouth made a round O. Then she made a lively little run at me. "My, oh my! Is it coortin' you're going?"

"Why not?" I said, and slung an arm around her.

Her dark-red head pressed against me for a moment, and then she shoved me away brusquely.

"Playboy! But you smell nice, whatever, and you had a

cold tang off you yesterday. I heard you sloshing water a whole half-hour, and ten minutes was the best you ever did. Near as bad as William Daunt, and he takes a whole hour. I don't like a man who is too clean, so I don't."

"And all the times you packed me off to wash my dirty face."

"There's dirt and there's clane dirt," she said.

"And clane dirt is no poison. Do I get any breakfast?"

"You'll get it. Let me see now!" she considered, a plump little finger to a shapely mouth. "A wake stomach has to be coaxed with soft things——"

"Try rodiron."

"——like a small plate of brown porridge with a sprinkle o' sugar and a ladle of cream."

I had that, and hammered spoon on plate.

"Friday that's in it," Julie said. "You'll get an egg."

But the egg was a big speckled turkey egg, and I pointed out that there should be no turkey eggs at this season. But it was an onnatural baiste of a turkey that wouldn't stop layin', Julie explained, fifteen eggs at a time, and on the hatch and off the hatch, and fifteen more eggs, seventy to date. Julie uncapped my egg with a knife, for the shell of a turkey egg was tougher'n a pig's ear, and all my fingers were thumbs, whatever. I was Julie's small boy back to her again.

I was sitting back sipping my third cup of tea, and smoking my first cigarette, when my mother came in. She looked a shade disappointed.

"Sorry, Davy——!"

"What are you sorry about?" Julie came in. "Amn't I able to look after him."

"You'll only get your share of him," my mother told her.

"I don't want to be quartered in dread I might die," I quoted the old ballad, and I went on carelessly. "Wouldn't it be a good thing if the three of us were living here together?"

"Where else are we living, in the name o' God," the literal Julie wanted to know.

"But just the three of us."

My mother understood, and moved her head sadly.

"No, boy! I spoiled all hope of that."

"But there's Beananaar?"

"There's no place top of earth." There was revolt in her voice.

"I could go to Beananaar?"

"No—never!" she said emphatically. "This is your—but, no—I mustn't say that. You may want to go away—far away." She moved her head forlornly.

"Where I go you go," I said.

She held her hands out, and her eyes pierced me.

"Do you mean that my son?"

"If it is what you want."

"It is all I want any more."

"Then we hold together till times and tides are done."

"Herrings alive! what else would we do?" cried Julie, who was not an entity by herself. She was my mother. She was me.

I knew what my mother wanted now, and I dropped the subject. I rose to my feet and drifted doorwards.

"I'll have a look at the curtilages this morning," I said.

"Careful, David!" my mother called after me. "There are some that may not be too loyal."

"Let them choose their own loyalties and welcome," I said over my shoulder, and shut the door behind me.

II

The back door was in the basement, but I did not go that way. I went out the front door and down the steps, and so round the gable-end to the annex that we called the Outside Room. Originally it had been the farm office, but after my father's death I had claimed it as my Sanctum. The door was wide open, and I went in.

It was a long narrow room. The length of it was the full width of the house. The front wall was practically all window, and from where I stood inside the doorway I could see the valley of the Doorn, and the roofs of Kantwell on the slope beyond. The casements were open, and a current of air drifted through freshly.

This room was as I remembered it. That mother of mine had preserved and aired it for me. I walked across the same red-brown coir matting, to the same flat oak desk below the window. A pack of clean blotting-paper was in the old leather pad, and the desk cabinet was stocked with stationery. There were all my old books on the shelves at the window side of the fireplace; and the grate was filled with fresh fronds of bracken, as it had been in all the summers I could remember. A corner-cabinet was in one angle between window and side-wall. One shelf of it would hold my old pipes; and in the afternoon I would prepare one of them and get some tobacco from town.

Along the backwall was a glass-fronted press holding my sporting tackle. The greenheart fishing rods would probably be dozed by now, but the steel-cored split-cane might still be useful. I would try it later on. On the bottom shelf was my double-barrel, twelve-bore fowling piece, and a point twenty-two rook rifle; but my short-barrel Webley revolver was no longer there. It would be at the Police Station. It had seen service. It had killed Robin Daunt. And it was my gun.

There were two cow-hide armchairs, a window chair and a swivel desk-chair, with a covered rubber pad on the seat. I am sitting on that pad now writing this with might and main. Gosh! I have a long way to go yet.

I would have plenty of time for rummaging, and I had other things to do this morning. But I sat for a minute or two in the desk-chair, elbows on the blotting-pad, and looked down at the Doorn River, and across the roofs of Kantwell towards the distant sea. Many a time I had sat like that, and, in the gloaming, watched for the lighthouse beam to go on and off, on and off, far out on the horn of the estuary. Then I used be carefree and devil-may-care; now

I was sobersided, and I had a duty and a purpose before me, and I was not at all sure that I was man enough to tackle them. I could but try. And a man who tries is not altogether worthless.

I went out to try. I did not go up through the garden-orchard, but took a handgate in the hedge, that led directly on to the farm road. I did not light a cigarette, and I no longer strolled. In less than a hundred yards I came to the white-painted double-winged gates leading to the steadings. I went through and round the end of a barn, and the big cobbled farmyard spread before.

Over there was the long, white-washed, low-roofed cow byre, every door open. It was still early morning, but the cows would have been milked an hour ago, and again out at pasture. And there were the four doors of the stable. No, not four any longer! Two of them had been broken open to a single wide arch, and, inside, I could see at least two green-painted tractors. The days of the Clydesdale and Shire were about over. Possibly there was no horse at Grianaan any more, or not more than one or two for odd jobs, and we used use four pair of plough horses. Behind the byre was the long roof of the hayshed, and the shed was packed with hay to the curve of corrugated iron. There were no cornricks yet, but the oats should be just about ripe. I must look into that. The mowing machines would be in the lean-to shed at the back, and there possibly might be one of those new Combines.

I walked up the concrete path by the side of the barns, and then by the dairy; but the dairy would no longer be a hive of activity, since most of the milk would go to the co-operative creamery. Recessed beyond the dairy was the Bothan, the eating and living quarters of the hired men. It was a stone house with small windows, and, in my time, it used have a roof of thatch, but the thatch was now covered with cor-rugated iron. A drift of smoke plumed from the single squat chimney. The full-door was wide to the wall, but the half-door was closed across to keep the chickens out. A murmur of voices came through.

I leant over the half-door, and the murmur stopped short. A dog barked, but there was no growl, and a black-and-white herd dog came out from amongst feet and looked up at me intelligently. I would make friends with that lad, but not now. I snecked back the wooden bolt, pushed the door open, and stood under the jamb.

"God save all here!" I gave the customary salute.

There was an unusual pause before the response came. "God save you kindly!" And it came in a woman's voice.

There were eight males and a female in the room. The female was a sonsy, rosy-cheeked, big-bosomed young one with the fine, bold face of the country virgin used to countering the quips of single men. She was sitting aside near a peat-burning range, and drinking steaming tea out of a mug. Her eyes were on me with warm interest. She put her mug down on the range and rose to her feet. She was the only one that did. That gave me a lead on the attitude I had to face. A showdown was in the offing, but not a physical-force one I hoped.

The men were all young—little more than youths—except the man at the head of the table. And that man was Bill Sheedy, the man who had been thrown out of Scanlan's bar the previous evening, the man whose evidence had put me inside a steel door. And two others I recognized as the lads who had been with him. The showdown was nearer. My heart was thudding hollowly, but a hackle was lifting too.

The eight were seated round a narrow table covered by a near-white cloth that had been made out of bleached one-hundred-and-forty-pound flour bags. They had just finished breakfast, and most of them were drawing at cigarette butts. The day being Friday there were a scatter of egg shells, and fragments of soda loaves, and the pleasant odour of the powerfully strong tea that farm hands must have.

In my father's time, and in my time after him, we used employ a round dozen hired men. Tractor-work would dispense with a couple of horsemen, and a couple more would go with the introduction of an electric milking machine. A big, mechanized farm could now be worked with six or eight fledgelings; and we deplore the depopulation of the countryside.

I looked them over slowly, and they looked at me and looked away again. Bill Sheedy plainly glowered, the others wore the vacant looks of indecision, or, rather, of youths who were under the thumb of a stronger character. And the stronger character was Sheedy. I spoke quietly and took one step forward.

"You know who I am—David Daunt. Who is foreman here?"

The lads looked towards Sheedy, and Sheedy's right hand flat on the table lifted a thumb.

"Are you foreman, Sheedy?" I did not lift my voice.

"I am William Daunt's foreman," proclaimed the light yet sullen voice.

"In future you take orders from me," I said evenly.

Sheedy brought his hand slap on the cloth.

"I take orders from William Daunt, and no one else."

"No one else?"

"No, by God! And that goes for others as well."

"Hold by that," I said agreeably. "You take orders from William Daunt only." I looked round slowly. "Any others of like mind?"

I got no answer, but two heads were hung. These lads were no tame serfs. They were not going to take sides as easily as that, I knew. Sheedy was not a character to win loyalty, and I doubted if William Daunt was.

I looked at the young woman. She came round to the corner of the table. Her face was flaming, and the light of battle was in her eyes. Murder! Was the young Amazon going to flare out at me? There was warmth in her fine voice.

"You don't know me, Masther Dave. Julie Brady's me auntie."

I put a hand flat out. "You were only that high," I said, "but you are Molly Cray. How are you Molly Bawn?"

I strode across to her and reached a hand. Her two hands

grasped mine and shook it with fierce loyalty. Her eyes were blazing behind unshed tears.

"Sir, oh sir! You are welcome. Ellen Furlong's darling son! Never you mind Bill Sheedy. Sure I'll wipe his mouth with the dish clout any time you want me."

She loosed my hand, stepped back and aside, put her fists on her hips, and her voice pealed richly.

"Out o' my kitchen, ye *bodachs!* Bogtrotters without manners, sittin' on yer hunkers and the young boss new home! Get out ye mongrel whelps. Get out I'm sayin', or I'll——"

They went, not in a panic, but sort of unhurriedly hurrying —seven of them and the dog, for something in Molly's voice sent the dog out with its tail between its legs.

Sheedy, the foreman, was of tougher metal. He would not be driven, to the loss of all face. He stayed in his chair, a solid bulk of man, his elbow on the table and back turned contemptuously. That was his mistake. For the young Amazon whipped the chair from under him, and he thumped solidly on the floor.

He was an active tough. He rebounded off the boards, turned at the same time, and his arm swung. It was an open-handed slap but wicked, and it smacked off Molly's rounded cheek, and sent her staggering.

Oh, damn! Molly you've done it. It's roughhouse now, and I'm in for a hiding.

But I did not hesitate. I hit him. I gave him all I had, with all the kick and steel I had in me: a swinging, shoulder-pivoted right to the jaw, and his head collided with the corner of the table as he went down. He rolled over, and the roll brought him to his feet in some sort of reflex action, and I smashed a savage left between his eyes. Maybe I was too savage, but I didn't think I could take Bill Sheedy so easily. For this time he rolled over on his face, and only came up to his hands and knees. I restrained a temptation to kick him towards the half-door, and I think he was expecting a root too.

"Get out!" I barked. "Out and take orders from William Daunt!"

He hadn't the final hardihood. He was on his feet, his back turned to me, and his hands up to his face. He stumbled for the half-door, where at least three heads were looking over. The door was opened for him, but before he disappeared he turned his head, his hand covering a bleeding nose.

"I'll hang for you yet, Daunt," he said shrilly.

I went back to Molly. Her eyes were batting and her hand was up to her cheek. I took the hand, and held it away. The livid palm mark was already turning red, and she would have quite a fair black eye by night time.

"Thank you, champ!" I said, "and sorry I wasn't quick enough." I patted her cheek softly, and kissed her under the eye.

"Oh God sir!" she said, shy for once, and drew away.

My left hand was stinging some, but my right hand was numb, and I began teasing sensation back into it. Molly dropped her shyness, took hold of my hand, and began softly massaging it.

"I don't want to use that medicine again, Molly," I said. "What about those boys?"

"Och sir! They'll ate out of your hand, and you after standing Bill Sheedy on his ear." She stepped back and swung a plump little fist. Her voice gloated. "Powders o' war! Such a wallop I never saw. Like the crack of a double-barrel gun, and Bill kicking his heels like a stuck pig, and the blood pumpin' out of his snout! Up David Daunt every whole time!"

Already Molly was adding trimmings. In a week my feat of derring-do would be Homeric.

"There's another Daunt too, Molly. William by name," I said. "Is he about?"

The very name sobered her. "He went into town early on, sir. But he'll be back. Ochone the day! He'll be back."

"He has a few things to say to me," I said.

Molly spread her palms sorrowfully. "Oh, sir, sir! You'll never be able to hold your own with him."

"No chance at all, Molly?"

"No, sir, not never!" She was very definite. "I know that you could break him in two with your bare hands, but what use is that, when he won't let it come to that. He'll twist and turn like a hare, and lead you on and on——" She pulled herself up. "But that's no way to talk, and he your——" She stopped again.

"Uncle and step-father," I finished for her. "You don't like him, Molly?"

"He'd gie me cause not to—if I let him," she said gloomily, and turned away to the kitchen sink.

"Cheer up, Molly Bawn!" I told her. "I know Uncle William is too smart for me, playing the game his way, so I'll not play the game his way."

"Play any way, and you'll need the mother o' God on your side."

"And my own mother, and good friends like Molly Cray," I said, and walked out.

III

I did not see Bill Sheedy any more that morning, and I thought it better to keep away from the farm activities. I went through the haggard, and found everything in perfect order. I stood in the mouth of the fold and looked over the cornfields. The oats were ripe for cutting, and the wheat was beginning to absorb the colour of the sun. The throb of a tractor came from round the curve. The harvest was at its beginning, and to-morrow I would begin to take my part in it. But that would depend. . . .

In half-an-hour I went back to the house from another angle, through a beech spinney, and by a side gate into the kitchen garden. And the kitchen garden was the one place that showed any neglect. Very few farmers pay any attention to the kitchen garden. It takes a suburbanite to maintain a rotation of vegetables and fruit for his household.

The farmer will indeed grow a plenitude of drumhead cabbages and late potatoes, and field carrots and swede turnips, and that's about all. He may have a drill or two of early potatoes in the kitchen garden, a cauliflower going to seed, a row of peas unstaked, but the delicate roots, like salsify, scorzonera, cardoon, are entirely absent.

It was that way with the kitchen-garden at Grianaan. The trees and bushes had not been pruned for years, and the fruit was small though plentiful. I had work in front of me this coming winter. I tried an Irish peach apple. It was juicy, but still too hard, so I threw it at a sparrow carelessly, and cursed myself for nearly hitting the little bird.

I did not go into the house by the backdoor. I did not go into the house at all. William Daunt might be in there, and I did not want to start anything indoors with my mother present. I went along the concrete yard, and into my Outside Room, and across to the window! I looked down across the lawn at the open gate, and I knew that my hour had come.

CHAPTER VII

NO PRINCE OF DENMARK

I

A brown station-wagon turned in at the gate and stopped. A man got out. He was tall and supple and lean in dark blue uniform, and I knew him for Joseph Yoseph, the guard of Jewish blood. The wagon came up the drive slowly.

I straightened my shoulders, drew in a long breath, and, again, my heart hollowed out emptily. I could wait in here in my own room? No, I could not. Out there was an opportunity and a situation made for me, and I must take advantage of them now or never. I shoved my silk shirt into the top of my pants, like a man preparing for action, but I went out to keep the peace—my peace.

I went quickly round the corner, and then walked slowly along the front of the house. I mounted to the second wide thread of the door steps, and turned round. But, before turning round, I glanced up at the window left of the door. A curtain had moved there yesterday, and a curtain moved there to-day. I lifted a warning finger, and the curtain was still. Then I turned round, and planted my feet firmly. This was my chosen stand for peace—or war. And my thudding heart might as well take it easy.

The station-wagon stopped well out on the gravel. William Daunt was at the driving wheel, and he had a passenger.

"How he got in I know not," I said, "but he'll never get out, and he can dam' well stick."

The passenger was Superintendent Jerome Farley. But he did get out. He was out before my uncle, and he got out without a wriggle, easy as a greased hog. He came round the

101

bonnet of the car, and his lazy brown eyes looked me up and down out of a massive face as placid as Buddha's. Buddha! that was it. And the black helmet of hair coming to a point on his forehead was strangely foreign. His voice was slow and casual.

"A nice brand of tailoring in Southland Jail! A bit behind the times!"

He had a good tailor himself. His suit fitted the great curves of him, but no seam strained anywhere. I would not bandy words with him. I knew why he was here. He had got my message from Tade Murphy, and had come along to see how I kept the peace. I hoped to show him.

William Daunt was out of the car now. He was not a small man, but Farley would have made two of him, and a bit of a third. My uncle took off a white panama hat, flapped it against a thick leg, and threw it back into the car with an easy, confident gesture. His bald dome, his fringe of blond hair, his mild brown eyes, his smooth, round-chinned face made him as benevolent-seeming as Satan on a job of ticklish tempting. He touched Farley familiarly on the sleeve.

"Come up to my room Jerome," he invited, "and let's talk this over with David."

"Wait!" I lifted my hand, but not my voice. "I have not yet invited Superintendent Farley into my house."

"What is that?" said my uncle astonishedly.

"You heard me."

"Nonsense, boy!" His voice had a brushing-aside tone. "Come along Jerome!"

He took a step forward, but Farley's hand and voice stopped him.

"This is not as easy as you think, William. Pause for a moment!"

My uncle's toe tapped the ground impatiently, but he did not move forward. Farley looked up at me, his face immobile, and his voice had no trace of feeling, one way or another.

"If needs be I can enter any house. On this occasion I await your invitation, Mr. David Daunt. Well?"

"It is my house?"

"It is your house."

"Then I cannot conceive any occasion on which I would invite you into any house of mine." That was meant to give it him between the eyes, but, reading it over, it sounds more than a little pompous.

"Good Heavens!" exploded my uncle. "I will not stand for this! I'll teach you manners, you young puppy!"

I am old for a pup, but I probably had no manners. That was good enough for William Daunt. He would try everything once. If he could overbear me now he could overbear me later and for always. He put a foot on the bottom step and threw a hand up and forward to brush me aside as if I were of no weight bodily or mentally. I waited till his hand touched my shoulder, and, then, I had his wrist with a snap that jerked his hand back. He swung his other hand at me, and I had that wrist too.

I gripped with all my might, only that, and nothing more. And I surely could grip. I felt the sinews ridge on my forearms. He had a thin skin and pampered flesh, and a grip like that can be paralysing. I hurt him. I saw his face wince and wince, as I applied pressure. He made one effort to wrest his wrists free, a weak effort because it only made the hurt intense. He tried to force me back by weight of body, but I was above him and firmly braced, and I brought his arms down across his body. He was helpless then; and I could have forced him to his knees. I didn't.

His face was below mine, and I could have bitten his nose off, but I repressed the urchin in me, held him helpless, and looked over his head at Superintendent Farley.

Farley had come up behind my uncle, but made no move to interfere. His inaction surprised me. And, then, he did something that surprised me more. He was looking up at the window left of the door, and he lifted a hand waist high, and shuttled it rapidly back and forth. There was no mistaking that gesture. It was a warning to someone to stay put.

I clamped my teeth shut on words that I wanted to say to

William Daunt, and acted, using all the force I had in reserve.

"Over to you, Mr. Policeman!" I said, and heaved my uncle up and back.

And the policeman retrieved him neatly and resiliently, stood him safely on his feet, and patted his shoulder.

"Take it easy now, William!" he advised mildly.

But my Uncle William was not inclined to take it easy. He held his wrists up, and looked at them. He blinked his eyes and looked at them again. No, they were not crushed into a pulp. Then he started massaging them wincingly, one over the other, and turned his head to Farley.

"Did you see that, Superintendent?" His voice shrilled. "He assaulted me. Look! that wrist is out of joint. You saw it—he assaulted me."

"The invitation was obvious," said the policeman calmly, and again patted Daunt's shoulder placatingly. "Don't put yourself in the wrong William. Whatever you do, don't put yourself in the wrong—you don't usually."

I could claim that I was the assaulted party. Farley had given me an opening to make that claim—so I didn't. I would wait for my uncle's next move.

He went on massaging his wrists, but his mind was working. His thinking machine wouldn't stay long off balance.

"But what am I to do?" he said petulantly. "He is keeping me out of my own house."

It was not his own house, but I would not open on that yet.

"He is keeping me out," said Farley, "and I do not choose to claim any right. I, certainly, cannot force an entrance."

"But then——"

"But then you are at liberty to say what you have to say right here, if you want me for witness."

The massaging motion slowed and stopped. Dominant methods having failed for the time, William Daunt would try on another tack.

"The boy is making things difficult," he complained with dignity, "but I suppose one must make allowances."

"Just a moment, Superintendent," I called. "Did my uncle bring you here as a witness?"

"He did, young man—a witness to a very reasonable proposal."

"Can I have you for a witness too?"

"A witness to what?"

"To a proposal of my own, and I don't care a cuss whether it is reasonable or not."

"I will listen to you at least," said the policeman.

"Fair enough! Let dishonourable—no, not that word— let dishonoured age begin."

"There you are, Superintendent!" cried William Daunt, almost triumphantly, and moved an emphatic hand. "You can see his attitude? I told you how impossible it would be for me to live under the same roof as this young man. Impossible!"

"Difficult at least," the Superintendent half-agreed.

"Well then!" said my uncle smartly. "Let us, if we can, avoid the difficulty or the impossibility. I am agreeable." He took two short quick strides away, and turned to face Farley. He would address his witness, and ignore me for the time. And his witness—as solidly planted as if he were squatting, touched his fingertips together on the curve of his abdomen, and listened in immobility. My uncle was completely reasonable, but allowed, just allowed, a trace of indignation to creep in at times.

"As I told you, Superintendent, I still hold that he should not have returned here to the scene of his crime. Good heavens! how could he? And there was no need. My wife and I could and would give him all the assistance he needed —or demanded——"

"There is that matter of his parole," murmured the god.

"Yes, I admit that." If possible he was more reasonable than ever. "Perhaps—I will admit it—I spoke over-hurriedly last evening. The shock, the rousing of bitter memories—

never mind! I reconsidered the whole situation in the long hours of the night. After all it was only natural that David should come here in the first instance. And being here he should be given time to decide where his new life might lie. But, and surely this is reasonable, being in this place of fatality, he should live a retired life. And with you to witness, Superintendent, I now offer him that retired life for as long as he likes."

"You have Beananaar in your mind," I said.

He faced me then, tapped forefinger in palm, and there was a satisfied note in his voice. "Exactly! Beananaar, and it was in your mind too. Where else can you live so quietly, and be in your own homeland? It is on its own road, and off the beaten track. My stepson, Charles Cashan, lives there alone, and he is completely under your hand. Fishing, shooting, an open-air life, and you can restore the tillage if you want to farm. That is my proposal and my offer, and I call on Superintendent Farley to witness it."

"I witness it," said Superintendent Farley, and added, "and a fairer offer I never heard."

Did that colossus know that I would hate to consider favourably any offer approved by him?

But, indeed, when all was said and done, it was a supremely fair offer. It promised me nearly everything I wanted. It would be easy to live with and rule Charley Cashan—and there was the third member of the team too! But no! that was beyond realization. Forget it! And yet, the prospect of life at Beananaar had the charm of an ideal. I might get completely attached to it, attached enough to agree to the breaking of the entail at Grianaan in exchange for Beananaar. And then William Daunt, a hale man still, would have the coveted place securely in his hands. And my mother! What about my lovely mother?'

My uncle was watching me benevolently. I took the stride down to the bottom step, and lifted a finger at him."

"Would you let my mother live with me at Beananaar?"

For the first time I saw the gleam of victory in his eye,

before he looked away from me. I was manageable after all, and I was now delivering myself into his hands. His eyes sought the ground, and his hand came up to smooth his round chin.

"This is very difficult." He spoke out of deep consideration. "This demands a sacrifice I never contemplated. Well! if a sacrifice has to be made for the sake of peace—peace but what a price! Yet she is his mother—and I only a mere husband." He lifted his eyes then. "Yes, your mother will live with you at Beananaar."

"And Superintendent Farley is witness to that?" I asked.

"I have heard you both," Jerome Farley said, and then his voice harshened for the first time. It is from that moment that my opinion of him began to change. He said: "It is a colossal impertinence that ye two would seek to make a chattel of Ellen Furlong."

"You mistake me Superintendent," William Daunt hastened to disclaim. "My wife is free to make her own choice. I meant nothing else. She is absolutely free to choose Grianann or choose Beananaar." He knew that she would choose as I chose.

I was tired of this bandying, and it was time I finished it. I put my hands behind my back, and lifted and sank on my heels like a serious young man.

"The issue is a simple one," I said impersonally. "William Daunt and David Daunt cannot live under the same roof. That is accepted by both. Then one of them must leave. I speak for Ellen Daunt. As is her right, she will live here at Grianaan, and her son David will live with her. William Daunt goes to Beananaar."

There! it was said now, and I would have to make it stick.

William Daunt couldn't believe his ears. He reared up.

"What nonsense is this?" he demanded.

"Let me be fair," I said, and I fear I was mimicking his reasonableness. "I cannot compel you to live at Beananaar.

You can live any dam' place you like, but not at Grianaan—not for one other day."

He turned with spread hands. "Superintendent Farley, will you please tell this fool—this madman—that he cannot do this."

Farley was looking down towards his toes, but I doubt if he could see them. Below the wedge of his nose I could see that his rather shapely pig's mouth was twitching. But, when he lifted his head, his face was again immobile. He pointed a hand at me.

"Let us get this clearly," he said slowly. "Are you, David Daunt, ordering this man, William Daunt, off these premises?"

"Thank you, sir!" I said. "Here and now I am ordering William Daunt off my premises."

He swung a hand widely. "Before coming to this outrageous decision did you look around you?"

"And before and after as well."

"Did you notice that you have returned to a prosperous and well-managed farm?"

"Did you notice a herd of Friesians that never milked a four per cent butter-fat," I gave back. "Have you seen the kitchen garden?—it's bloody."

"Lord, boy! have you no scrap of gratitude in your make-up?"

"Dam' the scrap! I am ordering my blood-uncle out of Grianaan, and I'll make it stick." In turn I pointed a hand at him. "I order him off this very minute, and I call upon you, as guardian of the peace, to assist me."

"Assist you?"

"Why not? You talk mightily about *your* peace. Look after your peace then. I order that man off, and if you don't put him off, I will, and to hell with your peace!"

"Man, man, yer a bonnie fichter!" said Jerome Farley softly.

My uncle shook his hands desperately, and the culture was no longer in his voice. "There it is Superintendent! He has threatened the peace. A threat from a man on Ticket-of-Leave! Put him back where he belongs—or my life is not safe."

"Don't worry! the peace will be kept," said the guardian-thereof easily, "and there is only one way to keep it at this juncture." He turned and took hold of my uncle's arm confidentially but firmly, and for a moment I thought they would come at me together. But no. "Don't forget yourself William," Farley said placatingly. "Remember your dignity! This nephew of yours is overbearing, but he raises a legal point that is beyond me. The peace is my concern, and to keep it you must go."

"Go!" said my uncle faintly.

"Yes! go and see your solicitor, and see him at once. That is the only course in face of this ultimatum."

"What an abominable situation!" said my uncle helplessly. He was completely deflated: he had had victory in his grasp, and, suddenly, it had been changed into defeat, and he simply could not understand how that had happened. And he was given no time to get his second wind.

Jerome Farley, still holding his arm, turned him about, walked him across the gravel and opened the door of the car. William Daunt got in blindly, so blindly that he sat on his fine panama hat.

Jerome Farley held the door open, and beckoned a finger, I turned to look. The Guard, Joseph, had come up the drive in case his officer needed him. He had waited at the grass margin not twenty yards away, had probably heard a good deal, and now came promptly to the beckoning finger.

"Joseph?"

"Yes, Super!"

"Words of not more than two syllables! Mr. William Daunt is leaving now, and the peace must not be broken. He will not come in that gate down there until further notice from me. Got it?"

"Until further notice! I got it, sir, and two syllables is right."

The car-door banged, but the car did not move for half-a-minute. Then the starter purred, gears clashed, and gravel spurted. The car swerved round, got two wheels over the grass-edging, straightened out, and streaked down the drive.

"Cripes! he'll never make the turn," said Joseph, "but, sure, if he takes the ditch to the river what harm?" But he made the turn safely, and turned left on the road to Kantwell.

Jerome Farley turned back to me, and moved a deploring head.

"Thanks for your assistance, Superintendent," I said genially.

"Blast your eyes! I won't be so soft when you come up for the second round."

"Soft, your grandmother!" I said rudely.

Someone chuckled softly at the head of the steps.

II

My tall mother, in her black and white, was standing up there. She stood poised, one foot forward, and if she took another step she would fly like a winged victory. There was a spot of colour on each cheekbone, and her eyes were shining, and pride was in her voice.

"I have got me a son, Jerome Farley. Haven't I got a son, Jerome?"

"God knows, no one will steal him from you," said Jerome Farley.

"David?"

"Yes ma'am!"

"You will do me a favour?"

"I will buy it, ma'am."

"You will invite Jerome Farley into your house?"

I did not even hesitate. I stepped aside, bowed, and my hand invited. "The inconceivable occasion, Mr. Farley!" I murmured.

"It was just round the corner," he murmured back, touched a finger on my shoulder, and went up the steps as if he were made of rubber. My mother took his arm with extraordinary familiarity, and they went into the hall, and through the door to the sitting-room on the left. I looked after them dumbly, and shook an uncomprehending head.

"They know each other this long while," said Joseph Yoseph behind me.

I turned round and looked at the long, lean, supple man. Now, that I had been told, I could recognize the Israel strain in him. He was the high-nosed, strong-jawed, indestructible type that can claim to be salt of the earth. Sometimes it lacks a sense of humour.

I found that I was shaking a little. I had been under a strain again, and though I had carried off things boldly and high-handedly—too high-handedly perhaps—my nerves were twittering like strings. There was one way to loose the tension. I pointed finger at the guard.

"Bad news for you, Joseph."

"Me, sir?"

"You, sir. Tade Murphy is talking of a libel action."

"That fella?" Joseph was derisive.

"He says he doesn't deal from the bottom of the pack."

"Why else is he teaching me the knack of it this past week?"

"Why, indeed?"

And then Joseph laughed. "Och! it's only a bar of fun between myself and Tade. But mind you, I can play forty-ones with the best of them."

"A fatal illusion, my friend! Look! I'm in to rescue my mother. You slip round and see Julie Brady. I haven't organized my resources yet, but Julie might have something behind her hand."

"I was thinkin' the same, sir," said Joseph, grinning. His eyes lit up. "And a bit of repartee with Molly Cray—she's a devil for fun."

"Ware the Gentile maiden, Joseph!"

"That's the worst of it, sir," he said, and scratched his poll. He leant forward and looked into my eyes, and his aquiline face softened. "God ha' mercy! if I stood in your place I wouldn't have a whip or a lash left in me."

"You would, brother. It is in your breed."

I turned away and went heavily up the steps, and there wasn't a whip or a lash in me any more.

I found Jerome Farley occupying the big couch at right-angles to the far window—the only seat that would accommodate him. My mother was alean in the embrasure, and she was being talked to amiably. But I could not be sure. His voice was usually amiable, but his subject matter. Oh, hell!

She reached a hand towards me. I went across to her side, put an arm through hers, and felt her possessive pressure. I wasn't yet ready to talk of anything that had happened, so I said:

"Not much of a hostess, Ellen Furlong!"

"You tell me, Daveen?"

"A mellow brown sherry for Superintendent Farley—his favourite tipple."

"I know what he likes, the poor man," my mother said. "Julie had the kettle boiling ten minutes ago. Ah, here she comes!"

There was a rattle at the side-door, and Julie came in trundling ahead of her a trolley, or a dumb waiter, or whatever it is called. It held a teapot under a cosy, one big cup and two smaller ones, a cream ewer, a hot-water jug, a sugar basin, and an enormous slab of the fruitiest fruit-cake ever made—Julie's own specialty. Fifteen, twenty years ago I might gorge on a cake like that—and often had. But who wanted to eat fruitcake at ten o'clock on a Friday morning?

"That's my fine girl!" said Jerome Farley, and he was purring. "And I've a nice job waiting for you too."

"Me, sir?"

"Yes. You're next to be warned off."

Julie leant towards me, and there was gentle mockery in

her eyes and voice. "Would he, Mr. Farley? You'd think butter wouldn't melt in his mouth, but isn't he the dangerous man entirely, entirely?" The bell in her throat vibrated.

"At what window were you listening, Julie Brady?" I asked accusingly.

She bridled. "Me listenin'! Would I do the likes o' that? But haven't I ears in my head? Will I pour ma'am?"

"You will not. Go and watch another policeman!"

"I'll watch Molly Cray, whatever," said Julie, and trotted for the door.

"Did Michael Paddian bring that salmon?" my mother called after her.

"He did so ma'am. A peel—five pounds."

"Salmon, did you say?" said the policeman. "No salmon has come out of the Doorn for three weeks—not honestly by Michael Paddian."

"The Galey River it was," said my mother, and lifted the cosy. I knew that big brown teapot. I had known it all my life, and it must have brewed puncheons of tea. I suppose it was the slacking strain that made my eyes sting, but it is the little things that touch a cord.

I was thirsty again, and drank two cups of tea, well-watered and without cream. Farley drank three large cups, two spoons of sugar to each, and a half-inch of cream on top. And he ate every scrap of that rich cake, daintily, without dropping a crumb. My mother drank tea too, but women will drink tea at any hour of the day or night.

There was talk, but I only listened. And it was the talk of auld acquaintance. Ellen Furlong and Jerome Farley were as chalk and cheese, yet there seemed to be an easy friend-ship between them. I tried to understand it. If he had been researching into our tragedy, he would certainly have approached my mother, and, formidable that he was, he would have got everything out of her. That was not a great deal, but he would have got her views, her feelings, her hopes, her grief, the whole panorama of the life we had led. And so he would come to know about Jean Harrington and me, and draw a certain conclusion. In that way he might get friendly with my mother, who was too fine in herself to mistrust people. It was that fineness that had blinded her to the character of William Daunt until too late.

She was excited and excitable this morning. She moved about the room touching things here and there as if she had a new affection for them. Once she did a little side-step of a dance.

Jerome Farley swallowed a wedge of cake, and reprimanded her mildly. "Don't be licking your chops, ma'am."

"I am, am I not? And why not? The good times are coming again to Grianaan."

"And maybe not so good a time down the line."

"Let it!" She would not be depressed. "It will only make the good times better. My son and Grianaan against the world!"

"You were listening, my lady. He nearly jumped at the offer of Beananaar."

"And you spurred him over that, Jerome dear."

"Ay faith!" The big man chuckled. "He took the bit after that." He poured some more tea, and seemed to be ruminating to himself. "There's another thing. What is it now? There's a long legal name for it. Restitution——"

"Oh! Restitution of conjugal rights?" She stopped in front of him. "He hasn't any. He can't have—not after giving me choice."

"He might plead that your son tricked him—and so he did."

She turned to me confidently. "You wouldn't let him, David?"

"Cut his throat back and front, I would," I told her.

"Ah! that reminds me." She went to the mantelpiece, took something from it, and brought it across. "Is that what you'd do it with?"

I took it from her. It was a good-class, boy scout's knife in a leather sheath, with a studded strap across the hilt. I unsheathed it. It was Sheffield steel: a short curved blade, a sharp point, and keen cutting edge. It would cut a throat or pierce a wame easy as winking. A drawing of a skull and crossbones had been scratched on the black hilt.

"Thank you, old woman!" I said easily.

"Where'd you drop it?" Farley asked softly.

"In his room—the bed valance hid it," my mother told him.

"Let me have a look at it?" He reached his hand casually.

I gave it him. I could do nothing else. He examined it indifferently, sheathed it, held it negligently between his knees and went on talking. When my mother was not looking he slipped it into his side pocket. I knew all about that knife, and I knew that it had no sinister meaning. But if Jerome Farley was barking up that tree, it was as good a wrong try as any to bark up.

My mother did not notice where the knife had gone to, and she had not time to say any more on the subject, for it was then that a clamour broke out in the passage to the kitchen. There were two women's voices, one commanding, one protesting. The door flung open.

Julie Brady came in sideways, and, with the energy of a terrier, she was hauling along her niece, Molly Cray; and Molly, a hand covering cheek and eye, was protesting that it was nothing at all—just nothing at all.

The Superintendent was lightly on his feet. Julie pushed Molly in front of him, and knocked the shielding hand away.

"Take a look at that, Mr. Sooper!" she cried triumphantly. "Wasn't that an unmerciful belt to hit an innocent slob of a girl?"

The Sooper took Molly's chin delicately in finger and thumb, and tilted her head. Her left cheek was inflamed, and the eye above it was turning nicely purple.

"I am to blame for that," I said from the window, and my mother turned towards me in a startled sort of way.

Molly noticed that startle. She drew her head away from the holding fingers, and turned to my mother eagerly.

"No, no, ma'am! Master Dave had nothing at all to do

with it. He was only lookin' on. It was the way I landed Bill
Sheedy on the floor for his bad manners, and he up and gave
me a sidewinder of a slap for I thank you. And, then,
Master Dave——" she stopped. Molly would not implicate
me in this at all.

"A nice, hefty I thank you," said the Superintendent
gravely. "And how were you to blame, Mr. David Daunt?"

"I was too slow," I said. "I gave Bill a bit of a push, but
the harm was done."

That was too much for Molly. She gurgled and choked,
and found her breath again. "That's right, sir! Just a small
bit of a push, and Bill's nose spoutin' blood, and if he hasn't
a lump on his poll he'll have a hollow."

"Some push surely!" said the Superintendent. "What do
you want me to do, Julie?"

"A month in jail would barely dissatisfy me," Julie
claimed.

My mother put an arm round her. "No, Julie, no! You'd
be shamed for ever."

"Would I ma'am?" said the trusting Julia.

"You would, darling. You know Molly? No man is safe
from her."

"Divil the wan!" agreed Molly's aunt.

"And she began it."

"Maybe a wallop was coming to her all right then. Look
at her now making for the door! an' the Jew lad in the
kitchen for a bit of fun. I'll put a stop to that, whatever."

The door banged behind the two, and Farley turned to
me.

"Care to amplify this tangle with Sheedy?"

There was no reason why I should not. I amplified. And
my mother's shoulder snuggled into me.

"Stop oozing pride, Ellen Furlong!" he chided, and
ruminated, head down. "I see! Sheedy will take orders from
William Daunt only, and that cooks Sheedy's goose. Two
birds with one stone this morning, and I believe the young
hellion lined them up for a cockshy!" He lifted his head.

"Keep out of this now! I'll get Joseph to chase Sheedy off the premises."

"Isn't your clothes-pole undergunned for Sheedy?"

"Not that you'd notice. The best light-heavy in the Garda team."

"Poor Bill Sheedy!" I said. "He is loyal at least."

"Yes, he'll take orders from William Daunt." He thrust forward his head. "And what orders will William Daunt give him?"

I shrugged my shoulders. "Uncle William is only a lath painted to look like iron," I said.

"Maybe so! But Bill Sheedy is not." He saw that my mother was troubled. "Sorry, Ellen! I only want to caution you that this thing is not finished. William Daunt wants Grianaan more than anything else in the world, and he'll try again—through another agent. Carry on! I'll be seeing ye." He brushed imaginary crumbs off his vest and padded lightly for the door. There he turned and nodded. "You'll have another visitor this afternoon, I'll bet a hat."

I saw him off from the front steps. He never looked back. Joseph Yoseph joined him from the corner of the house, and the big man took his arm, and moved a hand as he talked.

For half-a-minute I was easier in my mind about Jerome Farley, and then I was not. He was on my mother's side as regards William Daunt, and, necessarily, on my side. But after that! Damn him! Could he not let the dead past bury its dead? Or did he want the graves to yawn again? Or did I? That was my trouble. Did I?

CHAPTER VIII

A QUIET AFTERNOON

I

Jerome Farley was only half-right. Not one visitor, but two, came to see me that afternoon, and both were sent by William Daunt. Well, perhaps the second was not sent, but he came on information received.

My first visitor was Charley Cashan, but I was half-expecting him. He came not long after our midday meal, when I was comatose after stowing away too much grilse—or peel as we call it in the south. Julie Brady—my mother couldn't cook for tuppence—had her own way of cooking salmon. She skinned it, boned it, and stewed it in chunks in a bastable oven—or some similar receptacle in the bowels of the patent cooker—with butter, thick cream and onions. A couple of platefuls of that, and you were tied to the ground.

I was sitting at the desk in my Outside Room, leaning on my elbows, my glazing eyes looking sleepily down at the Doorn River wimpling between its green banks, and I had about decided to take forty winks on the old bed-couch behind the door. And, then, a pony and governess cart turned in at the gate, and came tacking up the drive at—yes—a snail's pace.

I knew cart and pony. The cart had once been a gallant vehicle of varnished oak-and-elm panels, with red-leather upholstery. But the varnish had faded to a grey-brown, and there was no upholstery at all. The harness brasses were green with verdigris, instead of a bridle there was a donkey's winkers, and the reins were a hempen hay rope. The yellow—almost white—pony had come out of Connemara, which betokens a sound breed, but it was about as old as the cart, and as fat as a dairyman's pup. I remembered it well, and many a time it had scraped me off under a whitethorn bush. Charley Cashan sat far back in the cart, so that the shafts sloped steeply upwards.

Pony and trap drifted round to the gravel front and anchored. Charley saw me through the open wing of the casement, and shook a fist threateningly. He got over the back door with an awkward swing of the legs, went to the pony's head, removed the winkers, and hung them on the hames. He addressed the pony with courtesy.

"You will nibble along the edges, Dandy boy. If you get a wheel over you'll upset, and that won't be nice for you and the offshaft broke in two places already. Mind I told you, now."

And as sure as I'm writing this down Dandy moved his head affirmatively. That was Charley's way with animals.

The pony slanted towards the grass edging, and Charley ambled round by the end of the annex. I didn't move. I heard him come in at the door, shuffle across the matting, and pull the windsor chair round to the desk-end. He did not give the customary valediction, and I did not look up. I said:

"A hell of an hour for a visit! What do you want?"

Out of the tail of an eye I saw him thrust his long jaw at me. "I want to cut your bloody throat for a start."

I moved a finger. "You can't—not any more. What'll you cut it with?"

He got that at once. The imitation savagery was out of his voice.

"Ah! did you find it yourself, Dave?"

I looked at him then: his long face, always pallid, his pale eyes, his clean-shaven jaw. He would not shave at all but for Jean Harrington who would not have frowsiness in her vicinity. He was still the Charley I knew nine years ago: a man of simple guile.

"What did I find myself?" I asked him.

"My snickersnee. You know? The bowie knife I brought back from foreign parts. I skinned eleventeen mules with it once one time in Idaho."

"You did not. You lifted it out of a boy scouts' camp at Bangor in the County Down. That was the original story. And you have never skinned anything with it, not even a rabbit. You'd have to kill one first."

"All right so! Where did you find it?"

"Under my bed. Were you out to cut my throat?"

"I would have, too," he said feelingly, "if I knew the way you were going to saddle me with ould William."

"What did ould William tell you?" I asked curiously.

"That he would be staying a few days at Beananaar to let you get eased in at Grianaan. Not for a moment——"

"A few days is right," I stopped him, and nodded towards the nibbling pony. "What's the chariot for?"

"He wouldn't give me the station-wagon."

"Wise man! It belongs to Grianaan, and I'll impound it first chance I get. Well, what do you want?"

"The ould fellow sent me over for a few of his things, such as——"

"Then you needed the station-wagon."

"He only needs his shaving tackle and a change or two. Look, Dave, wouldn't you take him for a dandy anywhere?"

"A very presentable man."

"And do you know, he still wears a nightshirt."

"What do you wear?"

"Nothing, me son! Me plain naked hide. But a nightshirt!"

"I wore a nightshirt for nine years. That's why I couldn't sleep last night; the pyjama pants kept slipping up my legs." I got to my feet and yawned. "Come along, and manhandle that shaving tackle!"

I led him round to the door of the basement by the side of the front steps. The door was open, and Charley had one look through, and swore wholeheartedly.

"Holy Saint Peter and the cock that crew! Are you sequesterin' him forever and a day?"

"And a day more. Take hold!"

For a couple of hours before lunch, Julie Brady and my-self, aided by Molly Cray, and directed by my mother, had collected every article not too remotely belonging to William Daunt. They tightly filled two ancient, humped steamer trunks, a hide case, and a travelling bag. I did not mind the old trunks but I objected to parting with the case and bag, until my mother assured me that they were really my uncle's.

Charley, sullen for once, helped me to manhandle the trunks and stow them crosswise on the seats of the trap. We piled bag and case on top, and there was no room for Charley anywhere. He was beginning to understand the situation now, and it brought a groan from the depth of his diaphragm. He came round to my side.

"Have you thrun him out for good, Dave?"

"Had to. I couldn't live under the same roof."

"And what about me? I can't either." He shook his head dolefully. "I can't any more. I got set in my ways, and I'll not share Beananaar with anyone."

"You'll just have to," I said heartlessly.

"Oh, yes! Charley Cashan must do as he's told. Very well so!" He reached a hand. "Give me back my stickeroo, and I'll skin a buck rabbit at the end of me tether."

"Let me know when," I said, and knocked his hand away.

He thrust his long head at me. "Blast you Dave Daunt! Couldn't you and Jean heal that dam' breach, and then I could have the Cottage back to meself."

"Go to hell, you fathead!" I told him.

"A nice, easy, downhill road! I'm on me way," said Charley heavily.

He did not trouble to replace the winkers where they be-longed, but took hold of the pony's top knot, and the two went meandering down the drive, both of them braking back against the slope—a matched team, and patient. But I did not know where the biped's patience might end.

II

It was well on in the afternoon when my second visitor arrived.

I had had a cup of hot tea, and it waked me up. I was sitting at this desk, and this big stationery book lay open on the desk under my eyes. Every page of it was blank then, and at this moment I have filled close on seventy pages with pencilled script. How many more may I fill? I don't know, I don't care; I've got into the rhythm of the blame thing.

I knew that my scars would not heal too easily; I knew that I would have long nights before me; I knew that many nights I would not sleep at all. It would be a good thing to have something to do to while away the time. I could not hope to bury the past, to ignore it, to smother it. It would only ferment and boil, and shrivel the soul in me. Let it be brought out into the open and examined, and let the winds of reason blow away the miasma that were always lurking.

First, I thought I would go back ten years, and slay the tragedy by chronicling it. No, that would not do! I would have to put things down on paper, that I would not want anyone to know, and no manuscript is a safe repository. Would I write of my nine years in jail, and of the great Michael Ambrose, who would come to live with me on his retiral in two years' time. That could wait too. Things had happened in the last twenty hours, and things might happen in the next twenty. Jerome Farley's movements and precautions had disturbed me, and he had implied that we were only at the beginning of things. Very well, then! I would put everything down from the time I got off the train at Kantwell station, and I would try to set it down honestly, without attempting polish or trying for effects. But, no doubt, I'll try for polish and tricks like every rogue of a writer. Some day, what I write may be of interest to—well to someone.

I stopped doodling on the left-hand page, and wondered how I would begin. And this is the way I began:

"I am writing this down in my Outside Room at Grianaan Farm near Kantwell-under-the-Hill, and I will keep on writing for three years——"

Three years! How sanguine I was! It might not be three months, three weeks, three days! How would I go on? I lifted head to consider, and there was a man in a dark suit walking up the drive, briskly, firmly, purposefully.

At first I thought he was one of Farley's policemen. Then I saw that his suit was not navy-blue, but black, and, then, the white band at his neck showed that he was a clergyman. A clergyman of serious intent, coming forthright on a serious errand. He was probably the Parish Priest of Kantwell, and, so, my parish priest—and William Daunt's.

William Daunt would, of course, be a leading parishioner, and a pastor of a flock naturally listens to a leading parishioner, and might be inclined to bring certain diffi-culties within the scope of faith and morals in favour of his parishioner. I would soon know.

I assumed more than I should. I assumed that this clergy-man was coming to see me at my uncle's request, and that he would take my uncle's side against me. Then I was in for battle, and so was he, by gosh!

I wondered why he came on foot, for surely he would own a car, and an elegant one. Or was this characteristic of the man: a brisk walk, with a cool mind, while an ultimatum was being cogitated. I would soon know.

He came briskly to the gravel curve, and was about to pass on to the front door when he saw me through the win-dow. He paused, hesitated, and lifted a finger briefly. And I was on my feet, made a tentative inflection, and gestured a hand invitingly. At once he pivoted and came firmstrided for the end of the house.

"Trapped, Daunt you devil!" I said. "That man's first word will be a chastening one."

I met him at the door. And at once I realized that he was

a man of cool—almost cold—dignity. He stood in the door-way and looked me up and down, and he took his time to it. Was he looking for the evil in me? I was, indeed, washed and shaven and shorn, and cleanly clad, but the prison pallor would still be showing. I was a Daunt and a Furlong —the best and worst blood in Irmond: saturnine, aquiline, dark-eyed, maybe deadly. Was he considering how to handle me: with a velvet glove, and iron hand under it?

I looked him over too. He was as tall as I was, but more strongly built. His clerical coat, rather long, was beautifully cut, and fitted his broad shoulders smoothly. He would have played an adequate game of football in his student days. He had a handsome, aristocratic, strong-nosed, longish face, that showed no signs of good and high living, and many celibate faces do show these signs. His eyebrows were black and strongly marked—almost shaggy— and the eyes below them were cool and blue and deep. This was surely a man of strong convictions, and he was of a calling that would insist on lesser men conforming to these convictions. God help poor David Daunt!

His voice was strong but modulated, and there was no trace of brogue. Probably he had been educated and ordained in Rome. He looked young for a parish priest, and, perhaps, he was only a curate. Nine years ago the old parish priest was over eighty. That man I knew well, and he knew me. This man did not know me, and I did not know him, but already I was forming preconceived notions of him.

"I am Eugene Connell, the Parish Priest of Kantwell. You are young David Daunt?"

Though he had no brogue he pronounced Eugene as we do in the south: Eujun.

"Not so young." I said. "Will you come in Father Connell?"

"Thank you, I will." He did not offer me his hand, and I at once misread that. As host, I should have offered mine.

I moved backwards into the room, and he followed, shoulders held stiffly. He looked round him, placed a shapely, stiff-brimmed black hat carefully on the couch, and looked round him again. With his hat off he looked older, for his hair retreated from his temples and was thin and grizzled, in contrast to his bushy black brows.

"A pleasant, workmanlike room," he said. "I have not been in it before."

He would not. The best parlor for him. And, then, he said:

"Your dear mother would not permit anyone inside that door until you were home again."

"It is what my mother would do," I said and swallowed pride. "Will you be seated, Father?" I moved a hand towards a leather chair.

He took it, but sat upright, hands over knees, and, if he were of another cloth, I would have said that he was not at all sure of himself. I pulled my desk chair round so that I nearly faced him. Ordinarily I would have offered him a cigarette and smoked one, but the thought did not enter my head. I was too watchful; cool enough, but wary. I waited. Was he hesitating for words or choosing them? At last he said:

"I should not have embarrassed you with such an early visit, but I felt that I had to come." He seemed to be the embarrassed one. That was natural enough in a man of culture faced with a difficult interview, with, probably, an ultimatum at the end of it.

Very well! I would take the bull by the horns, by forcing him to show his attitude right off. I said:

"William Daunt sent you, Father Connell?"

"No sir!" His shoulders stiffened, and he was on the point of bridling. Then he smiled faintly. "Your uncle did, indeed, speak to me at some length. It was only then that I learned of your homecoming. On my way out here I met Superintendent Farley. I rather think he waylaid me, and he talked too."

"Then you know all about me," I said drily.

He moved his head negatively. "As little as they do. What I want you to know is that I am here of my own volition as a priest, as the priest of this parish doing his duty as he sees it, God aiding."

This was a formidable man, stronger than William Daunt, able to meet Jerome Farley on his own ground. His God might be a stern God, but just. And he might assume that his God would think as he thought—all the fanatics do that. He would weigh me in the balance and find me wanting. Fair enough! Let him have the full indictment in his mind before he pronounced sentence and I spurned it. I put a hand up and forward to hold his attention, and I tried to keep all bitterness out of my voice.

"Before you do your duty, as you see it, priest of the parish, I want you to know where I stand, where I must stand. Wait please! I have served nine years of a twelve years sentence for killing a man, and I have to spend the remaining three years on parole. I must be careful. I must be law abiding. It is so very easy to put a ticket-o'-leave man back into jail! You could do it yourself at the wind of a word."

"God forbid!" said the priest.

"I was not careful this morning, Father," I went on, "and I doubt if I was law abiding. My uncle, William Daunt, insisted that I should not have come back at all. He might be right. It might be better for all concerned if I went into exile. I refused——"

"Did your uncle not accept your refusal?" he put in.

"He did. Indeed, he offered me an alternative: sanctuary at Beananaar out of the public eye. I refused that too. He told you so?"

"He told me so."

"I refused. I did more. I ejected William Daunt out of the house and farm that he had made prosperous. Did he tell you that?"

"He told me that."

"Did he tell you that the ejection was final?"

"No. He would not accept finality."

"You can accept it, Father Connell. He is not coming

back. Did he tell you that his wife will no longer live with him?"

"He gave her freedom of choice."

"She will live with me."

"Does she agree?"

"She agrees. But you can ask her. And that is about all. And now I await your ultimatum."

"No, no, no!" he said painedly. "No, no, no!" He had been sitting forward listening to me, and his austere face had given no sign of any emotion: displeasure or understanding. Now he sat back in the chair, and laid his arms and fine bony hands along the rests. He was no longer uneasy. The power of his calling was come upon him, and he would do his duty as he saw it. He spoke very quietly.

"You have been blunt and brief, Mr. Daunt, and you have managed to show yourself in the worst possible light. And, by the way, Jerome Farley puts a rather different complexion on the events of this morning——"

"But the fact remains," I put in.

"Yes, the fact remains, and you ask for an ultimatum— you demand one, as your tone implies." He moved his head slowly. "I don't stock ultimatums, my friend. They lead to evil—always. Once I heard one being fulminated. I was only a schoolboy then, and it was in my native parish. A certain priest, before the last gospel, leant his back against the altar and spoke of a scandal in his parish, where no scandal had shown itself in the light of day for twenty years. He spoke at length and almost obscenely about the enormity of that scandal, and then he gave his ultimatum. 'The young man,' he said, 'who is guilty of this sin of the flesh may be of the best blood in Ireland, but I will not have him in my parish. Here from this sanctified altar I order him to go, and never show his face again.' And that was that.

"It was not. A young man, at my very side in the gallery, rose to his feet, and his voice pealed from the rafters. 'I am the man you speak of, Father. I am of this parish, and so were my people generation after generation. They were here before you came, and they will be here after you are gone, and so will I.' "

He sat up in his chair, and his fingers met and tapped. "That was all, but, nevertheless, that young man was out of that parish within six months."

"You spoil your parable by a priestly ending, Father," I said. "Your priest was merely the stronger character—strong like yourself."

"The priest had nothing whatever to do with it," he said and fluttered a hand, "and I am only a reed shaking in the wind. It was his own pride that drove that young man. He was in love with the girl he had seduced, and she would not marry him; she would have nothing more to do with him." He paused and went on. "You are no longer a boy, and you may know. It frequently happens—not always—as I know, that the despoiled virgin comes to abhor the despoiler. That peasant girl would have nothing more to do with the son of the strongest farmer in the parish. His pride could not stand that, and, telling no one, he slipped away to New Zealand within six months. He died out there only last year, a crusty old bachelor. He was my elder brother."

"And the peasant girl?" I asked softly.

"She is a priest's housekeeper somewhere," he said indifferently, and added with some feeling, "and a dam' bad cook, so I'm told. She had a daughter—it should be a son, and he now a Minister of State, to round off the story—and the daughter became a Civil Servant and married one. She comes every year to visit her uncle—that's me. How's that for a parable?"

"What am I to learn from it, sir?"

"Pronounce sentence at your peril. Don't boast more than is reasonable, for pride carries a sting in its tail. Don't interfere with the course of nature—much; direct it in the course it should go, if you can, and if you can't pick up the pieces, and try and mend them. Sometimes you can. That is all."

"No, it is not all, priest of the parish." I leant forward to him. "What do you think will drive me from Grianaan in six months?"

He sat up straight then, and was inclined to be angry.

"Good God, boy! Do you think I came here to drive you, even by implication?"

"Then why are you here?" I asked obdurately.

"What? Did I forget to say? I am here to welcome you back to Grianaan, and to hope that you long enjoy it, you and your mother, in peace and goodwill." Then he smiled faintly, and his voice was sorrowful. "No wonder you are hard, David!"

I had been wrong in my estimation of this man. Had I been wrong all the time? Wrong about Eujun Connell, wrong about Jerome Farley? Holy murder! Was I also wrong about my uncle, William Daunt?

"I am a suspicious hound, Father Connell," I said. "Do you want me to live in peace with my uncle?"

"Yes, I do," he said readily. He lifted a finger for attention, and again smiled faintly. "I think you yourself were guilty of an ultimatum this morning, but I agree that you chose the only course to secure peace—peace in Grianaan."

"You mean—you mean——?" Surprise made me stupid.

"I mean, that knowing your uncle and his possessiveness, I know that you and he cannot live under the same roof. Well, he has his own farm of Beananaar. Let him live there."

That was concise and clear, and yet I was not satisfied because I was still troubled. I spoke hesitatingly. "There is another point that comes within your domain, Father——"

"Oh, I know, I know!" There was gentle mockery in his voice. "Who dare come between husband and wife? But if Ellen Furlong insists on living with her son what can anyone do about it? Accept the situation, of course. There is such a thing as legal separation, you know. That would put everything on a sound footing—settlements, allotments, all the clutter of law in modern life. And then you could begin to live. A little late, David, but never too late."

I rubbed the back of my head desperately and shut my

eyes. "I have the bad, suspicious drop in me, Father," I said. "Can you ever forgive me?"

"Forgive you? Forgiveness from me, a pampered sinner, to you who have suffered so much!" He covered his face with his hands. "Mother of God! Suffered so much, and you so young!"

"It was my own fault," I said quietly. "Don't grieve for me!" I reached out my hand, and touched his knee, and one hand came down on mine. "I did not suffer at all—after a time: Michael Ambrose, the chief warden, held me up, and laid a foundation for me that I could build on. I am building on it now."

"Splendid!" He loosed my hand and sat back in his chair. "You make loyal friends, David."

"Not so many, Father! I could count them on the fingers of one hand." And I did so. "Let me see! There's my mother, and Julie Brady, and, yes, young Molly Cray in this house; Charley Cashan at Beananaar, and——" I stopped.

"And Jean Harrington at The Cottage," said the priest of the parish.

"Her name is not mentioned in this house," I said.

"Some foolish nicety of feeling, perhaps! Don't you mind it. But hush! Someone is coming. Ah yes!" His voice livened. "It would be you."

III

Father Connell had good ears. I had heard no one coming. I turned to see my mother standing in the open doorway. She was carrying a silver tray. She was in a full-length dress, almost an evening dress, and her arms were slender and lovely. The ground of the dress was white, and it was stencilled with big, black, formalized blossoms. Her white hair was shining, and so were her eyes, and her tender mouth had a wistfulness that used not be there. And her voice had a throaty breathlessness.

"Oh, Father Eujun darlin'! Has my son been fighting with you too?"

"Woman, you were listening long enough to know," he said sternly. He was on his feet. "Come along in, and hear some more, and you may not like it."

I went and took the tray from her, and she touched my cheek with light fingers. I put the tray on the desk, and when I turned round the priest had a firm hold of her hand, and she was looking at him with a trepidation that was only half genuine. If she had been listening, and no doubt she had been, she would have heard the talk come round to Jean Harrington. Was that why she was interrupting us now?

Here Father Eujun turned to look at me. "Did I say that I never passed sentence on a sinner? I am going to now." He turned head to her and, judging by his face, he was about to scourge her with rods and scorpions, or is it snakes and scorpions, or, maybe, whips and scorpions? Scorpions, anyway! And his voice was stern.

"It is ordained that you, Ellen Furlong, live here at Grianaan with your son David and minister unto him. You hear me?"

"I hear you, Father Eujun," she said mildly. "I will do the best I can, and if I fail, I'll confess to you, and try again."

Father Eujun released her hand. "They always try again," he said, "like the man who always takes the pledge for life. But they always try again, thank God!"

Firmly, but respectfully, she pushed him down into the leather chair. "You'll be tired listening, Father, and your throat dry. 'Tis a drop o' nourishment you require. David?"

I turned and looked down at the tray. All it held was a crystal jug of crystal-clear water. Japers! was he only a water bibber? And where were the glasses? I looked at my mother and she lifted eyes to the corner cupboard within my arms reach. I had not opened that cupboard since my return. The key was in the lock, and I opened it now.

Yes, there on the top shelf, were all my old pipes, half-a-score of them, each head-up in its bracket as it should be. I would deal with one later on. And that brown jar with the patent lid might contain some shreds of tobacco. But the two lower shelves drew my attention. That mother o' mine had forgotten nothing. There were three bottles of our ten-year-old Southern whiskey, a bottle of Cork gin, limpid as water, a bottle of pale sherry, syphons of soda and tonic water, shapely goblets and delicately cut sherry glasses.

"The holy man likes a drop o' spring water in the native," my mother told me.

I poured into a goblet, and waited for him to say when. He didn't, so I added a *tilly*. He made me fill the goblet to the brim with water, and looked towards my mother.

"I would prescribe a gin and tonic as usual," he said.

"A couple of fellow topers, I see!" I said.

My mother mixed her own drink, because I didn't know how: a very little gin and plenty of tonic. I had a small sherry. I had never tasted the heavier alcohols. Michael Ambrose used make me take a bottle of beer to give him an excuse to take several.

It was then I thought of a cigarette. One wants a cigarette before tension, or during it, or after it. This was after it. I tendered the pack to the priest, but he moved a negative finger, and nodded towards my mother. No, he would not be a smoker. He would not yield to any of the petty vices, and a ball of malt was no vice at all. I lit my mother's cigarette, and inhaled deeply on my own.

"You were a pipe smoker?" the priest said, glancing at the corner cupboard.

"I start again to-morrow," I told him.

"Those pipes may have gone stale. You know how to treat them?"

I did, but I said politely, "Is there a way?"

"There is. *Slainthe!*" He sipped his drink delicately, and was eager to tell me. "Borrow a knitting needle from this lady——"

"There ends the lesson," I said. "This lady hasn't any."

He chuckled. "Julie Brady will. Heat the knitting needle red hot between the bars of the grate and—careful how you handle it—burn the old nicotine out of bowl and stem. Julie will bawl at you, but you'll have a smokable pipe. Don't use spirits; it softens and depraves the briar."

"But you are not a smoker, Father?" I wondered.

"A smoker! God forgive me! I'd smoke before breakfast, I'd smoke saying my office, I'd smoke in bed. I have to discipline myself after the fashion of old Father Finn of Drum—God rest him! I was his curate. Every evening, at six o'clock to the minute, his housekeeper entered his sitting-room. The four walls of that room were shielded in books—books on the floor, books on the chairs, books everywhere. One winter he made me read the history of Frederick the Great in fourteen volumes, and I've cursed Thomas Carlyle ever since. His housekeeper came in bearing his pipes—clay they were—a twist of venomous rat-tail tobacco, a kitchen knife, and a tin-pan for spittoon. I filled his pipe. I filled four pipes. And every time he made a bull's-eye on the tin-pan, the pan stood on its ear. No Ellen! I don't use a spittoon; I use a gentlemanly mixture of Virginia and Latakia made up for me by Tom Mitchell of Dun Laoire."

He took a silver hunter, without a chain, from his vest pocket. "Half-an-hour to my first smoke of the day." His glass was a quarter full, and he tossed it off in one neat movement, rose to his feet, and moved a hand benignly.

"I'll be seeing ye—I'll be seeing ye often. God bless!" And forthwith he marched out the door, his shoulders already back, and his feet brisk.

IV

I hurried out after him, and I walked at his side, or a little behind, as far as the front gate.

At the gate he turned and faced me. I sensed that trace of embarrassment again.

"Maybe I shouldn't ask," he said hesitatingly. "Do you practise the Faith?"

"Yes—but I'm a born doubter."

"Why not? Honest doubt is the buckler of faith." He hesitated again. "I may have no right in theology or rubrics, but on Sunday, if for—any reason—there might be some—you do not want to attend Mass——"

"What Mass is yours, Father?"

"You know, David, the modern generation of curates has no hardihood." He was warmly complaining. "I have two, and in the matter of fasting they haven't a stomach between them. I celebrate the last Mass—at eleven o'clock."

"May I sit under you, Father Eujun?"

That pleased him. "Do boy, and I'll not preach at you—noticeably. It is your mother's Mass also." He lifted a finger and again smiled faintly. "I know more about you than you think, David. I was coadjutor to old Father Kent for two years before he died. He was wandering a bit at the end." He saw my shoulders move, and went on quickly. "No—no! There was no breaking of any seal, nothing like that. But he was always talking about you, and the gay devil you were. I will tell you the last thing he said to me. It was on his deathbed. 'Mind the Highland lassie for me, Gene, and, take care, if you don't help that wronged boy I'll curse you out of the flames of Purgatory.' Queer how he coupled your names?"

"That was not queer, Father," I said. "But——"

I was going to say that I was not wronged, but he stopped me sternly.

"Don't think of lying to your priest, who only wants to help you!" His voice gentled again. "Can I help you at all, David brother?"

"You have, Father Eujun," I said, and reached him my hand.

He clasped it firmly, turned on his heel, and went striding briskly down the road towards the bridge, as gentle a tyrant as ever donned a blackcoat.

I turned and stopped. A hedge-sparrow curved in towards a bush ten paces beyond the gate, fluttered, and curved away scolding. I picked two round pebbles out of the gravel, lobbed one left-handed into the bush, and poised my right.

"Come! Come on out! or I'll blast you out. Ah!"

The bush stirred, and Joseph Yoseph stepped out on the roadside, and rubbed himself busily.

"By gum, sir! You have eyes like a hawk or ears like a weasel."

I was inclined to anger. This dogging and eavesdropping was getting me down. I blared at him.

"Have you good ears yourself, you damn'd Israelite?"

"Fair enough, sir," he said equably.

"Then go and report all you have heard to your great Gawd Buddh."

"Great God Buddh! Murder! But it fits him."

"Tell him that that man walking down the road and owning it is a better man than he is."

"Maybe he is, and maybe he isn't," said the loyal policeman. "That's a holy man, anyway, and I'd put my hands under his feet."

"What? You are not one of his flock?"

"I belong to no flock at all, Mr. Daunt." The invincible pride of race came into his voice. "If I did I would hold the faith out of which all the great faiths have sprung."

"You forget one or two," I said, and changed the subject. "You should have a black eye, Joseph."

"Two of them, and black enough they are."

"I mean Bill Sheedy——"

He laughed. "You ought to be ashamed, sir, and a nose on him to light a candle. Molly was telling me." He waved a hand up the road. "Bill is away."

"Easy as that! No trouble?"

"I was no more than standing by, you might say." He laughed again. "Molly Cray, the young divil, standing over him with the tongs, and making him empty out a sugar bag he had on the kitchen table. And she impounded a new pair o' socks and an American tie that didn't belong to him —so she said. Ay faith! and not a word out of him, and me hopin' he'd open his mouth so I could excavate his tongue."

"Poor Bill! He is loyal at least."

"I wonder is he!"

"Any of the lads opt out with him?"

"Nary a one." He shrugged his shoulders. "'Tis easy to forsake the fallen leader for the young and the bold. They're all up in the Cam field wearing into the oats."

"I'll be my own foreman to-morrow."

"And well able!" He looked at his watch. "You'll excuse me, sir! I have to be back."

"Yes. And tell your Tade Murphy that I'll thicken his ear for him if he don't watch out."

"Thicken the two of 'em when you're at it and God love you!" said Joseph.

CHAPTER IX

AND A QUIET EVENING

I

I turned in at the gate, and my mother was coming down the drive to meet me.

Tall and lissome in her black and white, she moved lithely—not springily—just lithely, sailingly, almost as if airborne. And, somehow, her shining white hair gave her a youthful look. She took my arm in her two hands, and swung me on to the grass, and there she swung me round twice.

"Look! Look you!" Her voice was a bugle. "Behold all that we own, you and me together at last. That white house, that lovely white house is ours—and Julie Brady, body and bones. And the steadings behind, and sixty cows at the milking, and sheds of hay and that slope of trees, and all the wide fields back to Beananaar. All ours." She swung me again. "And the Doorn River is ours, and Kantwell with its two spires and its old castle, and the Vale of Irmond out to the sea that you can see shining. They are all ours, because we are going to make use of them—you and me."

"Fair enough!" I said. "Where do we begin?"

"We'll try supper first," said my mother.

It was evening again, and I was only twenty-four hours home. Again the Doorn was wimpling black and gold and silver; the roofs of Kantwell were grey and purple; the tall arch in the castle ruins was strongly outlined; the vale was firmly etched in the clear evening light; the sandhills, far out about the mouth of the Doorn, held a light of their own; and

beyond was the sheen of the estuary. Ours to use and enjoy?
I wonder.

My mother was holding my arm, quietly now, and quietly
we strolled across the grass, and back again.

"What did you think of my Father Eujun?" she
asked.

"So he also belongs to you?"

"You had a long talk?"

"How much of it did you hear?"

"It is a woman's privilege—and safeguard—to hear all
she can," she said lightly.

"To know when to intervene," I could have bitten off my
tongue, and I went on hastily. "Why did he come on foot?
Didn't want to show dog on his first visit?"

"Rude boy! He hasn't a car."

"Come off it, old lady! Every parish priest and curate too,
has a car—and wheat and wine and oil, and beds of
asphodel."

"Not Father Eujun! He walks everywhere—and a cycle
has no dignity."

"A mean parish, Kantwell," I said.

"It isn't either. No, sir! We raised five hundred pounds.
You subscribed five pounds, unbeknownst. Was that too
much, Davy?"

"A little—say five pounds too much. Well, where's the
car?"

"We took out a driving licence for him, and we coaxed
him to take lessons from Tom Farrant of the garage. Tom
said he was the best beginner ever, if he wouldn't run over
stray chickens. Not that Tom minded the chickens, but he
had to pay for them then and there, Father Eujun having
no cash on him. And, then, we made a mistake. We handed
the money over to him so that he could buy the car of his
choice. No car! Not a smell of a car!"

"Hoarding! A saint must have one vice. He looks like a
hoarder."

"He hasn't a penny. Where is it? Ask the needy. Blast

them! Ask the scroungers who are only greedy. We are more careful this time."

"You are trying again?"

"Of course. He gets a touch of rheumatism in winter. We'll buy the car ourselves."

"He can sell it?"

"He'll try. But it will be licensed in the Bishop's name."

"I hope the Bishop is an honest man. One is, sometimes."

She glanced at me diffidently. "Joseph Yoseph was saying to Julie to-day that you might subscribe ten pounds this time. He is our treasurer."

"But he's a Jew, dammit!"

"That's why he's treasurer," said my mother reasonably.

"Ten pounds is out," I told her.

"Is it, David?" There was a small hurt in her voice. It was always easy to hurt her.

"It is, and I'll tell you why." I squeezed her arm. "We should have a bit of a car for ourselves."

"A car for ourselves?" she repeated softly.

"That station-wagon can be written off—for the time—I suppose. Too big anyway! And a little, wee, small bit of a car would do us fine."

She pushed me off, and her voice upbraided me.

"Little or wee, what are we to use for money?"

I knew the rogue. The way she pushed me off, the tone of her voice told me she was playing for a pleasant surprise. I could play too. I said:

"I have twenty pounds." It was jail money.

"You have not."

"I have so." I felt my wallet, and stopped short.

"It's all right boy!" she hastened to assure me. "You left it lying on your dressing-table—as usual—oh Davy, as usual! But no twenty pounds! It contained nineteen pounds, fourteen shillings and sevenpence, and a snapshot of a stern-faced man in uniform."

"That was Michael Ambrose."

"Oh! was that Michael Ambrose?" she asked with interest.

"He can wait," I said, and took her arm. "If we could scrape another hundred; you know—a second-hand two seater?"

She shook her head, and went on playing. "What do we want a car for anyway? Kantwell and the mart only over the river, and a short mile to Mass!"

"I would like one all the same," I said, humbly obstinate.

"Give me one good reason."

I moved a hand widely. "There's the Vale we own, and want to use. On a fine Sunday I would drive you across to the sea or down amongst the mountains."

"Oh Dave! Across to the sea or down among the mountains! That is strange."

"What's strange about it?"

I was not looking at her, but I knew she was looking keenly at me.

"Oh nothing!" she said, then: "A coincidence or—what is it?—a transference of thought, or something."

I shook her arm. "What are you blethering about?"

She seemed to be thinking aloud now. "Yes, God is good, and things might come to pass without me putting a finger in the pie. No, I must not. I would be afraid."

"Gin is out for you, my lady. And don't you be drawing a red herring across the bonnet of a poor, weeshy, second-hand two-seater, or, maybe, a two-door four-seater."

"I am not, David. Very well then! I did not want to trouble you so soon, but I'll go into my accounts with you after supper."

"Accounts—you?" I said scathingly.

"Yes, so! Look!" Her lovely arms made generous movements. "I have an account book that size, and everything down in it—in double-entry—I think."

"Go on out o' that! Book-keeping by double-entry?"

"I have everything down, anyway," she said proudly. "And you might find a ten pound here and a ten pound there."

"I doubt it," I said, and cheered up. "But what harm?

As you say, haven't we our feet to walk on, and haven't I got you?"

"Very well, then!" She changed the subject. "I wonder what Julie has for supper?"

"Gourmet, not quite gourmand!" I laughed, and she laughed with me. It was good to know that she was still interested in her food. She had always been a good, healthy meat-eater. She used relish even a calf's head—*tête de veau*, I believe, politely.

"I know you don't care for fish—not twice in the same day," she said. "Is lobster a fish?"

"Can't be—it's got claws," I said. "A crustacean—that's what it is."

"Julie might have a nice lobster salad for us," she said hopefully.

"She'd never think of it," I said, "but let us go in and see. You are starving me."

We went in arm-in-arm. Julie, at the cooker, shook her head at us.

"Such pride I never see. Walkin' up and down, like lord and lady, as if ye owned the barony!"

"We do," my mother said. "And if you did not waste your time watching us there might be something for supper. Have you anything?"

"Not a thing," said Julie. "Go away in and wash yere hands, and I'll see what there is."

We had lobster mayonnaise for supper. I knew I would not sleep after that second helping, but, then, I did not want to go to sleep too early. My mother had a second helping too, but objected to mine.

"It might be bad for you, and you not used to it," she said.

"I'll feed him in spite of you," proclaimed Julie, "and he half-starved already."

There had been no luxury dieting in Southland Jail, but Michael Ambrose had not half-starved me. A man should enjoy good food, but, also, he should not grumble when put

on short commons. Hunger should be a good sauce or a good
discipline. Once a week, Michael Ambrose, a countryman
like myself, used send me from his own table a dish of home-
cured bacon boiled with white cabbage, and floury potatoes
in their jackets. That was the countryman's dish. I had seen
white cabbage in our unkempt kitchen-garden, and Julie,
the darling, only needed a hint.

II

After supper my mother took me to her own room. My
mother's room was at one end of the passage, mine at the
other, and our doors faced each other. Her room had one big
window in the gable end, facing the morning sun; there was
no window in my gable-end.

Her room I had always treated as sacrosanct. I never
entered it without permission, and unless she was there before me. Now she opened the door herself, and drew me
softly in. The light was fading. Through the end window I
could see the valley of the Doorn, and it was lonely in the
half-light, the trees darkly ominous, and the ribbon of river
a wan silver.

My mother closed the door and felt for the switch. A pink
bowl glowed under the ceiling, and the landscape dimmed.
A woman's room softly toned in soft colours: pink or salmon
and smoky blues—I am not good at indoor colours—with
silken coverlets and downs, and flimsy draperies about a be-
bottled dressing table of three mirrors. The cream carpet
was soft under my feet.

She was very businesslike now. She went across and pulled
down the blind, and switched on a lamp over a faintly-
yellow walnut bureau by the side of the window. The bureau
was unlocked—she did not believe in locks—and she opened
the top-drawer and lifted out a thick account book—almost
a ledger—foolscap size. It was covered in a loose jacket of
tooled leather. She lowered the bureau flap on to its rests,

pulled in a chair, sat down, smoothed the brown leather affectionately, and opened the first page. I stood at her side, a hand lightly across her shoulders."

"I like that," she said simply. "I did not do it myself."

Whoever had done it knew form and colour. A formalized Gaelic scroll, twined with flowers in watercolour, made an oblong frame for a script that the old monks used in illuminated work. It read:

"These be the Accounts for David Daunt's Farm of Grianaan from the Thirteenth Day of August, 194– to THE DAY."

I knew who wrote that Script. I knew who had painted these flowers. I knew who had elaborated that scroll.

My mother tapped the page. "Yesterday was The Day, David son," she said deep-toned. "I am only giving you a glimpse now. You will take the book to your room, and go over it critically."

I swallowed twice, and found voice. "Over it, and over it! And who knows? I might come across a spare tenner."

She turned over a page, she turned over three, she turned over ten at a time. I had not much chance for any scrutiny, but I saw that the accounts were, indeed, in some form of double-entry, not too perfect, for there were numerous corrections and additions. And the corrections and additions were not in my mother's handwriting. The hand was not unlike my mother's: the same loops and broad m's and n's, signs of a generous and impulsive nature. I knew that writing.

"Your hand o' write varies a bit, good mother," I said casually.

"Oh, different times, different pens!" she said, equally casual. She was keeping her finger out of my pie.

Two-thirds of the way through the book, she slowed and stopped, lifted a page and peeped before she turned it. She put her two hands flat across the bottom half.

"And here is the final result, Mr. David Daunt of Grianaan, down to the last creamery cheque, the four pedigree

heifer calves we sold to the Kildare man, and the three ton
of maize for winter."

I put a hand across her two and pressed.

"I don't want to see it, Mother." My voice went up in
spite of me. "I don't want to see it at all."

"Oh, my dear son! But you must see it. I was looking
forward to this. Look! There you are!"

She moved my hand away with the lift of hers, and duti-
fully I looked. There was no pretence in my surprise.

"Holy Mother o' Moses! What bank did you rob?" I put
a finger under her nose.

The credit balance was well into four figures, and that is
all I will say.

She snapped playfully at my finger, and tapped the page.
"That, all that came out of Grianaan Geal, and there should
be more."

"A certain labourer was not worthy," I said, "but leave
it for now. Whatever will you do with all that bread—I
mean money."

"It is your money, darling, and all in your name in
the National Bank." She reached for my hand. "Some
on deposit, some in current account, and look! this is your
cheque book." She picked one out of a pigeon-hole. "One
hundred virgin cheques. You could use one to pay for that
bit of a car."

She loosed my hand, and looked up at me for praise. I
could not begin to praise her. If I started I would break down
and cry like a baby. So I walked across the soft carpet and
back again, and spoke judiciously.

"A strange thing, when a man finds himself with a lot of
money he hates to spend it. A car did you say?"

"Just a bit of a car, sir." She knew I was playing.

"No bit of a car," I said. "Not a second-hand two-
seater, not a two-door four-seater—it gives claustrophobia—not any sort of car. The car, madame, to suit your
elegance."

"To seat three in front?" That casual tone again.

"And three in back, and a lift for decent people—like tramps and scalawags. To-morrow I'll get a pile of catalogues from Tom Farrent."

She gestured her white pow. "There's a pile of them on my bedside table—latest models."

"How did you know——?" I stopped.

"Yes, David?"

"Nothing—just nothing." I put the cheque book back in its pigeon hole, took up the account book, and closed the bureau flap. "No fun going over figures by myself." I pulled open the top-drawer against her flat tummy, and put the book back in its place. "You are in for trouble ma'am over your long tots and cross tots. Say when did you learn to add——?"

I stopped again. In a corner of the drawer was a thick packet of letters—in their envelopes—tied with tri-colour ribbon. The address on the top letter was my mother's, and I knew the handwriting.

My mother drew in her breath, and put a hand out. I drew it away and closed the drawer. But there was no need why she should hold out on me. I put my arm round her shoulders.

"How long has Michael Ambrose been writing to you, mother?" I asked her quietly.

"Oh, dear!" she was distressed. "I didn't want to tell you for a long time. "For years and years, David—a note every month." She put her white head down on the slope of the bureau, and murmured. "I wanted to die—I might have died—but he made me want to live."

I put my black head down against hers. "What a brute I was!" I said.

"No, darling, no! I knew. I knew the trouble in your mind, and that you dare not write. But God is good! God is very good."

She was crying softly, so softly that I only knew by the quiver of her breath. I pressed close till her breathing quietened. Then she felt for my handkerchief.

"I am too happy, David," she whispered. "'Tis the way I am too happy."

"'Tis a happy complaint you have, ma'am," I said, and I was feeling as sentimental as hell.

"But you could make me happier still, David," she said. "A lot happier! But you'll have to find the road yourself."

But I knew there was no road that way.

CHAPTER X

BUT THE NIGHT HAS MANY EYES

I

I did not wake out of a nightmare that night. I did not go to bed at all, or, rather, I did not go when I should have gone. I padded back and forth across the carpet like an animal in a cage, but I no longer felt trapped. I could go out night-hawking if I wanted to.

To-morrow I would have to buckle down to farm work and farm stewarding. To-night I was free to do as I pleased: go out into the night, read a book, slip down to my Outside Room and have a drink. I contemplated a lonely cuss having a drink to himself, and then another drink. Well, I was a lonely cuss; indeed, I was lonely back of all in spite of all my pretences.

The years had driven me into myself, had inured me to abide secretly in a world of my own. In that world I could contemplate myself taking to secret drinking. I knew it was the resource and solace of lonely men, lifting the mind to a new plane where dreams could flourish. And I would be a lonely man all my days.

Curse you, you won't! I told myself. *You are only a male, and, some day, a woman's ankle, the swell of a breast, the turn of a head, the invitation of eyes will rouse the lust in you—lust not love, for love you have lost forever—and you'll marry and you'll have no more fine dreaming; and your only solace will be the mother that bore you— or drink in the night.*

But was I free even for one night? Was I not being watched this very minute by Jerome Farley's myrmidon out in the garden? Why? What had that formidable man in his mind?

To hell with it! I said, and walked across to the unblinded window. I lifted it as far as it would go and leant far out. The sky was cloudless, and the moon, hidden by the eaves, would be about full. Everyone will remember that wonderful late summer after months of rain, when most of us blamed the world powers for irretrievably shattering the seasons with nuclear experiments. And then the weather cleared, and there was not a drop of rain for weeks and weeks. Long hours of sunshine and heat, and balmy nights under one blanket. And when the rain came it was only in generous showers, to enrich the grass and swell the ears of corn.

And this was one of the balmy nights—and inviting. The moon was so bright that I could see the foliage of the fruit trees; and the shadows were black and firmly outlined. My eyes searched the garden, foot by foot, for a lurking figure or a suspicious movement. But Tade Murphy was a good scout, and, if he were out there, he would not give himself away. I leant forward, whistled softly, and beckoned welcomingly. Tade Murphy would not fall for that invitation either.

"I hope you're sitting on pismires, you hunk," I said loud enough for anyone to hear, and pulled down the blind. He could see my shadow through that, so I pulled the brown velvet curtains across. And then I was free no longer. I felt caged now.

I sat on the bed for a while, and considered all the ground I had cleared in twenty-four hours, and how much more I had to clear. Not so much! William Daunt no longer loomed big; he was, indeed, only a lath painted to look like iron, and the legal boys could deal with him. But Jerome Farley was no lath. Dammit! he had me caged in this room, and I had no freedom of action. What was he after?

He was not hounding me, or displaying his power over me. I knew that, now, after seeing him with my mother; and he had eaten my bread and salt—in the form of fruitcake. What was he doing then? Why was he watching me? He must be working on a hypothesis. Was it that I had not killed Robin Daunt? He had given me a single hint that he knew that I knew the killer. Was he out to get that killer as a sacrifice to his god, Peace? Could a second person be put in jeopardy for a killing already paid for? But he could prove nothing, or do nothing, as long as I insisted that I was the killer and had paid the price.

"*You can go to hell, Mr. Jerome Farley!*" I said aloud.

And, then, my blood tingled. Was there an Ethiopian in the woodpile? Charley Cashan had said that there was a fourth man on the prowl last night, and Charley would know. Was Jerome Farley using me as a decoy to get to close quarters with that fourth man? Again I spoke aloud. That, too, is a habit of lonely men.

"*Thank you, Mr. Farley! But I'd hate to be the bleating kid. If you are looking for an Ethiopian—or a tiger—I'll take a peep myself, and I'll do it in my own way, and I'll do it now.*" That was as good an excuse as any to get out into the night, and move in a certain direction.

I did not go out by the window that night. I would not have Tade Murphy or anyone else on my heels, for I must play this game alone. And it was a game I liked and could play: stalking the stalker. I had played it with river wardens when I wanted a salmon out of a moonlit pool, with game-keepers in the stubbed fields before we acquired our own game rights on Grianaan, and with poachers who, reasonably enough, would not respect our rights. I felt that I could outwit the policeman, but I was not so sure about Charley Cashan—if he were on the prowl. Charley, at night, was as cunning as a fox and as silent as an owl; but he was no beast of prey. By gum! if he interfered to-night I would belt the daylights out of him.

I used to have a dark tartan neckerchief or light muffler. Yes, it was still in my wardrobe, and it would do nicely to hide the white of my shirt. The boot cupboard was stocked with boots and shoes. Boots! yes boots too. Boots are made, now, for only sportsmen and farmers, and farmers mostly wear rubber wellingtons. I chose a pair of brown, leather-strapped canvas shoes with soles of raw rubber.

I didn't carry a watch, but, like most countrymen, I had an instinct for time. It would be on the minute of midnight or a minute after. My mother had put a green-leather travelling clock on my dressing-table. I went across to look. It said five minutes to twelve. That clock was a shade slow.

I sat on the bed again, and noticed that a spring creaked. I looked about the room and marked where the two chairs stood. I draped the pyjama jacket on my shoulders, and then moved round by the head of the bed, to switch off the light by the door. The room was dead-dark now.

I soft-footed along by the wall. This was the corner and the low boot press, and that was the fringe of the window curtain. Boldly I flicked the curtains apart, so that the rings sounded on the runner, and gave the blind a smart jerk to send it scooting up. The wan moonlight was reflected into the room. Anyone out in the garden would be looking into comparative darkness, and would only glimpse the light colour of the pyjama jacket. I moved across the carpet, found a chair, and kicked it. I said "Blast!" but not too loudly. Then I sat firmly on the bed.

The protest of the springs would carry to the garden, and if my mother was awake she would be listening for a sound like that. Now her son was in bed, and she could turn over and go to sleep.

I sat still, and there was no sound. Just one faint sound. I could hear the hurried ticking of the travelling clock, and I could see the phosphorous, green gleam of the illuminated dial. After ten minutes I eased to my feet, and the bed-spring made no protest. The knob of the door made no protest either, as I slowly put pressure on it. I opened the door to a slot against the steadying control of finger and thumb, and set one eye to the crack.

The hall outside was much brighter than my room. It was lighted from the roof by a rose window of light-amber glass, and the full moon was nearly overhead. The soft glow was like the reflection of the reflection of late-evening sunlight. I looked along the passage at my mother's door. It gleamed

darkly brown, and close to the floor was a thin line of light.
"Thu-thu-thu! Go you to sleep, darlint!"

It was as if she had heard that whisper. Her light went out,
and, in the stillness, I heard the rustle of silk as she turned
over. In that rustle I opened the door wide enough to slip
through, and closed it again along the guide of my little
finger. I moved down the hall flat-footed and silent. If you
want to move silently don't go on tip-toe, but smoothly flat-
footed, as prison warders move.

Along the passage to the left was the door to the kitchen,
and opposite it the door to the sitting-room. Nearer, on the
sitting-room side, was the curtained arch leading to the front
hall and the front door. But I was not going out by the
front door. As I approached the curtain I could hear the
muted tick-tock of the grandfather clock in the hall.

I got through to the front hall without moving the curtain
on its runners. The hall, lit by fan-light and side windows,
was wan silver. On one hand was the sitting-room, on the
other the apartment that William Daunt had made his own.
The grandfather clock ticked louder at my left shoulder; on
my right, wide stone stairs curved down to the ground floor.
That was the way I was going.

The ground floor was unoccupied, mostly unfurnished,
and had not been in use for a couple of generations. It contained the immense flagged kitchen with its huge old iron
range, and pantries and larders and store-rooms, and tiny
cubicles for servants' bedrooms, but no bathroom or lavatory.
That ground floor was a relic of the days when servants,
cheap and plentiful, were little above serfdom, and were confined to basements with gratings for ventilation. Contemplate the mentality of the ruling squirearchy who gouged
out underground quarters for menials in broad country
acres!

I went down silently on the stone treads, close to the wall,
and found myself in an empty passage running the width of
the house. Faint light came from a window at the front. On
my left stone flags led to half a dozen steps going up to the

back door, for the rear-wall of the house was semi-basement. Outside was the concreted yard and the orchard—and probably, Tade Murphy. That way I would not go either.

I turned right and shuffled forward, a hand on the dank wall. The front door was at the side of the steps leading to the main door. It used have wooden bolts, top and bottom, and a latch shoulder high. It still had them. I levered the bolts back against my thumb, and lifted the latch with a faint click. The hinges of this door would squeak like a ringed pig, and the slower I opened it the more prolonged the squeak. So I jerked it firmly a quarter-open, to a single short growl, slipped through, closed it to a muter growl, and flattened out in the angle between the wall and the parapet of the steps.

II

I was in a narrow shadow, for the parapet just hid the moon. The front of the house was in a white radiance, and gossamer shimmered on the grey-green of the lawn. I looked along the wall to the end of the house. Nothing stirred there, nor amongst the shrubs beyond. My mother's room was at that end, on the upper floor, but her big window was in the gable, and there was only a dummy window in her wall at this side.

There was a grass edging along the wall, inside the gravel, and I moved quietly along this to the corner; but I did not go round it lest my mother hear me. I listened. There was no least sound. I had to make the front gate now. I looked down the slope towards it, and, in the moonlight, the white posts were startlingly white. I could go down by the solid black bulk of the hedge, but I hesitated to use that shelter. Someone of evil intent might be watching me from there at this moment, and I did not want to tackle anyone in the dark. I did the bold thing.

I tip-toed across the gravel—you have to tip-toe in a hurry —and ran down the grass slope for the gate, taking my highest and longest strides to leave as little trail as possible in the gossamer. I went out the gate at a bound, and whirled behind the post to look back. Yes, I had broken the shimmering of the gossamer, and an observant stalker would notice that. But beyond this gate I would leave no trail.

Nothing moved anywhere. Last night Tade Murphy had come round one corner trailing me, and Charley Cashan round the other trailing Tade. And had there been a prowler trailing us all three? Not to-night! I listened. I waited till my breath eased and my heart stopped thumping, and listened again. And then, keeping to the margin of the road, I strolled down the curve towards the three-arched bridge across the Doorn. I was taking the long way round, and coming in from the rear. And I was in no hurry.

I had decontaminated a pipe that evening after supper and had found a pouch in the earthenware jar with some tobacco in it. I had tried the pipe already and found it sweet, and the tobacco not too stale. Now I filled a pipe at my ease, and was ready to light it by the time I reached the end-buttress of the bridge. There was a tall formalized pillar at the entrance, and I stepped behind it out of the drift of night air, and felt for my match box. But I had no time to scrape a match.

I stiffened, and pressed close to the pillar, pulling the muffler up about my neck. I was looking up towards the Grianaan gate, and I saw a man come hurriedly through and halt in the middle of the road. I stilled. Whoever he was, he could not pick me out at that narrow angle.

Even in that distance I could see that he was a big man. He was not Charley Cashan; I would know Charley's bulk and shamble in any light. He was too big to be Bill Sheedy. He could be Tade Murphy; but how the devil had Tade discovered that I had left my room? He might be the man I was looking for. And what was he going to do? And what was I going to do? I would not show myself unless he forced me to, and he could only force me by coming down this way; and if he came this way he was in for stormy weather.

He was standing very still up there, and no doubt he was

looking and listening. He got no lead. And then, suddenly, he seemed to have come to a decision, for he swung away and went striding up the road that led to The Cottage and Beananaar. He would assume that I had gone that way.

So long Mister! We may meet again.

I waited till the dark figure disappeared around the curve slanting away from the river. Then I crossed the bridge, but, to make sure, I went acrouch, and kept my head below the parapet. The far wing of the bridge had another formal pillar. Leaning against that I lit my pipe, using a second match to get it going well. I could see the white smoke pluming and fading in the moonlight. The glow of a cigarette can be seen a long way off; the glow from a pipe is scarcely visible.

I looked up towards Kantwell—blue-grey roofs and silence. The church steeples stood out against the pallid sky, and the tall arch in the castle ruins yawned darkly. There were yellow-lit windows here and there in the backs of houses in the Square: someone ill, someone sleepless, some of the boys having a card session. No one moved on the dark, oiled surface of the road.

I looked up at the moon. It hung poised and serene and aloof, high up, south by west, a full circle; and on the curve of it I could make out the lovely woman's face under its cloudy film of hair. Many people cannot pick out that face at all, but once found it is never lost again.

At the flank of the pillar a packed, clay-and-gravel path slanted off the main road, and angled down towards the river. This was the Town Walk in daylight and the Lovers' Walk in the gloaming. Do lovers walk in the moonlight after the witching hour? I do not know. I never did so walk, though Jean and I had been out at all hours—with Charley scouting before and behind. The walk meandered up the Doorn side for a mile or so, crossed the river by a swinging footbridge, went up through a spinney to the highway, and, so, back to town by the Grianaan road; a pleasant stroll in a pleasant valley.

I put another match to my pipe and went down the path to the riverside. I knew every yard of the way, every fence, every stile, every kissing gate where I had never kissed. Hands in pockets I meandered along, drawing softly on my pipe, or taking it from my teeth so that I could breathe deeply. I was no longer the hunter or the hunted. I no longer wanted to play tag with anyone, friend—or killer. I only wanted to be in tune with the night. I would just circle round by the swing bridge, and be in bed in an hour's time. I might look at The Cottage in passing, but I would look for no one there. I might go on and look at the ivied walls of Beananaar, and get home across the fields. Or I might climb a small hillock that I knew, and rest on a mat of pine needles under whispering larches. That was all.

I strolled on, letting body and mind drift easily. Unless you are after game—or after a man—there is no ease in watching every step, every bush, every stir, listening to every sound. Neither Tade Murphy nor Charley Cashan, nor that problematical third could know that I had taken this side of the river to get round to The Cottage or Beananaar. Later on I might meet Tade on the road. But, by the Powers! if Charley Cashan showed as much as a nose I'd leave him as noseless as Quoddle.

In places the path ran along the top of an embankment above the river, and the water, down below, gurgled and chuckled and sang its remote song. In the shallows I could see every amber pebble agleam in the moonlight. The deep pools were like plates of polished black steel. Across the river were my own fields. The herd of Friesians were in their night pasture, a little further along than last night. Again they were lying down, chewing the cud, and I paused to listen to the subdued, sibilant grind of three score little mills. Again the bull was on his feet. He was up near the road and didn't see me, but I heard the rattle of his nose chain.

In places the path went amongst trees: alders on the river bank, beeches on the slope; and in the comparative darkness I had to move carefully because of the root-crotches. Once or twice a waked bird cheaped and fluttered away; and once a weasel—no! a stoat, there being no weasels in these parts—snaked across the path on some deadly errand of its own.

The path had changed hardly at all over the years. It was a right-of-way through private property, and rigidly confined within narrow limits. Two difficult stiles had been replaced by kissing gates, and that was about all. And I saw no lovers, and I heard no suspicious sounds.

Half a mile up was the bathing pool widening below a low cascade, and, another half-mile further on, the valley narrowed to a gorge, and the straitened river chafed angrily, in black and white, among quartz boulders. Once a strong swimmer had been broken to pieces in trying to make that gorge.

Here was the swinging foot-bridge. It was a crazy contraption slung on overhead wires, with two flimsy side-wires for hand-guards, and laths, three by one, for foot-walk. It had never drowned anyone off it, as far as I knew. It used be a feat in my young days to navigate the bucking length of it without touching the side-wires. I didn't try that feat to-night.

I knocked out my pipe, and pocketed it, reached a foot out along the treads, and felt for the side-wires. I went across cautiously and slowly, watching my feet, waiting on the up and down sway, repressing a desire to hurry. I could see the roily boil of the water below me. The far bank was higher than the near one, and, to keep a reasonable level, a way had been gouged out between two tall boulders. I took a last long stride on to firm rock, and a step between the boulders.

And a big man stepped out in my face from the flank of the upstream boulder, and gripped me forcefully by the coat lapels.

III

He was Charley Cashan, and he was laughing triumphantly into my face.

I was never so startled in all my life, and I had seldom been so angry. And as the startle faded, the anger boiled to explosion point. The lout had beaten me at my own game. If he would stop laughing I might control myself. But he only did that to jeer at me.

"Thought you could get away from me, Daveen! Not in a pig's ear!"

I didn't try to wrest myself free, but I drew in a long breath for steampower.

"I couldn't get away from Mr. Cashan, couldn't I?"

"Not never!" He gave me a possessive shake, and thrust his long jaw at me. "I could hold you here till the dawn o' day. I could drown you in Poul Dhuv behind you if I wasn't so fond of you." His grip tightened and he pulled me close. But I was not going into his bear's hug.

"Fair enough! fond fellow," I said. I went with his pull, and drove my left deep into his midriff. His breath exploded, his hands slipped loose, his head came down, and I brought my right up in a full jolt to the chin. He went down on his back, bumped his head, rolled over on his face, and began to kick steadily.

I was immediately sorry. No, I wasn't! I was only half sorry. There was a wallop coming to him, but I had hit him twice too hard. Charley was strong enough to rend me, but he couldn't hit a dent in a pat of butter. Even at wrestling, unless he got in his bear's hug, his reflexes were so slow, that I could always trip him. I had clouted Bill Sheedy that morning, and felt better for it, but there was no need to give Charley two kicks of a mule. And, anyway, he might well be vain of his night skill; and his bit of boasting had done me no harm. But, all the same I was only half sorry.

I had got away from him all right, and I could walk off about my business if I wanted to. No! there were one or two things I wanted to ask Charley, and I might give him another clout if I had to. I leant against one of the boulders, massaged my knuckles, and waited.

Charley was recovering. He drew air into his lungs with a cock-like whoop, propped himself on his hands, shook his head, and lifted to his knees. He looked up at me, and his attitude was strangely prayerful.

"What did you belt me with, Dave Daunt?" A childlike question!

"Belt you! Did you see me hit you? Did you feel me hit you?"

He opened his mouth, and shut it. He sounded perplexed. "I didn't see you and dam' the thing I felt. A flash in me skull, and there I was scrabblin'." He looked up at the faint-starred sky. "It couldn't be a flash o' lightnin'. Was I long out?"

"I could have pitched you into Poul Dhuv, and I had a dam' good mind to. Why the devil did you manhandle me?"

His praying-mantis hands apologized. "Och! that was only a bar o' fun. What did you do to me?"

"A trick I learned from a Hindoo in Southland Jail. Feel your chin?"

He winced. "If that wasn't a wallop what was?"

"Sore about the middle?"

"I haven't drawn a sound breath yet."

"And your poll?"

"Gor! what hell's trick was that?"

I took a step towards him. "I couldn't hit you in three places at once, could I? Get up and I'll show you how it's done. It's known as three-point contact."

He scrambled to his feet and backed away hurriedly.

"I'll take your word for it. Stay where you are, and God love you."

I backed against the boulder, and felt for my pipe. Charley was not yet steady on his feet, and found a fragment of rock to sit on. He rubbed below his breastbone, and had a doubtful cock to his head. I filled a pipe.

"Did you see Tade Murphy to-night?" I asked.

He forgot his hurt to snigger. "That fella! Lying doggo in the black currants and the flies atin' him. I had one eye on him and the other cocked for you."

"How did you know I got away?"

He hesitated, but he was an honest slob. "I didn't. That was a smart bit of work—out be the bottom door wasn't it?"

"Why not? How did Tade know?"

"Ah-ha! you fell down there." He was cock-a-hoop again. "You left your window raised and your bed as it was. If it was me I'd ha' heaped bolster and pillow cunning to deceive."

"Well?"

"Tade was taking no chances. After ten minutes he hopped on the parapet wall, and snapped his flash across the room to make sure there was no one in the bed. 'Blazes! the divil is gone again,' says he, and lepped and ran. I saw him up the road for The Cottage."

"And then?"

"I remembered me lessons. Do you mind me an' you an' Jean long ago. We might have the same end to the road two nights running, but we never took the same road twice to get to it. So all I had to do was meander along down through the cows—the bull knows me——"

"His dumb brother he would! But you couldn't know the end of my road."

"Couldn't I?" he said derisively, "and it drawing you like a magnet? And wasn't I right too? Was that why you hit me —or did you?"

"Stay where you are and I'll show you," I said warmly. I stepped away from the rock, and he got to his feet. If I took another step he'd run. I pointed a finger at him and spoke fiercely. "You'll stop following me round, Charley Cashan. Do you hear?"

"I hear. But what else is Tade Murphy doin'? What else is the Jew lad doin'?" So he knew about Joseph too.

"That's none of your business," I told him.

"It is so my business." He threw his hands and his head up, and I saw the moon glisten on his pale eyes. "Jerry Farley has something in his mind. Isn't that why he has a watch on you? And amn't I a better watch than any *bockagh* of a p'liceman? Do you think I'd let any bastar' get near enough to put a hand on you?"

That gave me a fresh thought. I said, "Any sign of your third man to-night?"

He shook his head. "No! Nary a sign or smell. Maybe he knows I'll put the fear o' God in him."

"Like hell he will! If he's not on the prowl there's no need for you as a watch dog." I took a step forward. "Get out of here, and back to your kennel!"

He reached forward a beseeching hand, and his voice was beseeching too, almost pitiful. "Wait, Dave, wait! To tell you the truth I wanted to see you to-night I don't know what to do at all, at all, and you are the only wan I can turn to. Haven't I you back to me again? You never saw me wronged, Dave Daunt, and you won't now."

He got to me that time. "What is it, Charley Boy?" I asked quietly.

"The ould fella—Bill Daunt."

"Has he done something to you?" My temperature began to mount.

"Himself and Bill Sheedy. You know the little nest I made for myself up-by in the house at Beananaar?"

"I don't. You tell me?"

"Two rooms, and the only chimney that'll draw smoke. And a fine bed, a splendid gran' mahogany bed left me be Jean Harrington her own self. And all my books and manuscripts, worth pounds and pounds—a million after I'm dead and gone. And everything there under my hands. Mind you, to look at it, you would think it was the remains of a jumble sale; but I could put my hand on anything I wanted with my eyes shut. Do you know what them two thieves did?"

"Evicted you, begod?"

"That's a mild way of putting it. They thrun everything

o' mine, barrin' the bed, out into the passage. Every dam' thing, higgledy-piggledy, mixum-gatherum, *tree-na-kale!* Oh, holy Moses!"

I thrust my chin at him. "And you stood by and let them, you fat craven?"

"I did not. An' if I was there itself, what could I do an' Bill Sheedy hoppin to lambaste me? Mind to-day when I was across at Grianaan for them toilet requisites? Lor! Dave! if you saw th' ould lad's face and he speculatin' the pile o' luggage!" He gurgled, and was serious again on his own grievance. "When they got me out of the way that's the time they did the dirty on me." His voice was helpless and hopeless. "And what can I do agin the two of them: Bill Sheedy was always able to peg the daylights out o' me."

"Could you not find other quarters in that big house?" I reasoned.

"I suppose I could—I've picked a place a'ready. But 'tisn't that." He lifted a hand, clenched and shook it. "What I can't stand, what I won't stand is fat William sleepin' in Jean Harrington's bed. Sure I never slept in it myself."

"You never——" I took a stride closer to see his crumbling face. "You never slept in that bed?"

"Not wan time, never! Sure a bit of a pallet in the corner is good enough for me."

"I see, I see! That bed was a sort of a high altar?"

"It was Jean's bed wasn't it? She'd slept in it, didn't she?" He made smoothing motions with his hands, and spoke confidingly. "I always kept it nice and tidy: the linen sheets tucked in, and the silk covers without a wrinkle; and in winter I used put a hot-water bottle in it against the damp. It was ready——" He stopped.

"Ay Charles! Ready, aye ready!" I kept my temper in hand. "What do you want me to do then?"

"What you are well able for." He gestured a tame fist. "Didn't you run William Daunt out the gate this morning? Didn't you stand Bill Sheedy on his ear, and to hell with your Hinjoo, and his three-point contact? Didn't you?"

"I did. Do you want me to put Uncle William out of Jean Harrington's bed?"

"I want more than that." He gestured his fist again. "Me and you ag'in the world! And can't we play the game the way them two dealt the cards? Are you listenin'?"

"How do you play it?"

"They threw my things out, didn't they?"

"And you want to throw William Daunt's things out?"

"Why not I?"

I waved that aside. "A silly game, Charles! You can't throw William Daunt's things about. It is his house, you know. He'd love to put Jerome Farley on to us, and back to jail for me, as a breaker of the peace."

"Blast him! so he would."

"And blast you too! Do you want me back in jail?"

"Oh gor' Dave! Don't say that! But what about my darlin' bed?"

"It is your bed beyond a doubt. We can take that back all right."

"And lose it again when your back is turned?"

I knew Charley of old. He was hugging himself. He had some asinine scheme in mind, and I would have nothing to do with it.

"Out with it, old gluggerhead!" I ordered.

Charley chuckled happily. "I was only tryin' you out, Dave. Sure I have a plan o' me own to beat the band." He thrust his face within a foot of mine. "A darlin' plan! I'm putting it into the new play I'm writin'——"

I shoved his face away. "If it's that sort of plan I'll not touch it," I said firmly.

His hands besought me, and his voice hurried. "But wait, wait! Wait till you hear. This is Friday night isn't it?"

"Or Saturday morning."

"Then to-morrow is Sunday?"

"Wise fellow! And next day Monday."

"And Monday it is. Monday is the D-dam' day. Are you listenin'?"

"I'm listenin'," I humoured him.

"We are goin' to do this in a' absolutely law abiding and decorous way. Now, then, ould William has gone up to Limerick to see his solicitor. He is coming back on Monday, and I heard him arrangin' with Bill Sheedy to meet the late train with the station-wagon. That means he don't get back to Beananaar till eleven pipemma. And what does he find?"

"He finds that the bed has walked out on its four legs."

"Eggs-actly! I've it all planned. I got a room picked, with a strong oak door—they are all oak. I'll nail the window down, and I'll put a patent Yankee lock on the door—I'm handy that way, and you'll give me the price. And there you are! The two Bills arrive home, and the bed is gone. Down the passage they come raging, to find a locked door. They knock, they shout, they kick. 'Who's that?' says I in a mild way. 'Open up you so-and-so son of a so-and-so!' And I open up—just like that. And in they come, and there's the bed. Ho-Ho!"

"Eggs-actly, Mr. Cashan! And Bill Sheedy clouts you thorough to behold; and the bed is gone again."

"Not on your life, Dave!"

"Why not?"

"Because you'll be sitting on the bed." He leant, and patted me affectionately. "Right on top of the bed, Dave!"

"Like a sultan in his hareem!"

"Like the lord of the situation! You'll do that for me Dave, won't you? It's the last thing I'll ever ask."

"You'll want my help to shift the bed too?"

"No! You'll do nothing at all to give Jerry Farley a hold on you. About ten o'clock you'll evade Tade Murphy—if he's still on the watch—and I'll have everything ready again your coming. Are you game, Dave?"

"Will you be game, you fat coward?"

"I'll be no coward Monday night, and you'll see that," said Charley, and there was a strange hard note in his voice.

"A tame ending to your melodrama, Charles," I said. "Don't you want a bit of blood-and-murdher?"

"No—no! In the play I'll have skin and hair flying, but this has to be done quiet and lawful for your sake, and not a whisper of a word to anyone. Are you on?"

I lit my pipe, and out of the side of an eye saw Charley's restless feet and restless hands. It took me some time to make up my mind, but I made it up, and I knew what I was doing when I spoke quietly.

"I will be there at ten o'clock on Monday night."

"Good man yourself!" he cried triumphantly.

I thought he would embrace me. But I shoved him roughly aside, and set foot on the path curving up through the spinney in the half-dark.

Charley came up to my shoulder, and went on a little ahead. He was very solicitous of me now, ready as it were to hold me up lest I dash my foot against a stone. "There's a corrig of a rock stickin' out there, and don't bust your toe all to glory." I did. "Didn't I warn you? Hub over to the right—there's a root to cripple you." I missed that root. "Come on now, 'tis easy footin' to the stile."

I went over the stile between two hawthorns, and stepped out on to the Grianaan road in bright moonlight. The fork to The Cottage and Beananaar was only a hundred or so yards further down. Charley was at my side. I knocked my pipe out on my palm and pocketed it.

"I might have offered you a fag, Charley," I said.

"I gave up smoking years ago."

"Don't you smoke the clays you get at wakes?"

"Smoke is bad for the sight at night time, and it ruins the scent altogether."

"What scent?"

"Sure every man has a scent. I could trail you anywhere my eyes shut. Do you know, you have a different smell to-night? You didn't smell at all nice last night."

"The prison smell that was, the smell of death-in-life. Well here is the parting of the way, and I'm off to bed."

I stopped at the fork, and looked up the Beananaar branch. The road, reddish-brown between the black bulk of bushes, was empty and silent. If Tade Murphy was about anywhere he was not showing himself. I couldn't see the gate of The Cottage in its escalonia hedge. Charley touched my sleeve, and pointed a thumb.

"You'll be coming up for a collogue with Jean?" Was the oaf poking fun at me?

"Go and boil your fat head!"

"Ho-ho-ho!" He was plain jibing now. "Don't think you can fool me. You took the long way round, but you're home now. Come on up! She'll be sitting at her window waiting for you—an', maybe, a rub of perfume behind her ear."

"Thank the Lord, I clouted you," I said.

"I'm easily clouted, amn't I?" said Charley softly.

"Yes, you are." I pointed a finger at him. "You are just plain jealous Mr. Cashan."

"Jealous?" he wondered.

"Yes! You may own a bed, but you don't own the woman that gave it to you."

"Holy God!" Words failed him for a moment. Then he moved his head in heavy assent, and his voice rumbled heavily. "Maybe I am jealous, but you got it the wrong way. Women are the divil; they break the friendship of men. Jean Harrington is nice, but she is a divil all the same; and she is apt to steal you away from me, and what would I do then in my—predicament?"

The big baby could always get inside my guard.

"Never mind, old son!" I said. "Jean will be in her beauty sleep, and we'll not waken her. Come on! I'll see you as far as Beananaar and take a peep at that room of yours."

"And waken ould William?" said Charley doubtfully.

"Let him wake, then," I said, and turned into the fork.

IV

I walked on slowly, hands in pockets, head down, and deep in thought. I was developing a strange theory, adding a piece here and a piece there. I had played with that theory before, but I was not playing now. Charley Cashan shambled along at my right shoulder.

The escalonia hedge was on my left. I did not look at it. I passed the dark-green gate without a glance.

And then, a voice I knew spoke out in fierce disappointment.

"Slinking by! What have I done to deserve this, blast ye?"

'*My heart would hear her and beat had it lain for a century dead.*' That was the line that came into my mind. I turned slowly. Jean Harrington was leaning far over the garden gate, and the moon was shining on her. I said nothing at all. I just looked, and felt that the night was a decent sort of night after all.

She opened the gate smartly and came out on the road, and her every movement was warm with indignation. She was in a short, walking dress and light-coloured short-sleeved blouse; and, thrown on her firm shoulders, was a scarf of some light material—chiffon or mohair or something. My gosh! She was indignant and hurt, and her voice showed that.

"You two bohunks were out on some play? You were, you know you were! Why was I left out of it? What have I done? Why didn't I know? Did I ever let you down? Why wasn't I asked? You always asked me."

"No ma'am," I said softly. "You just came, and you were always welcome—Jeanathan."

"And welcome no longer!" She would not be placated. "But don't think you can give me the cold shoulder, Mr. David Daunt!" She flung round on Charley, who was steadily backing up the road. "As for you, Charley Cashan, you chicken-stealer, you hanger-on-to-coat-tails, you—you gluggerhead of a baboon, I'll not have you taking my place.

Do you hear me?" She thrust a hand at him. "Get out of here! Begone! Away with you to your own hole-and-corner!"

Charley put his hands over his ears, turned, and went off in a shamble that was almost a trot. Probably he'd slink over the hedge when he got round the curve; and I hoped that he'd run into Tade Murphy and get booted home. He did.

I turned to Jean. She was still the impulsive, warm-hearted, possessive Jean, but, for a woman who had sadly dismissed me twenty-four hours ago, she was behaving inconsistently. And now she was beginning to think so herself. Her mouth opened, and she put a hand up to cover it. The moon was shining into the golden lustre of her eyes, and it made the copper of her hair darker. And I felt the vibrancy of the vital force in her, and shied away from it. Using her own idiom I said:

"Puir auld Chairlie! a flea in his lug—maybe twa!"

But she was quite heartless about Charley. She swung her head.

"Och! he's used to that. I only wanted to get rid of him."

"And so you did ma'am, but there was no need to explode a bomb at him."

"Stop it, Dave! I wanted to talk to you."

"Were you waiting for me?" I took a step nearer.

We were face to face. I was in love with her. I couldn't do anything about that, and I no longer wanted to do anything about it. I wasn't shying away any more. I just wanted to take her into my arms. She sensed that; and she turned aside, and moved a hand.

"Let's walk for a bit. You'll do the talking."

This was better. We walked slowly, two feet apart, down to the fork and back again. I don't know how many times we did that ambit—if ambit is the right word. The bright night and its peace wrapped us round. We had the world to ourselves. I did not even think of Tade Murphy.

"I did want to see you, but it was only feminine curiosity,"

she admitted. "Just greedy for news at first hand! I walked
down as far as the Grianaan gate—and turned back. And
then along came you and Charley. I saw red for a minute.
One day home, and you were at your old tricks."

"No Jean. I met Charley—casually," I said, "and the
old tricks are no good any more."

That troubled her. A sadness came into her voice, a gentle
sadness without trace of rebellion. "Indeed, the old tricks
are no good any more. We cannot begin again. Never mind,
David! Do not tell me anything——"

"Hold your hosses! Dammit, woman! Me, I don't want
you to pine away and die of feminine curiosity. What news
did Charley give you?"

"I didn't see the tough. I was in Kantwell, and there were
rumours."

"Such as?"

"You were back and a devil on two legs, same as ever.
And you were you know—I mean a bit of a devil on two
legs. Your uncle had left Grianaan and gone to Beananaar,
but only as a temporary arrangement, to give you time to
settle in and take over the reins. Was it as easy as that, David,
or was there any truth in the wee sma' rumour that William
Daunt was out for good?"

"You'd like to know, wouldn't you?" I half teased her.

"You needn't tell me," she began, and then blazed. "Of
course I want to know, you thug!"

"Fair enough!" I said, "seeing that you are largely re-
sponsible for what happened this morning."

"Nonsense David!" But she was not a scrap surprised.

"Not a bit of nonsense, and you know it. Look, Jean! You
and I met last night and we teamed up. Straight off you en-
lightened me on the situation at Grianaan." I reached a
hand and just touched her firm forearm. "You told me all I
wanted to know, all I must know to carry on——"

"I might be wrong."

"You might keep your mouth shut and not interrupt me,"
I said rudely. "When I left here last night I knew what I must

do to keep the peace at Grianaan. And that very thing I did this morning."

"Did you——? Sorry Dave!"

"I did, and don't start running a temperature. Listen to me!"

And pacing up and down I told her everything, well nearly everything. I did not tell her anything about Tade Murphy and Joseph Yoseph, and Jerome Farley's ideas. That would be coming too near home, and might distress her. Everything else I told her, from last night up to and including Father Eujun's visit. And at the end she said quietly but warmly: "Thank you, David, my dear!"

She hadn't interrupted me once. She hadn't chuckled, or protested, or commanded or commented. But she had come closer and taken my arm confidently. And I did not press her hand against my side. Now, silence settled between us, and I waited. She chuckled softly.

"David Daunt is home, and get out from under! You fooled me last night. You disappointed me, you were so meek and mild, and so wanting peace. And this morning——"

"Didn't I keep the peace, dammit?"

She shoved me away playfully. "Bill Sheedy might not think so. It's all right, Dave, and I'll take my share of credit. You had to show your hand right from the start, and prove that William Daunt didn't really count. You can carry on now, as we say, without let or hindrance. What's 'let'?"

"How would I know, schoolmarm?" Then I said casually, "There's still a small job I have to do for Charley."

"Let Charley do his own jobs," she said, I thought, heartlessly.

"He never could," I said.

"If he wanted to. He lives in a world of his own, where he does all the jobs. He has got a hard shell, and William Daunt cannot put a dent in it."

"He has got his Achilles heel all the same." I was still casual. "Say, did you ever present him with a bed?"

She chuckled again. "He told you about it? I did." We were opposite the cottage and she gestured that way. "He used sleep in there on a frowsy pallet, and when I left Beananaar I left him a good bed—my second-best bed—same like Ann Hathaway got. I know, I know!" she said wisely. "It is the best bed in Beananaar, and Uncle William has taken it for himself. Charley wants you to get it back for him?"

"Something like that," I said carelessly.

"Don't Dave! Ignore William Daunt. If Charley Cashan is not man enough to keep his bed let him go back to his pallet."

"Let him, begobs!" said I agreeably. I didn't tell her that Charley had never abandoned his pallet. I was cutting her out of one of our plays.

We were in front of her open gate, and, abruptly, she turned in and shut it between us. She put her hands on the top bar, and with no stress in her voice put me a half-question.

"Your mother has not once mentioned my name, David?"

"How do you know?" I played for time.

"Of course I know. She is a possessive woman—and so am I. She wants you for herself alone."

"And to keep my books for me," I added. "Do you know, she is dam' good at book-keeping by double-entry?"

"She could be," Jean agreed.

"Teach your grandmother to suck eggs," I told her, "but thank you all the same." Then I said abruptly, "Will you take her for a drive on Sunday? I'll have a car after that, and I'll take ye both."

"Oh dear! Oh dear!" There was distress and longing in her voice. "I don't know what to do. I don't want to interfere at Grianaan, but I know there is a tie between us, David. But I am afraid. I spoiled your life, David."

"Stop that, Jean!"

"But I did. I was a hot-headed young fool. I took nine

years out of your life, and I can do nothing to restore them. And I want to do so much! But I can't—I can't——"

There was hysteria in her voice. I put my hands over hers and gripped, and felt the tension, and felt it slacken. I used all my will.

"Listen Jean! All that is over and done with. Let us not kick against any pricks. Let us just carry on as we are, and let the years work out our destiny for us. Time is on our side Jean, and let us give time a chance."

"Thank you, David!" Her eyes were on mine, and I could see the glisten of tears. I could have drawn on her hands, then, and kissed her. But I only smoothed down her firm forearms, and let her go. She turned and walked straight-footed to her door, which was ajar. She did not look back but lifted a hand. "Good night, my dear!" she called huskily.

"One hell of a night!" I said in my throat.

Chapter XI

THE TIGER PROWLS

I

I plodded down the road for Grianaan, and my feet were heavy, so was my head, and my heart was not light. Jean Harrington did not know what to do, and I did not know either. I stopped and stamped a soft sole on the road. *I do not understand her*, I said aloud. *I can only understand her by disbelieving what I saw with my own eyes. But take your own advice, damn you! Give the years a chance.*

I did not lift head till I reached the white gate of Grianaan. I looked up at the house serenely shining in the moonlight; I looked across at Kantwell in grey and black; I saw the light-house winking far out on the estuary point; and finally I looked back up the road. A tall man in grey was striding easily towards me, his feet making no sound. He was Tade Murphy, coming in the open at last. He halted in front of me, and shook his head reprovingly.

"You don't make things easy, Mr. Daunt."

"Should I, Mr. Murphy?"

"Maybe you shouldn't then," said Tade agreeably, but with meaning. If he had a job in hand, he could not do much about it if I stayed in bed.

"Fair enough!" I said. "Have a cigarette? Go on man! You've been on the watch long enough."

He hesitated, and took one. "Man alive! I was wanting a couple of puffs," he said.

I held a match for him, and saw his wide cheekbones and strong, flat chin. He straightened up, and inhaled deeply, and so did I.

"Any interesting talk to-night to interest your Old Man?" I asked casually.

"I wasn't listening," he said definitely. "What I heard last night was enough for me, and I wouldn't listen again for any man living."

"Tell your Super that?"

"I told him. And what did I get?" I saw his grin. " 'You were a shameless eavesdropper right enough,' says he, 'and I'm ashamed of you.' And I couldn't tell whether he meant it or not."

I was still casual. "You saw me go straight to bed last night, didn't you?"

"Japers, sir! I was on top of the wall in one lepp when I saw you haul mad Charley out from under the bed." His hand moved oxterwards. "I was on to him every minute after that."

"But he is on my team, you know."

"When I'm on duty Mr. Daunt, I wouldn't trust the Pope o' Rome."

"I suppose you know that Charley was the third man on the prowl last night?"

"I guessed it anyway."

"He says there was a fourth man."

"And who might he be?" asked Tade promptly.

"Charley didn't know. A poacher who could see in the dark? Tell your Super. He might have an idea."

"Thank you, sir, I will."

"Did you see Charley to-night?"

Tade laughed outright. "I was near enough to hear young Mrs. Daunt take the hide off him before sending him off naked." He lifted a finger. "But he didn't go far before he stopped. I was paralleling him inside the fence, and at the bend of the road he dodged between two bushes for a peep. Do you know what I had in my hand? A solid lump of a divot I heeled out of the edge of the ditch. 'Go back to your bed, peepin' Tom,' says I, and let him have it on the side of the head. Gobs, sir! I didn't think he could do it, but he lepped the width of the road, and he was runnin' before he landed."

"That fixed Charley for the night," I said with some satisfaction.

"I made sure it would. I wouldn't have him snooping when I wasn't. I pursued him right up to Beananaar and round to the bank. I was at the corner of the byre when he was crawling in through a window." Tade rubbed the back of his head and laughed again. "Man dear! I was tempted, and I fell." Tade spread his hands wide and high. "Crawling through the window he was, and his—rear elevation that size. I'm a Tipperary stone-thrower, and I had a solid lump of a pebble in my hand. What else could I do but let him have it? Only twenty yards, but dammit! I missed him by an inch, and bang! the stone went through a pane. He yowled and clumped on the floor inside; and there wasn't another cheep out of him."

The two of us laughed heartlessly. The fool's troubles are always risible.

"Not a very happy night for Charles!" I said. "But he'll learn to stay put this time." I moved a hand gatewards. "Seeing me to the corner of the house?"

"Why not I?" said Tade.

We went up the drive together, Tade watchfully taking the side nearest the hedge. We went round the back of the Outside Room, and I stopped at the door.

"Let us take it easy," I said, and touched his sleeve. "Come in and take the weight off your legs."

"That might be no harm," Tade said.

I felt for the bunch of keys my mother had given me, opened the door, and put finger on switch just inside the jamb. Tade followed me in, shut the door, and stood with his back against it. I went across and switched on the anglepoise lamp on the desk. Tade was at my side in long strides.

"You will excuse me, sir!" he said, and flicked the heavy tweed curtains across the wide window. "Better be sure than sorry," he said.

"Sure and sorry, I don't like," I said, and fitted the key into the corner-cupboard door. "You are not a teetotaller? No! A small taste of Paddy to shorten the night?"

"I dunno should I? Well, just the one finger."

"Don't worry about your reflexes," I told him. "I'm going to bed, and you can sit under a vine and fig tree—if you must."

I poured three muscular fingers of whisky into a tumbler. "No water handy, try a splash of soda. There you are!" I poured a finger for myself and added a good dollop of soda.

"Health and life!" he toasted, "and long may you reign in Grianaan." He took his drink continently.

I wasn't used to whisky or whiskey. Mine was drowned in soda-water, but a heat and a bite came through that was contrary to my human chemistry.

Tade Murphy coughed delicately. "'Tis a good dram that makes Tade Murphy cough," he said. "You don't care for it yourself?"

"You'll drive me to it yet," I said, and I exploded a little. "How long is this damn'd baby-sitting to go on?"

"And a fine healthy baby, God bless him!" said Tade easily, and added seriously, "The Super doesn't do things for fun."

"He thinks there is someone on my tail but he is only guessing, and who has he in mind anyway?"

If I had hoped to draw something out of the guard I was disappointed.

"I don't know," he said evenly. "Myself I'm plain puzzled. All I know is that I have to watch you like a hawk, and report movements." He leant to me persuasively, comfortingly. "And another thing I know: you are well-liked in Kantwell. No one has any ill-will against you——"

"One or two, Tade?"

"And you drew their teeth, and, if you didn't, there are plenty to draw them for you. All decent people are glad you're back. You'll remember that football team you raised. Some of the lads—no younger than yourself—play yet, and I heard talk to-day of you being made a vice-president. Slainthe again, sir! and we'll clear your feet."

Tade emptied his glass, and set his hand against another drink.

"Are you for the window to-night?" he asked.

"No! I must go in as I came out."

"Maybe you don't want me to know?" he said half-coaxingly.

"Come and I'll show you," I volunteered.

He snapped off the desk lamp, went ahead of me to the door, and snapped off the light there. Then he opened the door. He was standing with his broad back covering me when I stepped out. I pulled the door softly shut, and listened with him. There was nothing to hear.

We moved soft-footed round the end of the Outside Room, and then he let me go ahead along the grass margin close to the wall. The moon was still clear and white-shining, and the lower door, by the side of the parapet, was no longer in shadow. I stepped in front of it and lifted hand for the latch.

"God'll mighty! I'm a dumb cluck," Tade Murphy exploded, and pulled me forcefully aside.

"Blast, man!" I twitched my shoulder.

"Steady Mr. Daunt—steady! This is my job. Has that door been on the latch all the time you were away?"

"Had to be. Ah! I see your point. You've got your torch, and we'll take a look-see."

"You'll stay put," he said in his throat, and his firm shoulder held me away from the door. He whispered urgently, "If a man was laying for you could he choose a better place?" Then he made light of it. "Och! there is nothing in it, but I'll run my flash over the place to make sure."

Tade was not as confident as he sounded, but he did not hesitate. He faced the door and braced his shoulders, his electric torch in his left hand, and his left coat lapel thrown back. For a moment the moon gleamed on the butt of a long Webley. The latch clicked, the door went wide-open with a grate, and the light of the torch flashed along the passage.

But, even as the light flashed, possibly half-a-second before it flashed, the back-door, up the steps into the yard, banged shut—not a loud bang but a definite one.

"By God! the bastard was there," said the guard savagely, and leaped through the door.

II

Tade Murphy had made a mistake in leaping through the door and blundering down the passage. If he had at once rushed round the end of the house, he might have got close enough to identify the lurker. Well, I might get a glimpse myself.

But I did not go blundering blindly. Not any more. Some-one meant business that time, and he might still be meaning it. I sidled quickly along the wall and round the end of the Outside Room, which was in shadow, and peeped out from the corner.

And I did catch a glimpse. There was a rustle far up the garden, and a dark figure went over the back wall nimble as a cat.

In daylight I would not hesitate to run him down, if I were able. But not at night over rough country. I knew all I wanted to know, and the lurker might be only trying to lure me on.

"If that was an invitation I am not accepting it, brother," I said softly, and I added savagely, *"God have mercy on you, you hound! I will not."*

I heard the back door being pulled open, and I sidled back to my place at the open door by the side of the front steps. I was hardly there before Tade came driving round the corner. He was angry and frustrated, and his teeth were grinding. He wanted to go asearching, but he would not leave me unprotected.

"Charley Cashan was right," he said. "There was a

fourth. Oh, hell! if I had a scrap o' sense we could have trapped him." He moved a hand widely. "See anything this way?"

"No one passed this way," I said heavily, and touched his arm. "Take it easy, son! You did fine, but you can do no more to-night. I'll crawl off to my bed like a sick hound."

"By the lord! we'll make someone sick," said Tade Murphy.

I turned into the open doorway, and the guard was at my shoulder, his flashlight splaying out ahead. He bolted the door behind us. We went down the passage together, and he went up the steps and bolted the back door. He was making no mistakes now.

"Like locking the stable door, and the horse away," he growled, "but we'll take a look round."

We did. There were no electric fittings down here, but Tade's flashlight probed into every corner from the doorway of each room: the immense kitchen, pantries, sculleries, disused bedrooms, we missed nothing—and found nothing. There was plenty of dust everywhere, and plenty of traces in the dust; but, as I told Tade, I had been down for a look-over in the morning; and traces meant nothing. One thing I did observe and kept to myself. The iron lever used in lifting the range lids was lying on top of the range. It had not been there in the morning, for I had looked for it to find if the lids were rusted in. It would be an adequate blunt instrument. I did not touch it. I knew too much already.

Back in the passage I said: "I'll let you out the back door."

But Tade was very thorough this time. "There are too many ways in and out of this house," he said. "Up you go!"

He flashed his light on the bottom step of stone stairs, curving up to the front hall. I made no protest. I led him up the stairs where the tick-tock of the grandfather clock greeted us uncaring, and through the curtain, and along the dimly-glowing hall to my room. I softly opened the door, and felt for the light-switch, but before I pressed it I looked back at my mother's door. There was no line of light along the foot of it.

"Sleep sound, Mummy!" I whispered. "It will not be long now."

I switched on the light and went in. My mother was sitting on my bed.

She crinkled her eyes at me: brilliant eyes, but tired eyes too, and the skin of her face was drawn tight over the firm and shapely bones. She was wearing her creamy voluminous dressing-gown.

My mouth opened, and I had not a word to say, but I was thinking furiously. My mother was fighting to remain calm.

"There is something I don't like going on here, David," she said very slowly, and her voice only trembled once.

My back was turned to the policeman, and cautiously I lifted a silencing finger to my lips. She rose to her feet, and I went over, and took her firmly into my arms, sending comfort to her with all my will. My black head was against her white one, and I whispered softly into her ear, but I did not care whether Tade Murphy heard me or not.

"There is nothing queer happening, Mummy. What is happening is the most natural thing in the world, and I know it now. Listen!" I shook her a little to make contact sure. "In two-three days all this will be over, and you and I will be able to carry on the same as always—the same as always, Mummy. You can be sure of that now."

She sighed deeply. "Yes, Davy!" she whispered back trustingly.

"You will go to bed so—and sleep and sleep."

I led her out, and she came without a protest, just lifting a hand like a benediction towards Tade Murphy. She did not speak again. At her own door she smoothed a slow hand down my cheek in her old gesture. And that was all.

When I got back Tade Murphy had gone. An exit by the

window would not trouble him. A whistle that imitated the double-note of a blackbird's song came through and a light flashed twice. I lifted a hand, switched off my light, and sat on the side of the bed where my mother had waited for me. I did not go to bed for a long time.

III

I had a good deal to think of, and I thought of it all. I went back ten years, I went back two days, I went forward three days, and I did not care to contemplate the third day. I was not sure of anything—not really sure—but I was sure enough to take a chance, a chance dangerous as a rattlesnake, but if I did not take it I could never lift my head, or get another chance to clear my feet.

After a while I considered the present. My mother had known that I had gone out, but she would not know where. Had she waited here to question me? But she had not waited to question. Had she come to guard my room? Was she in Jerome Farley's confidence? Was she too on the watch? Then, she had been in my room for a long time. She would have heard Tade and me come in and go out again. Had she heard the stealthy movements of someone else? She would have heard the muted bang of the back door. If she were on the watch she would have seen the prowler go over the parapet and up the garden. It was bright moonlight, and would she recognize the prowler? But, if she had, why had she said no word to me or the policeman? Instead she had gone to her room with scarcely a word. Then she must have some reason of her own—or she was acting under orders. I left it at that.

Another thought! Tade Murphy was an able scout, and carried grey matter under his thatch. If the prowler had fled by the garden he would deduce that my mother had seen him, and probably recognized him. But Tade Murphy had made no attempt to question her. I did not give him much time. I did not want to give him any time, and he would see that. And he had not stayed to discuss the point with me. It was obvious that he was leaving the questioning to a sterner man. His duty was to tell everything to his chief, and his chief would not hesitate to question even my mother. And she would tell!

Fair enough! Jerome Farley would question me too, and I would have a few things to say—and a request to make. I must now play the game as it lay, and the end could not be far off. I might be dead at that end, but if I died Jerome Farley would know enough to clear my name.

"*A clear name is not much good to a dead man*," I said gloomily, and went to bed.

I slept as sound as the rock of ages.

Chapter XII

CARDS ON THE TABLE?

I

Saturday afternoon I went into Kantwell for pipe tobacco and cigarettes—and for another purpose too.

All the morning I had worked with Molly Cray building stooks in the cornfield; and, after a while, Joseph Yoseph turned up, peeled off his tunic, and joined us in the work. He was interested in Molly, and she in him, and they would keep shouldering each other, until finally she shouldered him into a half-built stook, and the stook went over, and the two of them with it. Whereupon I chased her off to prepare the midday meal in the bothy.

The sun was again busy making a countryman of me. The backs of my hands were colouring nicely, and, looking down my nose I could see the first faint freckle. The farm lads, to show their growing goodwill, had decided not to take the half-day off. The oats would be shedding its grain, and the weather might break.

"Fair enough!" I had said. "Time-and-a-half to five, and double time thereafter! One of you keep tally."

I had midday dinner in the kitchen with my mother, Julie Brady ministering unto us. Chicken and bacon it was, with white cabbage and floury potatoes, and apple pie like Julie made, and coffee and cream. Julie deplored that I had lost me appetite altogether, but I about tied myself to the ground.

"Any visitors to-day?" I had asked casually.

"No one in particular." That was my mother, equally casual but Julie would have none of that.

"And is Jerry Farley no wan in particular, and the dacent man eatin' us out of house and home?" Her voice belled. "Will you take a look at that lady there? Did you ever in all your life know her to keep her mouth shut, and like a split in a stone it was?"

"Julie Brady," said my mother warmly, "if your mistress keeps her mouth shut you should not open yours."

"And did I open it once?" cried the outraged Julie. "Sure all I said was that if I had a double-barrel gun I'd put a couple o' buckshot where they'd make sittin' down onaisy."

I had forgotten that Julie's room, too, overlooked the yard and garden, and that Julie was as wakeful as a bird. She had seen someone last night, and so had my mother. However, I did not pursue the subject any further. I did not need to.

I rested for an hour. Then I shaved and showered and put on clean clothes: a comfortable flannel suit and an open-necked nylon shirt. Then I strolled into town. My mother accompanied me as far as the gate, and she was a shade anxious.

"Don't mind what anyone says or looks," she said. "Should I come with you?"

"No ma'am. This is no longer an ordeal." It wasn't. The big ordeal was yet to come.

As I strolled down the slope towards the bridge, I saw a figure in dark-blue taking the curve ahead of me. Joseph Yoseph had left the cornfield, and was on duty again. He leant an elbow on the parapet and waited for me.

"Saturday, Joseph!" I said.

"So it is," he said, a little perplexed.

"And you've broken your Sabbath day?"

"So I have." His saturnine aquiline face smiled at me. "And haven't you a parable in your Testament that says what a man might have to do on the Sabbath day?"

"Am I your ass or your ox?"

"Whatever you are, you'll fall into no pit if I can help it."

"You have a tongue in your head," I said, "and God help Molly Cray!"

"She's one gay divil," he said, and smiled almost fondly.

"Duty before divilment! I'm going to Spillane's for some 'baccy. Are you coming?"

"I'll look on you not too far off," said Joseph.

I took a longish, narrow cardboard box from the skirt pocket of my jacket—the poacher's pocket.

"Hand that in to your Superintendent in passing?" I requested. "It's only a stick of dynamite."

"It 'ud take more than one to make a dint in him," Joseph said.

I lif ᵊd the lid to show him. "It is what is known as a blunt instrument. Ask him to look it over, and say I'll be in to report later on."

I lit a cigarette, and went up into the town ahead of Joseph, but instead of crossing the Square I turned left and entered the Catholic chapel, first dipping a finger in the stone basin of holy water. That church had been designed by Pugin and was finely proportioned. Far up the aisle votive candles gleamed on their stand. A ruby light suspended from the high-up groin glowed before the sanctuary. Shawled figures, here and there, swayed and prayed. An old man was doing the Stations of the Cross, pausing to contemplate and moving on again.

I knelt behind the last seat, remembering the Pharisee and the Publican. Did I flatter myself that I was not a Pharisee? I was not humble enough for the Publican, and so I did not ask for mercy. I said the Lord's Prayer. *Forgive us our trespasses as we forgive them who trespass against us.* I paused there. *I bear no enmity. I do not ask for Justice, for Justice is only Vengeance. I want—God! I do not know what I want. You know.* I said the Prayer to the Woman, and felt a strange peace.

I crossed the Square by the flank of the Protestant church, and round the curve into Main Street. At Spillane's I got me some tobacco, and ordered a supply to be sent to Grianaan. I went on to Tom Farrant's at the Motor Garage, an old friend of the family, and a friend still. I looked over his stock, and was pleased with a long, stream-lined American car. I walked round it three times, and Tom chuckled.

"I like that one, you old robber," I said, "but my mother will come in and decide."

Tom rubbed his hands. "The sale is made so, young David. Ellen Furlong walked round that car three times a day for the last month. You are your mother's son."

I met friends, many friends: friends of my own generation, friends of an older one, youngsters grown to manhood who had looked up to me as a County footballer in the days of their adolescence. I was well received everywhere. I had two beers and refused several. Nine years blunt the point of tragedy. "The evil that men do lives after them." Robin Daunt was dead, and men remembered that he was evil. But I was alive, and had paid for the ill I had done, and I was going to carry on in spite of hell and high water. It was spirit that counted with these men. And wasn't I Ellen Furlong's son? And who would dare say a word against the young widow, Jean Harrington?

I had my second beer in Jerry Broder's bar with two members of my old team. And it was there that Bill Sheedy came in. He stopped inside the door and glared at me, tempted to brazen it out. He was not drunk, but he had drink taken, as we say. His nose was an inflamed bulb, and there was blue-black under both eyes. His eyes were the pinkish-white of the belly of a salmon too long in fresh water. He thrust his slack mouth at me, his face sheerly wicked.

"Get outside, Sheedy!" said Jerry Broder from behind the bar.

"Ah-ha! Mr. David Daunt and his friends!" he jeered in his high voice. "But he'll be alone some fine day, and I'll know it."

Big John Walsh, who used play centre-field with me in the old days, took one stride forward, and Sheedy turned and went hurriedly out the door. He had not the final hardi-hood, and that lack might make him supremely treacherous.

"Don't worry about Whitey Sheedy," said big John, turning to me. "He'll get his marching orders if you say the word."

"Leave him be," I said. "He is loyal in his own way."

"Ay! and if he's not careful he'll take his loyalty where it belongs, and that's the hot hob o' hell."

I knew what he meant.

II

I made my way back to the Square and the Garda Station. Joseph Yoseph was at the corner and moved away in front of me. The Station Sergeant was in the big room as before, but he was not asleep this time, and he was not alone. Three or four of the boys were busy doing nothing, and greeted me cheerfully.

"Conduct only fair to middling," I said. "I've come to give myself up."

"Go on in and tell him," the Station Sergeant said. "He's waiting for you in a hell-of-a-temper."

Already he had the desk-flap lifted. He led me round the table, and put a careful hand on the knob of the brown door. "We have to take him quiet as a mouse," he whispered. He then dunted the door with his fist, thrust it open, shoved me two paces through into the cool blue room, and banged the door shut.

"Blast it!" I said.

"If that was Murty Conners I'll splade him," said the quiet voice of Jerome Farley. "Sit down! I've a good deal to say to you."

"I have something to say myself too." I walked across the druggeted floor, and sat in the windsor chair at the corner of the black-topped table. I looked at Jerome Farley, massive in his massive chair, and saw no sign of a hell-of-a-temper. Buddha was right! With that impassive, moulded, yellow-skinned face, and expressionless brown eyes, helmet of hair, and solidly-corpulent body he could sit cross-legged and immobile under a pagoda. But who might worship him?

"Smoke if you want to," he said. He had his pipe in his dry fingers, but it was unlighted. He rubbed the bowl at each side of his nose, a fashion with some smokers, and looked at me mildly. He placed a hand on the thick file on the table before him, and his voice was placid.

"Forty-eight hours home, and you have added pages to this file of yours! When do I write *Finis?*"

"You do not know, but I can guess," I said. I was teasing tobacco for my pipe.

"Guess what?" he queried softly.

"At something seen through a glass darkly."

"Guess wrong, and I write *Finis* surely. There will be nothing else to write."

"And little to right." I pointed my pipe stem at a cardboard box on the table. The lid-lifter was lying on tissue paper, and the paper showed grey smudges. "Has fingerprinting reached Kantwell? Find any?"

"Not yours, son. You are one of the select many whose fingerprints are common currency. Tell me about this gadget?"

"I was looking for it in the basement-kitchen yesterday—mere curiosity. It should be on top of the range. It wasn't. It was there at two o'clock this morning."

He considered that, his face expressionless, and moved a hand. "Leave it! It is not evidence yet, since no one attacked you. Anything else?"

"If my mother won't talk, Julie Brady is unreliable. She suffers from night-blindness."

He pointed at the cardboard box. "I no longer need your mother's information, or Julie Brady's. Is that all?"

"The rest can wait. You have a lot to say to me?"

"So I have, and the time has come to say it. I did not expect it to come so soon, but things have moved rapidly, thanks to your night-hawking——"

"Just a moment!" I said. "There is Bill Sheedy——"

He fluttered a hand. "Forget him! He was under observation too, and he was not your third man—or fourth man, if there was a fourth."

"Carry on!" I said.

He threw his cold pipe amongst the dead matches in the ash tray, leant his abdomen against the table, and opened the file.

"I am going back a long way. I am going back nine years, or more." He turned pages, and tapped a finger. "This is a transcript of your evidence. You committed perjury."

"So the verdict implied," I said equably.

He went on in his remote easy voice. "Briefly, you heard a shot in a plantation a few hundred yards back of Beananaar. You knew about firearms, and knew it was not a shot from a fowling-piece, or even a twenty-two rifle. It was a pistol shot, and for a reason of your own, you wondered, and went to see. You found your cousin, Robin Daunt dead on his back behind the plantation, a bullet in his heart, and your short Webley lying on the grass near him. Your Webley, Mr. Daunt! You picked it up to make sure. And so Bill Sheedy found you. The only fingerprints on the gun were yours. That should have hanged you."

"It dam' near did," I said.

He inclined his massive head. "As you say. It was the dead man's disastrous reputation, his wife's unhappiness, your mother's popularity and your own, too, that just turned the scale. There was no clear evidence of premeditation. You had a habit of toting that Webley around with you to the danger of the State's lieges. Yourself and Jean Harrington used shoot target matches with it, a shilling a side."

"It was a source of income to her," I said foolishly.

He lifted head and looked at me, and his voice was slower than ever. "Yes, she could shoot. Surely she could shoot. In your evidence you implied that the gun must have been stolen from Grianaan. But you had a match the previous evening, and you left the gun at Beananaar."

I pointed a finger. "That is not in that file," I said harshly.

"No, that evidence was not given." He picked up a pencil, turned over a page, and tapped the paper. "There was another bit of evidence that was withheld too. The two together would have hanged you."

I was warned now. I scraped a match, set it to my pipe, and looked through the smoke at him. "You are only theorizing, Mr. Farley."

He sighted the pencil at me. "You'll know how good the theory is. Take a look at it? You went across to Beananaar that morning at ten o'clock. You met Jean Harrington, and she was weeping forlornly." He spread his hands on the file and a heaviness came into his voice. "Forlornly and despairingly! and she was only a girl, twenty years young. Her mouth was bleeding and her eyes blackening from a savage beating given her by her husband. He accused her of being your mistress."

"That was a foul lie." My eyes were stinging, and I was sorry that Robin Daunt had died so easily.

"A foul lie, yes! But how nearly true all the same? She was desperately unhappy, and you were desperately loyal. You tried to make life livable for her by carrying on as in the old days—you and she and Charley Cashan. But what would the husband think? Leave it! You went away raging that morning. You would find Daunt at the world's end, and you would break him in two with your bare hands."

"And I would," I grated.

"But you did not find him for two hours. You had time to cool off, you had time to decide on an easier way of killing. Your gun was handy at Beananaar, and you were found standing over Daunt's dead body, your gun in your hand. That bespoke premeditation—and a noosed halter. How is that for a theory?"

I relit my pipe. "Let us accept it and call it a day," I said. "You can't put me in jeopardy again."

"The day is long yet," he said. He pushed back his chair, placed his left ankle on his right knee, and joined his fingertips on the curve of his abdomen. He was Buddha all right, and his theories worse than any Karma. "Take it easy," he said. "I am going to trouble you now."

"You cannot leave it alone?" My voice was not as calm as it might be.

"No! not now. Assuming—only assuming—that you did not kill Daunt, I'll give you a theory of who did, a theory of what happened to make you take the rap. Listen! You heard the shot, and reconnoitred as before, and found Robin Daunt dead. But there was someone there before you. Jean Harrington was standing over her dead husband, and your gun was in her hand: your gun that had been left at Beananaar where she lived. Wait! You took the gun from her, and sent her away, chased her away, said something that sent her running, and, then, you wiped the gun clean of her finger-marks. And so Bill Sheedy found you. Fair enough, as you say yourself?"

I put my pipe on the corner of the table. This theory was so near home, that it made me cold as ice and cool as marble.

"That's some theory," I said. "You are implying that Jean killed her husband?"

"No, I imply nothing. It is what you assumed."

I waved that aside. "Very good! Let us take a look at your theory?"

"Go on."

"Have you studied Jean Harrington, Superintendent?"

"I'll say I have." He lifted hand and moved it three times. "She is Highland, she is proud, she is warmly tempered. She would not stand insult and manhandling. She would be as resilient as a slip of steel. She would face that devil again, but this time she would have something to protect herself. She had, and she used it. Well?"

"Yes, you know something of Jean Harrington," I said reasonably. "I will even admit that she might pull trigger in defence or on impulse. But——" and I slapped the table "——would that woman you picture let me—or anyone else —take the rap for her? Would she, you hellish tormentor?"

He dropped his leg and leant forward on the table.

"Would she, you self-tormentor?" he asked softly. "That's the question that nearly broke you in Southland Jail. That is the question that will not let you sleep at night, that sends you out to wander, and be drawn as by a magnet. Until you answer that question you cannot live any life worth while, here or anywhere else."

"I will not admit the question," I said a little desperately. "Why are you baiting me?"

"Because it is the way I have to work. That question of yours: would Jean Harrington let you take the rap? has worried me too. It has worried me for seven years." He smiled faintly. "I am a vain man, and I refuse to stay worried. And then I met your mother. And by the way," he said matter-of-factly, "I love your mother, but so does everyone, and that's all right. I got to know Jean Harrington too, and I could not fit her into any theory except one."

"What—another one?" I asked with some sarcasm.

"No—not another one! Into the theory that she knew you had killed her husband."

I sat up and forward. "Dammit, man! that implies that she is guiltless?"

"So it does, but leave it. I kept an open mind. You mightn't think so, but I have a lot of the woman in me: cruelty and intuitiveness. And I had a feeling that there was something hidden in your case. I said to myself: *I don't care whom I hurt, if I make Ellen Furlong a happy woman again.* Sheer vanity and selfishness! I began at the beginning. I asked myself: *Who would kill Robin Daunt?*"

"A good many if all tales be true."

"Let us stay at home. The weapon used points that way. You would kill him?"

"I would."

"And Jean Harrington?"

"She could—I admitted that."

"And the third member of your team, Charley Cashan?"

"If I told him——"

"Or Jean Harrington? He is her slave."

I moved a hand. "But he would not use a gun. He's utterly gun-shy."

"As you say. What about Bill Sheedy?"

"Robin Daunt's door-mat?"

"Pity you did not say worm or robot! A worm turns, and a robot becomes the creation of Frankenstein." He leant his corporation against the table-edge and lifted one finger.

"What about William Daunt?"

"His father?"

"It has been known to happen—for lust or lucre. Your blood-uncle is a cold-hearted—not cool, for he is not strong enough—a cold-hearted schemer under a benevolent facade. He was out of Beananaar—against his will. His unbeloved son, Robin, had a scandalous stranglehold on him, and made him give up Beananaar and any entail rights he had on Grianaan, and, in doing that, the son might have invited his own death. For William had an apple for each eye: one apple was your mother, the other was the ancestral freehold of Grianaan. He might win your mother, but, now, two lives stood between him and entailed Grianaan: yours and his son's. You've heard of killing two birds with one stone, and you know what happened. He married your mother, and practically owned Grianaan. He made one mistake, the mistake of a conceited man. He thought he could scare you off. You don't scare easily——"

"You are scaring me out of my skin," I put in.

"I'm doing my best. Well, I've only one other name on my list of candidates." He leant elbows on the table, and looked down at it. "That is your mother's name," he said in a low voice.

I did not say a word. I would not be drawn. Speaking of apples I was the apple of my mother's eye, and I had lost the apple of mine! I would not consider the possibilities. I lit my pipe steady-handed and waited. Jerome Farley leant back in his chair and put his arms along the rests.

III

Jerome Farley went off on a new tack.

"If you had killed Robin Daunt there was no more to be said—or done. You had paid. To get moving I had to work on the hypothesis that you had not killed him, and I had to put flesh and blood on the bare bones of that. Where did that lead me? It led me to consider what manner of lad David Daunt was. I found out plenty about a young hellion and his team mates, but I found nothing sordid. I found out about a man who would play a game to the end, given the right incentive. And I set out to find that incentive. Do you see where I went from there?"

"Not even as through a glass darkly."

Again he clasped his abdomen. "If you did not kill Robin, the killer was still under the glimpses of the moon, and the killer would soon learn that I was reinvestigating. I made no secret of it. I did the very opposite. I questioned and re-questioned all concerned with the case; I questioned scores who had nothing to do with the case, but knew all of you intimately. I set rumours afloat. People began to wonder, and they are still wondering. You can feel the tension in the air. Everyone is asking: what is going to happen now?"

"And what is going to happen now?" I asked cynically.

"What we are going to make happen." He lifted a finger. "The killer was safe as long as you were in jail and he—make it 'he'—kept his mouth shut. There was a dead-end to the road. But as soon as you got out of jail—ah then!" He reached for his pipe, saw that it was empty, and slapped it back on the table.

"I am out of jail," I said. "What then?"

"Then the killer might panic—only might—and decide to get rid of you at the earliest possible moment. The earlier the better, for he would know that I would get hold of you, probe you, make use of you, rouse the gorge in you, thresh things out of you until you were only a husk. Blast it all!" he swore mildly, "have you any grain in you at all?"

"Some corn won't thresh," I said humbly.

"You'll thresh all right, if you get the right incentive." He moved a finger again, and his voice was smooth as silk. "And the right incentive is the hope—the hope only—that Jean Harrington did not kill her husband."

I leant forward, put an elbow on a corner of the table, and looked him in the eye.

"Very well Superintendent Farley!" I said coolly. "What do you propose that I should do?"

He moved his massive head heavily, and for once his voice lifted. "I'm damn'd if I know." He thrust a hand at me. "It is you who must propose to do something. My hypothesis being that you are not the killer, then the killer has every incentive to kill you. That is why I have you watched and warded. You are a difficult man to watch, dam' your eyes! but that is no harm so long as you don't get yourself liquidated. You might induce the Ethiopian in the woodpile to show his black hide."

"And then?"

"I don't know!" He shook his head like a baited bull. "I don't know at all! He must be tricked into the open, and he must give himself away absolutely. And that is your job, Mr. David Daunt."

"Foul enough, you shirker!" I scathed grimly. "And will you kindly give me an idea as to how I am to find him?"

"Fair enough to that!" he said readily. "Let us consider who would want to kill you! Who would?"

"Isn't that much the same question as: who would want to kill Robin Daunt?"

"No, it isn't! Your mother, for instance, would not kill you." He fluttered a hand. "Forget about your mother, boy. Ellen Furlong would not kill anyone, though I could give you ten reasons why she might."

"And Jean Harrington?"

"Yes! she could kill you. There are three motives for getting rid of you: greed, fear, and vengeance——"

"Jean would come under the head of vengeance?" I said mildly derisive.

"Why not if you killed her husband? She might love him back of all. Tanning a woman's hide does not destroy the core where love abides. A woman, a dog, and a walnut tree—you know the old saw? Any tinker and his wife will confirm that."

" 'And the colonel's lady and Judy O'Grady are sisters under their skins,' " I quoted.

"Maybe, though Kipling juxtaposed the classes for the sake of the rhyme. The colonel's lady was in the bottom drawer compared to an O'Grady, of the best blood in Ireland."

"And talking of Jean Harrington, you are sleeping out and far to-night, the colour-sergeant said."

"Have it! There is our Mr. Sheedy? He said he'd hang for you, according to Molly Cray."

"The man who threatens seldom comes to hanging."

"But you slew his idol—or so he thinks. There is no doubt about the idol-worship. You treated Sheedy with contempt and contumely, and the man in the basement last night behaved true to Sheedy's character. Well?"

"All right!" I said. "You can have Bill."

"Can I have Charley Cashan too?"

"For tuppence. Fear, greed, vengeance—which?"

"Connote greed with possessiveness."

I considered the immobile face of the man, and spoke slowly. "I see your point. Charley worships Jean, but, like all worshippers, he has a strange fear of the worshipped. I am his buckler. And another thing." I lifted a hand. "Tade Murphy chased him into his kennel last night, and Charley is a good deal of a craven. He'd stay put. Anyone else?"

"The best wine for the last: William Daunt?"

"Fear, greed or vengeance?"

"All of them. If he killed his son, fear. If you killed him, vengeance. And a greedy possessiveness till the cows come home. You threw him out. If you die, his beloved Grianaan is his by entail, and the first fine careless rapture being long over, he'll get rid of your unprofitable mother. Are you aware that he has gone up to Limerick to take steps towards a legal separation? That hints some premeditation."

"Splendid!" I said. "Let us hang Uncle William."

"Not so easy—if he gets Bill Sheedy to do the dirty work."

"By the powers! so he might. This is a new thought, and you had given me plenty to think about already."

"Call it a day then." He leant his great body across the table, rested on his forearms, and folded one dry hand over the other. He looked at me for a long time, but his expression did not change. Then he drew a breath that was almost a sigh, and his voice was heavy. "I don't like saying it again, but to get anywhere you must take a chance. The Ethiopian in the woodpile——"

"Wrong!" I said a little bitterly. "You mean a tiger on two legs? You are for making me the decoy-goat tied at the foot of the tree."

"Something like that." He moved a slow head. "The tiger-man must be lured into the open——"

"That is easy. He must be lured to talk before he strikes, and that is not easy."

"And if he strikes first there is an end. I should never have asked you."

"You asked me nothing," I said, and leant towards him. "I am taking that chance. I have to." My voice tightened. "It means everything to me, and you know it."

I rose to my feet and turned towards the door. His quiet voice stopped me. 'Was there not something you had to say to me?"

"So there was. I nearly forgot."

That was a lie. I had not forgotten for a single moment.

Chapter XIII

AND ONE UP MY SLEEVE

I

I sat down again, and Jerome Farley watched me placidly, but no doubt he was busy with his thoughts. I spoke easily as if the matter was of no great importance.

"It's like this. A ticket-of-leave bloke like unto me, under the thumb of a man with a fetish for peace like you, has to be mighty careful not to break the law, or go within an ass's roar of breaking it."

"No, sir!" He tapped the table firmly. "In no circumstances will I look the other way for you—nor will any of my lads."

"It's not that. It's merely that a friend of mine wants me to stand by him in a small job he has on hands, and there might be a wee sma' risk of breaking the peace."

The policeman settled himself back in his chair, and embraced his abdomen, as if this session was to be a long one. And I slouched in my chair as for a spell of gossip.

"Don't run the risk, then," he said calmly. "Let Charley Cashan—it is Charley is it not—that helpless slob?—let him do his own jobs."

"Yes, it is Charley," I admitted. "The whole thing would be plain ridiculous if it were not so pitiful."

The policeman grunted. "Go on! I'm listening."

"Remember when you ejected William Daunt for me?"

"Say that again, please?"

"When you induced William Daunt to turn tail, he went back to Beananaar, Bill Sheedy following later on. There were at least half-a-dozen rooms to choose from, but William

Daunt chose Charley Cashan's, where Charley has all his treasures piled; and William and Sheedy threw Charley's lares and penates—ain't I well read—out into the passage. All but the bed. You heard about the bed?"

"What's wrong with it?"

"It's not a bed. It's more than a bed. It's an altar. Charley used doss on a pallet; and Jean Harrington, when leaving Beananaar, presented him with this marvellous bed —her second-best bed same like Ann Hathaway. A mahogany affair, with spring-mattress, and sheets of fine linen, and silk and down coverlets—a miracle of a bed. Charley still sleeps on his pallet. He says his prayers—if any—to the bed: dresses it, airs it, warms it but never sleeps in it. That is Charley. And now William Daunt snuggles his plump carcase in it. That revolts Charley. Dammit! it revolts me. We won't stand for it."

He lifted a forefinger. "Are you sure it is his property?"

"I am. Confirmation by Jean Harrington."

"Has he other quarters in Beananaar?"

"Yes, he has another room prepared."

"Then, why don't the blame fool take his bed back?" said Farley impatiently.

"For one thing, Bill Sheedy would bust one on his snout. Charley is craven."

"Oh, I see! Charley wants you along to bust one on Sheedy's snout?"

"No, sir—not necessarily. We have evolved a plan—a darlin' plan."

"Wait!" He sat up and considered me. "Who evolved this plan—you?"

"I certainly did not." I spoke very definitely. "I had no hand, act, or part in it—up to now. If you ask me, it is a dam' foolish plan. If I were in Charley's place, I'd report to you——"

"You would like hell!" He put an elbow on the table, and propped his great jowl on his fist. "Go on! tell me about this plan."

"As silly a plan as ever was, and, mind, I said it! There is really no harm in it, and it suits Charley's dramatic sense. He's putting it in his next play. As you know, William Daunt has gone up to Limerick. He'll be back on Monday by the last train, and Bill Sheedy is to meet him with the station-wagon. They'll get back to Beananaar about eleven p.m. And what do they find?"

"Any donkey could answer that," he scathed. "The idol-bed will be in Charley's new quarters."

"You have the soul of a policeman, and forget all about the dramatic refinements. Charley will have a room prepared, the window fastened down—and that reminds me, he'll have to patch a pane after Tade Murphy's bad shooting—and there will be a Yale lock on the door. The two Bills will find the bed gone, and what do they do?"

"Kick the door in, lock and all."

"No, sir! Charley will open the door to them, mild as buttermilk. And behold! David Daunt, peace-deputy to Superintendent Jerome Farley, sitting on that noble bed like—like the great gawd Buddh."

"And, as I said, Bill Sheedy gets busted one on the snout?"

"That will be entirely up to Sheedy. And you might absolve me later on—if necessary. Well?"

I sat back, lit a cigarette, and waited. He sat back too, and lifted an ankle to rest on a knee. He looked down at his neat brown shoe, and seemed to be deep in thought. I inhaled smoke, and grew impatient.

"Dammit!" I said, "I'm not asking you for the moon."

He lifted slow eyes to mine and his voice mused. "You know, Cashan's plan has its points. At any rate you get the bed back without starting a rough house; and William Daunt puts himself in the wrong if he uses force after that. What time did you say?"

"I didn't. Daunt gets back at eleven. To make sure I'll be there at ten."

He spoke slowly. "Would it not be better if Daunt found Guard Murphy sitting on the bed with you?"

"And spoil—Charley's play?"

"What you really want is for me to take Tade off your tail for that evening? Is it not?"

"Have it so—and let the play develop."

"I don't see why I should play with you two urchins, but I'll see to it," he said, mildly resigned.

"Thank you, sir!" I said, and rose to my feet.

He brought his foot down. "Just a minute!" he said, and pulled open the middle drawer of the table against his tummy.

"What troubles me," he said very seriously, "is that you will be without a guard on Monday evening, a nice opportunity for your two-legged tiger. Well, you'll have to guard yourself, that's all. Take this back."

He fumbled in the drawer, brought out a brown, short-barrel Webley, and reached it to me, butt-first. I took it cautiously. My initials were scratched on the underside of the grip.

"Yes, it is yours—the killer," he said. "I cleaned and loaded it this morning."

"You were dam' sure of yourself," I said.

For the first time he chuckled softly. "No, son! I was sure of you."

I broke the gun, and looked at the butts of the bullets. It was fully-loaded. I picked up a bullet, looked at the blunt wicked nose of it, hefted it in my hand.

"I play fair," Jerome Farley said mildly. "These bullets are lethal." A sudden thought seemed to strike him. His voice was no longer lazy. "You spoke to Jean Harrington about that bed?"

"I mentioned it."

"Tell her about Charley Cashan's plan?"

"No, and will you teach your grandmother to suck eggs?"

"Get out of my sight!" said Jerome Farley.

I dropped the Webley into my poacher's pocket, and went.

II

I paused at the head of the stone steps, and looked across the square. The sun was again low, and again the shadow of the church spire lengthened on the tarmac, and pointed the road to Grianaan. Joseph Yoseph stood at the corner near Scanlan's bar. Jerome Farley spoke quietly at my shoulder.

"What's in your mind for to-morrow—Sunday it is?"

"Last Mass with my mammy," I said, and looked over my shoulder at him. "Anything in your mind?"

He looked up at the high, clear sky. "It will be a fine, sunny day, I'm thinking. The sort of day your mother used be going down to the sea at The Bar o' Bal, with a certain young widow—and Charley Cashan trailing along."

"Fair enough! you ask the young widow to give me a lift, and I'll trail along too."

"Yes, I will do that," he agreed surprisingly. "And Charley?"

"I'll get rid of Charley for you," I said in a murmur.

He put his hand on my shoulder for a moment, and his voice was gentle. "Yes, we'll play it your way, and your way I don't even half-know yet." His voice hardened for once. "You used be quick on the draw, I'm told. If you pull that gun, shoot to kill, and don't hesitate. Off you go!"

I cut across the angle of the square, and Joseph Yoseph, ahead of me, drifted towards the chapel. At the mouth of the bridge road I paused to look back. Jerome Farley was watching me from the Garda station steps, and distance did not dwarf the squat massiveness of the man. He waved me away, and I shook my fist.

You are letting me stake my life on the board, I said in my throat.

I walked past the open door of Scanlan's Bar, and heard feet shuffle in the sawdust. Out of eye-corner I saw Charley Cashan hurrying, but I just kept pacing steadily on. He came up to my shoulder, and made complaint feelingly.

"What the hell-hurry are you in? I was waiting for you."

"Why?"

"You might stand me a pint o' stout for the road."

"How many have you had?"

"I had the price o' two——"

"Two are enough to make you sleep sound to-night," I
went on casually. "You didn't sleep very sound last night, did
you?"

"Oh hevvin's alive!" He nearly wailed. "That bastar'
Murphy put the heart across me. That fella was out for
murdher, and I'm tellin' you."

"Not Tade Murphy, you gom!"

"Tade Murphy, gom or not! A lump o' sod, a ton-weight,
off the side o' me head, and, as I went in the window, a
corrig o' rock off the back o' me poll—and a lump there
a'ready."

"Bah to you, Charley Cashan! A divot and a pebble for a
craven! You for a guard, and your fourth man laying for me
in the basement!"

"That was no fourth man," said Charley simply. "That
was only me."

I checked, missed a step, and went on steadily again. I
knew that Charley had been in the basement last night, and
I had been erecting a theory on a flimsy foundation. That
temper of mine began to smoulder.

"So that was you in the basement last night, Mr. Cashan?"
I said with restraint.

"It had to be me or a skunk, hadn't it?" Charley said
reasonably. "Well it was me."

"Look behind you, Charley!"

"I looked. That Jew tough is followin' us up."

"Fine!" I was still restrained. "You will now tell me, and
tell me good, what you did last night and why? If you don't,
I'll call up Joseph, and by the great horn-spoon——"

"Wait now! Wait, wait!" he appealed, his hands urgent.
"What else could I do? When Tade Murphy knocked me
in the window with a lump o' rock off the back o' me skull, I
lay on the floor for a while gathering my senses, an' the

first clear thought I had was you, and you going in home in the black dark. I knew you'd left the bottom door open, and some skunk might know, too, and lay for you. I couldn't lie still after that. I wanted to, but me conscience drove me. Over I had to go and reconnoitre in fear an' tremblin'! Me very skin was crawlin' in that bloody basement, but, with the aid of a butt of a candle I had, I made sure no wan was hidin', an' when I found a crooked bit of iron to fit me hand I was as brave as a line. I was on the verge of clearin' out when I heard ye at the door, and I skedaddled be the back steps, Tade's flash on me heels. Did the devil see me?"

"He didn't say," I said, and raised my voice. "You were within an inch of your life. Why did you run, you donkey?"

"After the way he treated me? O' course I ran, and hadn't I a good start?"

"Not with a bullet in your tail." I stopped and faced him. "Listen Charley, and take heed! In future speak out loud before you move or jump. If Tade Murphy don't shoot you I will. Look!"

I held the Webley in the flat of my hand, the muzzle pointing at his midriff. The sound he made was almost a squeak, as he flapped a nerveless hand and backed away from me."

"Gor! is it loaded? Is the safety catch on?"

"Six lives in it, Mr. Cashan." I broke the gun and showed him the ominous-gleaming butts.

"Murder! An' I seen you hit the ace o' hearts at twenty paces!"

I snapped the gun shut, and jerked it down in the marksman's throw. "Bang! Bang! And your toes up."

"Put it away, Dave darling!" he besought me. "Put it away, and God love you!"

I dropped the gun back into my skirt pocket, and walked on. Charley sidled up to my shoulder. He was breathing hard.

"That lets me out." His voice quavered. "Tade Murphy and the Jewman can do their own watching. Be the gobs!

You'll not see me after the fall o' dark, an' that murdherin' weapon in your pocket."

"It will be in my pocket Monday night too," I told him. "Or do you want to call off that silly play of yours?"

"No-no-no!" he protested hurriedly. "I want to show the ould fellow where he gets off. But you'll not be needing a gun."

"I'll tote it along. It gives a nice comfortable feeling."

"But—oh! all right so!" There was a note of anxiety in his voice. "You'll be able to evade Tade Murphy, will you?"

"Of course. Up through the farm-yard and across country. I will be with you at ten sharp. You'll have everything ready?"

"Sure. The window tight, and the lock on—and you'll pay me when I ask you." He stopped and threw back his head, and his laughter pealed, mocking and triumphant. "The divil in all his glory! Wait till you see ould William's face. Man alive! I'll astonish nations."

"Fair enough, Charles!" I said, and put a careless question. "What do you do on Sunday?"

"Jean Harrington hauls me off to Mass in spite of me," he said, as if it were a grievance. "And we go to the sea fine days."

"You and I will go to the sea to-morrow," I told him. "And I'll probably drown you. So long! I'll be seeing you."

I turned in at my own gate, and plodded heavily up the drive.

Chapter XIV

I AM AFRAID

I

I did not see Jean Harrington that Saturday night. I wanted to see her, but decided that now was not the time. I was in a low mood, and might want to seek strength in her arms. But I could not stay indoors. The night was fine and clear and balmy and inviting, and I could not hold myself in. I did hold myself till nearly midnight, and then slung out the window. I did not look for Tade Murphy, and if Charley Cashan showed his nose I would see how close I could clip it with a pistol shot.

I marched boldly round the gable-end, down the middle of the drive, and out on to the road. There I paused to fill a pipe and light it, and then, still at midroad, strolled slowly up the gentle slope. The moon was slightly gibbous on the wane, and the bushes cast black shadows; and the night was so still that I could hear, far below, the aloof murmur of the Doorn, running over its shallows.

The herd of Friesians were in their night pasture, and, again, the bull paralleled me inside the fence, his nose-chain clanking. I stood between two bushes, and looked down at him, and he snorted at me. He was a big fellow in white and grey, taller than our native beasts, but not so massive: a dangerous brute if you had fifty yards to make the fence, and he was on your tail. The urchin in me wanted to tease him. I had, as a boy, teased a placid Polled-Angus by racing into his paddock and out again over a clay fence, until, thoroughly exasperated, he had taken the fence after me, and I had to climb a lucky sapling and hang on until rescued by the herdsman and his two dogs. The herdsman had given me a small leathering, and my father a real one to drive his lesson home. I blamed the bull, and the next time I teased him I had a nice tree handy, a catapult and a pocket of buckshot. I surely made that bull gallop, and, my pride restored, took my next leathering with equanimity.

I saluted the Friesian and went on. At the fork of the roads, I paused, and, then, took the right-hand branch. I stopped outside the gate of The Cottage, but did not lean over it. The small house was dark and silent, and I felt that it was withholding itself from me, shielding something within it that was explosive, but dare not explode. Under the moon the windows shone blindly, and nothing that I could see moved behind them. Yet I felt that something wanted to rebel behind one of these windows. And I knew that I could walk across the grass, and that a window would open. I did not. I lifted a hand slowly, turned away, and walked on up the road. I felt the bitterness of gall in my mouth, and my heart was as rebellious as the heart of a man in a lost cause, who will fight again.

I went on as far as the farmhouse of Beananaar, less than half a mile away. The road sloped gently upwards between flowing folds of grassland, and the house nestled in one of the folds. Behind it, a quarter-mile away, was a thick shelter-belt of spruce. On the flank of that belt Robin Daunt had been killed.

The house was barely twenty yards back from the road, and at right angles to it: a one-storeyed, inordinately long house under a roof of heavy slates, and with walls ivy-clad to the eaves. Beyond it, like the cross-bar of a T, was the long line of byre and barn, but no cattle would be in stall at this season. The half-acre of ground round the house used be well-kept and flower-bedded within a low drystone wall, but, now, as the moonlight showed, it was utterly ragged and unkempt, and there were breaches in the drystone wall big enough to admit a straying tinker's donkey.

I climbed cautiously over an angle of the wall, and went

shuffle-footed along it amongst fallen stones. The whole
length of the back of the house was facing me: a door in the
middle, and four windows at each side of it. The windows,
half-hidden by the trailing ivy, gleamed blackly in the moonlight. There was no sign of habitation. It was a house as
nearly derelict as makes no matter.

I turned the top angle of the wall and moved on to the
gable end of the byre where a bed of nettles grew thigh-deep.
One frond brushed a careless hand, and I felt the warm sting.
I could see the end of the house at a wide angle. There were
two windows in it, and one of them would be the window of
Charley's new room. I leant against the wall-corner, and
looked for a patch of cardboard. And, then, from over the
top of drystone wall behind me came a tense whisper.

"'T's all right, Dave! It's only me." The whisper grew in
urgency. "Only me, I'm telling you—Charley Cashan! Gor!
Keep your hand away from your pocket, or I'll have to
flatten your head with the stone in me fist."

I was so startled and angry that I could have blazed at him.
But another voice rapped with deadly purpose.

"Lift your hand, Cashan, and you're in hell!"

That purposeful voice came from the back of the byre
where there was a door out to the haggard. It was Tade
Murphy's fighting voice. A stone struck stone as it fell.

I turned in time to see a head disappear, and, then,
another head loomed and disappeared. That was Tade
Murphy's voice again.

"Up you get you hunk! Come on! Up and over!"

Charley came heaving over the wall as if helped by a
root behind, and Tade Murphy came with him in an active
vault, grasped him by the neck, and thrust him into the
angle between gable and wall. An adequate man, Mr.
Murphy! His hands went rapidly over his victim, and his
voice grated.

"Blast your soul to hell! do you think I'll stand for your
meddling?" The voice softened suspiciously. "Very well, Mr.
Cashan! I'll pay you off this time."

Charley, tight in his corner, lifted protecting paws, and made fervent appeal.

"Sure I was only helpin' you, Tade darlin'. I knew where you was all the time, and I was guardin' the other flank."

"Fine, Charley, fine!" Tade's voice was too pleasant. "Aren't we all friends here, and let us be nice to each other? What would you want me to do to you, Charley boy?"

"Let me go back to me bed," said Charley promptly.

"The very thing," said Tade agreeably, "and a little something to remember me by as well." Forthwith he jerked Charley out of his corner, knocked his guarding arms down, and brought round an open-handed, right-armed swoop to Charley's jowl. There was a smack as of wet leather, and Charley sat down among the nettles. He was up again, hastily, and massaging hands and face desperately.

"Goramighty! I'm burned to a cinder," he complained with anguish.

Tade Murphy was relentless. He clutched Charley two-handed, and heaved him out on the grass.

"Go back to your bed, you son of a gun! Go on or I'll——" His hand moved oxterwards.

Charley went. And he did not shamble. He went in long loping strides, his shadow flitting on the grass before him. At the near window he looked over his shoulder, and saw Tade's lifted hand. The window went up with a complaining squeak; Charley, with an activity that surprised me, went through in a frog's leap; and the window crashed down again. Peace settled round us once more. Charley Cashan had not been notably lucky in his night prowling. But he would not be warned.

"He's a glutton for punishment," I said.

"Punishment! That was no punishment." There was still some heat in Tade's voice. "Begobs! if there was no witness present, I'd ha' kicked his backbone up through the roof of his skull. The dam' fool coming at you suddenly like that, and a rock in his hand!"

"A defensive precaution!" I said lightly.

Tade drew me back from the exposed corner, and stood facing me.

"Any other bit of pastime in your mind, Mr. Daunt?" he asked ironically.

"Sleep!" I said. "You could send me back to my bed, too, but not by the same method. You know, 'Sleep's worth all the rest of them.'"

"'But love is the best of them,'" he quoted back at me.

I leant against the gable-end, and looked at this big, gallant lad who was doing his best for me. The moonlight was gleaming on his well-opened eyes, and made planes of his strong-boned face. I felt contrite.

"I'm sorry to drag you round after me, Tade," I said. "I have no consideration at all."

"Keep it up," said Tade cheerfully. "It is the game I like."

"And you play it."

Tade moved a thumb. "Do we keep to the road? Some-one——" He stopped.

I knew what he meant: Someone might be ready to talk to me now.

"No," I said. "I am going across country to get the lie of the land. Coming?"

"If you've no objection," said Tade.

II

So we went back to Grianaan across the fields: pasture fields acres wide in hawthorn hedges. There was a thick felt of grass everywhere, though the farm was well-stocked. In one field alone I estimated two score beasts: white-fronted Hereford bullocks that would be butcher-fat in October without any hand-feeding.

There used be a well-defined path between Grianaan and Beananaar. I had worn that path myself. It was still there, but not so well-defined: angling across fields, crossing clay

fences over rough stiles between bushes, running along thick
hedges, curving over low slopes, and finally dropping down
on Grianaan by the back of the steadings. I took it easy, and
Tade Murphy moved back and fore like a gamedog. The
night was as mild as milk, and the coolth of the dew and the
gossamer seeped through the canvas of my shoon. In one
field we put up a covey of partridge, almost treading on the
close bunch of them, and once we roused a brown hare out
of its form. The rabbits would not be out until the dawn.
We did not speak at all.

At the head of the final slope, we sat side by side on a stile,
and smoked. The bulk of the Grianaan buildings was below
us, asleep on the hillside; and below that, in the valley
bottom, the Doorn River was black and silver in moonlight
and shade; beyond were the huddled roofs of Kantwell,
and beyond and far beyond spread the vale of Irmond and
the lighthouse winking far out on the Estuary. A land worth
fighting for, as Ireton the Roundhead had said away back in
1649.

"Manalive!" said Tade comfortingly. "There are grand
times ahead of you in this grand place."

"And I'll share them if I get a chance—I might not," I
said. The mood of despondency was coming on me again.
I could not get my teeth in anywhere, and I was only guessing wildly.

"Say Tade, do you read detective stories?" I asked.

"I do, faith! But I have to hide them from the Super. He
says I should be reading for promotion."

"Have you read Dashiell Hammett?"

"I have so. The knight-errant school: Raymond Chandler,
Rex Stout, and my darling Eugene Manlove Rhodes."

"Read 'The Thin Man'?"

"The lad who did not exist at all?"

"Exactly. Our man does not exist either."

"Jerry Farley thinks different," said the guard, "and I'll
put my money on him. Someone——"

"I know. Someone or something is trying to break me, to

drive me away. I won't drive, but I'm afraid of breaking. I broke before."

"Take it aisy, boy!" said Tade Murphy who was years younger than I was. "That's not a bad sign. A man is inclined to weaken near the end of the road. But when the end faces you, you will not break in a million years." He touched my sleeve. "What you want is your bed. Let's go."

We flanked the steadings, and went into the backyard by the side-gate. There I took Tade's arm, and led him along the wall to my Outside Room. Tade chuckled.

"There's something in your mind," he said, "and I'm guessing good at it. God increase your store!"

I closed the door behind us and switched on the light. Tade hurried across to draw the heavy curtains, and I opened the cupboard. To-night I poured two equally stiff whiskies, and added a little soda. Silently I lifted glass to Tade, and took a deep mouthful. It did not revolt me this time. I needed it, and it steadied me. *I must watch this*, I told myself.

"*Slainte! agus bas in Erinn!*" Tade toasted me.

"Death in Erin!" I said. "And it might not be far off."

"Far and far," said Tade. "Sure you're not three days home yet, and things are moving. I feel them. Do you know, I'm a seventh son—not the seventh son of a seventh son, but I can see things once in a while. Looking at you, there is sunlight in my mind. 'Tis the dawn of day for you, David Daunt, and your sun is rising. He-oro!"

I felt the lift of his mind. "Thank you, brother," I said.

Tade did not stay long. He took his drink in two mouthfuls, and coughed his delicate appreciation.

"I'll take a turn round the policies," he said. "Don't stay long up."

I moved a hand towards the desk. "Half-an-hour. I've some work to do. You'll see me going in by the window."

He went out and pulled the door fast-shut behind him.

III

I sat at the desk, and put my head in my hands. I was still at a low ebb, but the alcohol, moving in me, told me that I must rise out of it, and carry on. For how long? Only three days home, and was I being hounded? Was this William Daunt's final method? Was I hounded at all? I could not say that I was. Damfool Charley kept blundering in and out, and that was all. And Jean Harrington?

You love her. Take her and go! Both of you are civilized enough to ignore primitive opinion. No, you are primitives yourselves and the blood and doubt will break ye. To hell with it!

After a while I took out my short-barrel Webley, and laid it on the table. I talked to it, but, maybe, that was the whiskey talking.

"Killing is your business, and you killed a man. You are not a defensive weapon. There are no defensive weapons—not even atom bombs. When your work is done it is only then that defence begins. You will do no work for me. I will not kill with you. You will not kill at all. Never!"

I pushed the gun away, and drew it back again, and looked at it for a long time. Then I broke it, and shook the bullets out on my palm: blunt-nosed, leaden ones, ominous, wicked ones. I hefted one. It was lethal. . . .

I said half-an-hour. I sat there for an hour. Then I reloaded the gun, and slipped it back into skirt pocket.

It was bed time.

I went in by the window. I was sluggish, or was it that drink slowing my reflexes? but, anyway I failed twice to make the proper vault and pivot. The third time I went back to the garden parapet to get impetus, and Tade Murphy chuckled softly above my head.

"Man, man! 'tis hard to be getting old."

"You go to hell, Tade!" I said, "but watch this first." And I went through that window like a hawk swooping.

I did not go to bed at once. I opened the door noiselessly, and looked along the passage glowing softly under its amber

roof-light. There was a thin line of light along the foot of my
mother's door. She would know that I had gone out, and
now she was waiting for my return—waiting, and wondering
why her son had to go out into the night—and where?

I moved flat-footed along the passage, and tapped softly
on her door: one, two—one-two-three, our old signal knock.
I did not hear the murmur of her voice. There was no sound
at all. I opened the door inch by inch, and slipped through.

She was propped up on her silken pillows, and sound
asleep in her silken bed, breathing softly, evenly, her delicate
white hands folded over an open book. Her reading-lamp,
turned aside, made a nimbus of her white hair, and showed
how gentle and lovely was her face—and how mournful,
how heart-stabbingly mournful.

I took two slow steps forward, and she opened her eyes,
and smiled at me. She was not startled in any way. She
reached a graceful arm, and I took her hand, and she drew
me down until my black head found the hollow of her neck.

"I am back, Mummy," I whispered.

"Yes, boy! you are looking for your road, and you will
find it."

"I don't know, Mummy. I'm afraid. I'm frightened. I
did not kill anyone, Mummy."

"I know, my son. I always knew that." She smoothed the
back of my head and neck, and her voice crooned deeply.
"My poor hurt darling! My own wee little cry-baby! Sing a
song of sixpence, a pocket full of rye—sell it all for twopence,
and never say die."

That was her old habit. No nursery rhyme was sacred to
her, and to this day I could not give the authentic version of
most of them.

My breath was fluttering and she could hear it. She said
no more, but pressed her cheek against my head, and went
on soothing the back of my neck. I drew in a long breath,
and swallowed the knot in my throat, and my voice was a
bass murmur.

"Whatever you smell, ma'am, I had only one small drink."

She chuckled softly. "You are never afraid, Daveen."

"No ma'am, not any more!" I straightened up then, and patted her hand. "And next time I take to the road, I'll bring you back a pound weight of happiness."

She crinkled her eyes at me. "I'm happy enough, boy, but I'm greedy. I want that pound, and it will be your pound too."

I suppose I knew what she meant.

Chapter XV

SUNDAY BY THE SEA

I

I had not seen Jean Harrington in daylight since coming home. I had seen her twice in the quiet heart of the night litten by a moon at the full; and what the full moon does to a woman has been poetized about since Adam looked on Eve outside the precincts.

In deceptive and transforming moonlight Jean Harrington was "delicate and rare", her hair a glory, her eyes lustrous, her face unlined, her mouth generous; young and vital and desirable as ever—and a spice of devil in her still. But what would daylight show? Daylight, the just, the unfair, the giver, the destroyer! She was twenty-nine years old. She had suffered a woeful tragedy. Surely the years and the woe would have left their marks and traced their lines.

I saw for myself on Sunday morning.

My mother and I went to late Mass. We started out in good time, and we walked arm-in-arm. She was tall and queenly and oozing pride in her black and white, with a scrap of black chiffon to cover her cumulus of white hair. Women are commanded to cover their hair in church. They use a bit of lace, or a triangle of kerchief, or a couple square inches of hat to meet the rubric, and the cure is several times worse than the disease.

Myself looked almost respectable in dark worsted. I would never be anything other than a long, lean, tough-looking customer, but the prison pallor was almost gone, and the prison shamble with it; and I was prepared to look any man in the eye—or woman either.

We met some people coming from the earlier Mass, mostly farmers from the hinterland, and mostly in motor cars. The jaunting-car of my youth was a thing of the past. And then a car slowed down, came over to our side of the road and stopped. We stopped too.

The car was a four-seater, tourist-model in good shape. The hood was down to welcome sun and air, and Charley Cashan slouched in the back seat. He was in his ancient Donegal tweeds, but his shirt was new and white and without a tie. He looked at me coldly out of a fishy eye, and tenderly rubbed the back of his pointed dome. But I had no eyes for Charley Cashan.

I always look at hands first, and my eyes were on Jean Harrington's red-gloved hands holding the wheel. As a girl she had good-sized useful hands, almost masculine, but in red French gloves they were delicate and shapely. But, then, women's hands look best in gloves. That is why women wear gloves—even walking through fields. And is it not a fact that women are more alluring clothed than—well than otherwise?

My mother turned me aside to face the car. She pointed a finger stabbingly, and her voice was all reprimand, disapproval—and falseness.

"Jean Harrington! How could you? My son home for three days, and you——" her voice went prim "——but perhaps you do not know my son, David?"

"Why is this my dear friend, David?" said Jean softly in her quiet Highland voice. "How are you, David? Why you look splendid—just splendid." Her voice had a small thrill in it then.

She kept her hands firmly on the wheel, and her golden grey eyes were frowningly intent on me. I suppose she was looking for daylight signs, too, as I was.

"I am fine ma'am," I said, "and thank you kindly, and, what's more, I'm thanking God for the sight of my eyes this fine autumn morning."

And I was. This was no slip of a girl. This was a mature

woman, lovely and unlined and young—yes, young—her copper hair shining with health under a scrap of chiffon, her eyes brilliant, and a touch of colour in her cheeks brought there by my words and tone. This was a woman who respected her body, who cared for it, who arrayed it, who kept it youthful and vital for a purpose of her own. Something went out from me to her, from her to me. We belonged.

Slowly she drew her eyes away from me, and, then, the old imp came alive in her. She wrinkled her nose at my mother.

"Go boil your head, Ellen Furlong!" she said deplorably. "Your son, David has talked to me for hours—and then some. Haven't you David?"

"There was talk anyway, ma'am," I said.

"Oh, indeed!" said my mother.

"Yes, indeed!" said Jean. "As if you didn't know! Of course you knew."

"How could I——?"

"She got it out o' me—twice," said Charley Cashan from the back-seat.

"You're a tell-tale hound, Charley Cashan," Jean thanked him. "Jerome Farley was the man."

My dear mother was not a scrap embarrassed.

"But couldn't you come over and let me talk to you about him?" she wanted to know.

"You had to savour him first. Look, darling! You'll have him late for Mass."

The car was purring softly. I had a hand on the top of the door, my eyes on her hands, and I spoke without looking up.

"My, oh my! oh my! I haven't had a plunge in salt say water for—years and years. Dear, oh deary me! how I would like my head under a wave, and the white bubbles going up in the green before my eyes, and they open."

A red hand came down on mine, but did not press. She did not speak for a while. Then she sighed in surrender, but her voice was brisk.

"Right, Davy! I'll be along as soon as your mum has had her post-prandial nap."

"Post-prandial has my money, and thank you Jean! Haul the Cashan along. I want to drownd him."

"Be the sorras!" said Charley feelingly. "I'll go be myself, and keep a mile away from you."

Hand and foot moved, and the car slipped away smoothly. My mother and I walked on up the slope, her arm again in mine.

"No seaside for me to-day," she said, a quarter sorrowfully. "Not after Jean Harrington told me to boil my head."

"But not for the four minutes required," I said. "You're coming all right, old lady, and you'll like it."

"Ah, well! I suppose I'll have to get used to being ordered about," she said cheerfully, and started humming softly to herself.

We met some more friends and acquaintances before and after Mass, and no one turned back on me. The men of our congregation had a custom of gathering in groups about the chapel rails ten minutes or so before the Service began to talk of crops and football and running-dogs. So I did not go in with my mother. I had not seen women in bulk for nine years, and I noted that, at any age up to sixty-plus, they had grown more subtle in displaying their charms. But they displayed them, which is a mistake, I think, for a male should be allowed to use his imagination. Fashion is a slavish and vulgar thing.

Father Eujun was not saying this Mass to-day. Probably a newly-ordained priest was deputising for him. Father Eujun was walking up and down on the gravel by the side of the church, reading his office: a tall dignified man completely aloof from the groupings of his flock—or so he seemed. But I noticed that the groups were quiet and easy in his presence, and accepted him as they accepted heat, light and air. I did not think he saw me; but when the parish clerk, in his black soutane, came out to ring the bell, Father Eujun shut his missal, and came straight across to where I was chatting with some of the old team. He put a hand on my shoulder, and his voice was dignifiedly warm.

"It is splendid to see you here, David my friend, very splendid, indeed! What was Jack Walsh saying about that girl's ankles?"

"They'd be better hidden, Father Eujun."

"Fair comment! But the dictates of fashion are stronger than mere male criticism. Come over some night soon David? I have a book for you." He pressed my shoulder and walked statelily away.

"You wouldn't think he had an ear on his head," said Jack Walsh. "Thanks be! I didn't say what was in my mind about that girl's collops."

The Service was a Low Mass, and was over in less than thirty minutes. There was a five-minute sermon on the Virgin, and the young priest quoted in a voice that pulsated with feeling: *I was exalted like a cedar in Lebanon, and as a cypress on Mount Zion; I was exalted like a palm-tree in Cades, and as a rose-plant in Jericho.*

Listening to him, I could not keep another woman out of my mind, and I recalled a verse of a Scots love poem:

> "I canna sing for the song my ain hert raises.
> I canna see for the mists afore mine e'en,
> And a voice droons the hale of the psalms and paraphrases,
> Crying Jean—Jean—Jean."

It was a satisfying Mass for me, and brought me peace. I needed an interim of peace, for I knew in my bones that I had an ordeal coming soon. Kneeling or standing or sitting at my mother's side at the front of the clerestory I did not use my missal, but watched the priest's hands, and followed his ritual. He was a young priest, full of the symbolism and mysticism of the Sacrifice, and his movements had the slow rhythm of drama.

I told myself that I would call on Father Eujun, and argue doubts with him, and ask him why the ordinary churchgoer was not better instructed in the symbolism of the Mass and its ritual. Knowing these one does not need his book of prayers, which is, indeed, better than a praying wheel, but not so very much.

At the end of the Last Gospel—"*In the beginning was the Word, and the Word was God, and the Word was with God*"—in my new mood of peace I made my own small petition and confession of faith.

God helps those who help themselves, and I will try to help myself all I can, God willing. Not vengeance, not gloating, not blood on my hands. Only a little happiness for this woman at my side, and a small bit for myself. Let it not be too long O Lord, for I am a weak vessel.

II

We walked home too. Julie Brady had an early lunch for us: duckling, green peas and apple sauce. She had been to an earlier Mass, and was brightly confident how our day would go.

"Eat up now and have your rest for yourself," she said to my mother. "No one knows when that girl Jean'll come tearin' in like the wind out o' the mountains." Her chuckle was a silver bell. "That's right too! A breeze o' wind in a sleepy house." Her eyes opened at me. "Do you know this, Davy? This is a sleepin' house most of the week, and 'tis only when Jean Harrington comes that the house stirs itself and wakes up, and has an ear listenin'. Off you go for your forty winks, Ellen Furlong! You'll get your coffee later."

"I will not go, Julie," my mother said indignantly. "I never sleep at all—but I may as well go and powder my nose."

Jean arrived within the hour. From the sitting-room window I saw the car turn in at the gate. I had not actually been watching out for her; I was merely smoking a cigarette and keeping an eye on the prospect. I threw the cigarette out on the gravel, and was at the head of the steps when Jean, of long practice, made a swooping three-quarter circle on the spurting gravel, and stopped dead at the foot of the steps—like a cowpony coming in with a flourish and braking, fore-feet planted.

Full of dignity, I strode down to ground level, my eyes looking down my nose, but before I could open the door she was out in a whirl of shapely legs and shapely knee caps. She caught at my hand, and her eyes were merry.

"At your orders, Squire Daunt! Anyone would know you own this house."

"I own it, my wench. Where be your tame yellow pup?"

"Charley?" She flung her copper hair. "Threw him out at the gate to catch a bus. I wanted a spare seat." She laughed. "He don't trust you no more. Och! never mind him." She swung me round to face the house. "Look at it! Isn't it a fine bit of a house, this house of yours?"

"It is asleep in the sun," I said. "Go thou and waken it?"

"Watch me!" She raced up the steps, her flimsy flowered dress lifted—but already I knew she had good legs—and into the sitting-room. Her voice rang, and rang again, through the house.

"Wake, wake ye, Ellen-for-short! Julie, Molly! I want ma coffee. Whaur's ma coffee?"

I walked up the steps silent-footed, holding myself in, careful not to meddle with the mood that had come upon this quiet house of mine. Julie was right. This house that had been asleep was awake again, as it had been awake years ago. And it would remain awake, given a chance. And my withers were wrung.

Jean Harrington was hugging Julie Brady, and Julie's silver bell was pealing. Molly Cray came in pushing a coffee trolley, and made a skirl of her own.

"Here's to love among the corn!" said Jean knowingly, and Molly skirled again.

My mother came in chuckling softly. She had, indeed, powdered her nose, but the soft brilliance of her eyes showed that she had had her forty winks as well. This was an old ritual; this had happened hundreds of times over the years; this was how Jean Harrington had kept this house alive and sane. Would she, could she go on? *Careful son! Keep out of it now. Don't disturb the mood, and some day you might slip into it as by right.*

So I sipped my coffee and held my peace. Only once did I catch Jean's eye, and her smile was strangely wistful for a moment. But gaiety was the mood she had decided on for that day—even if the gaiety was not quite genuine, and it wasn't. There was something of the Indian Summer about it, and winter, inevitably, on its traces. Right! Let us have our Indian Summer!

We drove across the Vale of Irmond to the sea: ten miles of road almost rule straight. My mother sat in front with Jean, and talked about a car that we might have next month, or the month after. Actually the American car was coming on Wednesday. Molly Cray and I sat behind, each in our own corner. Jean, after a whispered talk with Molly, had made her come along. She was a trace shy in her corner, and I respected her shyness. I filled a pipe, and admired the smooth nape of a white neck in front of me, and wanted to caress it with a finger; and once I caught a golden eye in in the driving mirror, and it winked at me.

On our right a low heathery hill swelled slowly, and sent a long flank down to the estuary; on the left, bent-grown sand dunes fringed the horizon and hid the sea. Over a final rise we dropped down to the shore at the Bar o' Bel. The village was white-shining, windblown, and sandblown. Two tall seasonal hotels reared themselves out of it. Wings of summer villas were spread wide, from black, green-topped cliffs on one hand to yellow sand dunes on the other. The sough of the sea was everywhere.

Molly Cray disappeared. We established my mother in a canvas chair on the green lawn of the low promontory splitting the bathing strand in two. She had a book and magazines, but I do not think she did any reading. She held court, she inhaled ozone, she dozed a little. Jean and I clambered down to the yellow strand, and hired a couple of bathing boxes. I was out first and walked leisurely across towards the line of breakers. The air caressed my back and shoulders, and the fine dry sand was warm between my toes. I wanted to run and plunge but I would savour this slowly.

The day was still and sunny and faintly hazed, the sea a subdued blue-green, and far out the straight ten-mile line of the horizon was laid down between the strong, black horns of the Estuary. A quiet sea, gently lifting and falling, and that lift and fall, with two thousand miles of sea behind it, checked and toppled and broke in dazzling white along the miles of clean sands. Pink and white bodies dived under the breaking line, and dark heads and brilliant heads bobbed up in the smooth water beyond. The first ripple washed over my insteps and made my breath flutter.

A man ahead of me was wading easily out towards the white surge: a tall, slender, golden-skinned, perfect figure, back muscles rippling. He dived under a breaker, and came up facing me, tossing the black hair off his brow. He was Joseph Yoseph. Perhaps he was on duty, but Molly Cray would not be far away.

A lithe figure in red, and red-capped, swooped and whooped by me, water splashed and pin-pointed me, and Jean turned, beckoned, threw herself backward, and let a wave break in white over her. The water was surging green and white about my knees. I dipped a finger, signed the Cross as of old, and walked straight into a breaker. I braced myself, kept my feet, and waded slowly until the quiet swell lifted me by the chin. I ducked my head under just once, blew through the water that brimmed my lips, and kept myself afloat in an easy breast stroke. I only wanted to soak. The sea tasted salt on my lips, and the water that had been chill for a few seconds, had now the cool tang of fine wine.

Jean Harrington's red-capped head broke the water near me, and a long arm touched my shoulder caressingly. We turned over on our backs and floated side by side, the soft sway of the sea cradling us, and the soft sough of it in our ears. The water was so buoyant that we had scarcely to move a fin. Jean, her head back, spoke up into the sky.

"Our fifty-yard sprint? No!"

"Not to-day, lassie! I'll soak sea-salt to dissolve the last sordid taint of durance vile. Bet you couldn't say that—straight off—and keep afloat."

"Forget durance vile—you must Dave," she said seriously enough.

"Not if it adds a savour to good times. Good times? How do I know?"

"I don't know either. Mother of Heaven! if I only knew——"

An animal bellow came to us from not far away. I moved palms and lifted head to look. Dark and bright heads and tanned bodies bobbed and cut the water here and there, and one big body heaved itself up amongst them, and a mouth opened to bellow at us again. That was Charley Cashan. He smashed the water with hands and torso, and came surging towards us.

Charley was like a sea-pig in the water: he was at home in it. He had no accepted method of progression. He just moved animal-like where he wanted to. A dark head was shouldered out of his way and went under. And then Charley went under. This was a trick of his. In the water he was as playful and mischievous as an otter. He would swim twenty yards under water, and, before you knew, there was a grip on your ankle and down you went. But he would never hold you under.

I was in no mood for horseplay. I turned over on my side, and got ready. I knew exactly where to kick him. For some reason—probably pressure concussion—a wallop is more disabling under water than out of it. I waited. But Charley came to the surface in about the same place where he had submerged. He had been a full half-minute under. Half his body bobbed out of the water. He was spluttering, and I could see his staring eyes.

He splashed flat, took a couple of strokes, and again went under. He surfaced almost immediately, and did not hesitate for a moment. He yelled fearsomely, and threshed his way towards the beach, tumbled through the breakers on to his feet, and splashed into shallow water. Joseph Yoseph, grinning broadly, breast-stroked across our front. Charley Cashan had met his match.

"Whatever is wrong with the sea-pig?" wondered Jean, treading water at my side.

"Bit by an octopus I expect."

"Stood on a crab, more likely." She touched my shoulder. "In long enough for a first-dip, young fellow? Out you go!"

We took the breakers arm in arm, and, arm in arm walked through the shallows that now felt almost lukewarm. I smoothed the little roughness of gooseflesh down her forearm. Charley was waiting for us ankle-deep, and he was looking apprehensively out to sea. His big, hairless torso was ridged and folded with fat and muscle.

"Goramighty, Dave!" he panted. "I was nearly drownded. Look!" He lifted a smooth-skinned leg. There was a red band, almost a weal, above the ankle. "I was down three times."

"Twice! A kraken beyond a doubt," I said heavily.

"What the——?"

"A man-eating octopus from Palestine. See him waving a tentacle out there!"

"You and your Semite playboy can go to hell, Dave Daunt!" He stamped out of the water and away up the beach.

"It couldn't be a giant octopus, could it?" wondered Jean, who sometimes displayed a national sense of humour—or an endearing lack of it.

"Why not?" I said, and put an arm across her smooth shoulders. "I would I were a bit of an octopus myself and eight strings to you."

"Oh Dave! You darling fool!" she said softly, drew away from me, and ran light-footed towards the line of bathing boxes. I watched the fine woman's build of her, and proceeded leisurely.

We dressed, and sought my mother on the green lawn fronting the old Norman ruin. She was lying back in her canvas chair, her long hands folded on her flat stomach. She roused out of a half-sleep and smiled at me lazily. I sat down with my shoulders against one knee, and she smoothed a soft and not toil-worn hand down my neck.

"I was watching," she said. "You have the nice Furlong hide. Give it all the sun you can."

Jean Harrington sat at my mother's other knee, and kicked off her shoes to get rid of the sand. And my mother ran her fingers through the tangle of copper hair. Jean sighed deeply, and my mother patted her shoulder comfortingly. Quietly I reached a hand across my mother's knees, and ran my fingers through that copper hair as my mother had done. But Jean knew, and moved her head negatively. I gave a small tug, and drew my hand away.

"'Tisn't even good wool either," I said.

"Wool don't make a good net," murmured my mother.

Jean crowed, "Dame Ellen, do you mind the time he tried to write a story?"

"I do, Jeanathan. How did it begin?"

"Oh God!" I said.

"This way," said Jeanathan. " 'Gillian the Dark, son of Cathal, son of Con, met Fionula of Urda at the King's dun of Mullaghmore, and his heart became entangled in the meshes of her red hair.' That was it. Ho-ho-ho!"

"Don't hold it against me," I appealed. "I never wrote another word after that attempt."

"You are writing now," my mother said. And so I am.

And Jean said softly, "It was a lovely story. I have it still."

Quiet settled down again. The three of us sat there, saying nothing, not needing to say anything, contented with ourselves. A brief contentment, I knew. It could not last. But given one hypothesis it might last our time. Jerome Farley wanted me to put that hypothesis to the test and I was going to do it. I could only take a chance, a chance thin as a thread, deadly as a king-cobra.

Later on we strolled up into the village to my mother's special tea shop. Women will drink tea at any hour. So will I. And, then, my mother said that she must visit a couple of cronies, and drink some more tea, and would we please take ourselves out of her way, and go for a walk above the cliffs, or amongst the sandhills, and not get hit with a golf ball, and, if we needed a drink, there was the lounge of the Clan Morris Hotel that had only a six-day licence and, in any case, was not supposed to sell hard liquor on Sunday.

So we took ourselves off, and went for a walk, shoulder to shoulder, amongst the sandhills.

III

We left the scatter of villas behind us, and crossed the corner of the golf links that is—or are—of championship class, and Jean pointed out the mound whereon my mother had rested twenty years ago, and we laughed again, as we had laughed many a time.

My mother, sitting alone on that mound, had seen two small white balls on the short grass some distance in front of her. There was no one in sight, no one at all, and my mother thought someone had dropped them, and that they would be very nice for her small son David to play with. So she went across, and picked them up, and put them in her bag, and returned to her seat. And, then, two golfers came round a sandhill, and started to look for their balls where no ball could be hidden. My mother did not know where to look, and she could not proclaim herself a thief. She said nothing. The golfers, too, said nothing—aloud. They dropped balls and played on, and a voice came back to Mother. "Dam'it to hell! You couldn't believe your eyes, she looks so respectable." I had played those balls quite a time with a hurley-stick, but they led me into vice. I became an addict, and was down to a two handicap at the age of nineteen, when I reformed and took to plain poaching.

The rounded tops of the sand dunes were thinly grown with bent, but the hollows and wide reaches were carpeted with a close-growing grass that makes the finest greens and

fairways in the world. We saw no rabbits, the pest of seaside
links, but many traces of old scrapes. A man-introduced
disease called myxomatosis had exterminated the rabbits,
Jean told me. Some hellish scientists experimenting on
microbes for the final war?

Jean spoke out of a blue sky. "I'll bet you a'e bawbee you
can't tell who is following us at a distance?"

I considered that. "Your grammar is hellish," I said, "or
you are cheating. You thought I'd say Charley Cashan.
'Who are' not 'who is'."

"Bet's off!" said Jean promptly. "Yes, Joseph and Molly
Cray. These two are fond of each other, Dave. How did you
know?"

"A man in love knows these things," I said carelessly.

"Yes, yes!" said Jean hurriedly. "Ah! they are slanting
away now."

"They'll not go far," I said. "We go this way."

We flanked a big dune, and came out above the sea, well
away from the risk of sliced golf balls. A little along we found
a handy green bank, and sat down with our backs to it, our
shoulders not quite touching. A yard beyond our shoe soles,
the bank shelved steeply to a ridge of shingle, and beyond
that was the pale tan of the long strand within its white
fringe of sleepily-breaking, sleepily-soughing rollers; and
beyond was the slow-moving blue-green sea out to the horizon
line between the guarding promontories.

A mood of quietness was on us now, and we did not say
anything for a long time. I did not even think of filling a pipe.
I felt strangely in abeyance—abeyance is a good enough
word. And then Jean slipped her arm through mine, and
spoke as if the time had come for speaking.

"I did not see you last night, David. But that's wrong. I
did see you."

"You mean I did not see you, though I passed your way.
Paso por aqui!"

"To see Charley?"

"I saw him."

"I knew that you would not come back my way. But I was at the gate. I went as far as your gate. And then I knew what I had to do."

"What have you to do, Jean?"

Her voice was calm and sure. "I am going way, David."

"You are going way, Jean?"

"I must, David."

"And I must stay."

"You must stay, and I must go."

I had nothing to say to that. I could not use any pressure on this woman. Her surrender would make me a betrayer. Perhaps, to-morrow, perhaps next day, perhaps in three years' time—but not now.

"Where are you going, Jean?" I asked then.

"Dublin."

"That is not far away."

"A million miles, Davy," she said sadly.

"Just about, but I could jump them in the wink of an eye."

"So could I. Every night I'll jump them." And then her voice hurried to explain. "You know, I have done scripts for the Radio Eireann people, and a broadcast or two. There's a job going, and they are agreeable to give me an interview and an audition."

"The job is yours, Jean."

"I think so, David," she said simply.

"When do you go up?" I put no stress on that question.

"Day after to-morrow, to make arrangements." Her voice was steady. "This is good-bye, David. I will not see you again —for a long time."

I tried to keep the harshness out of my voice: "So you say, but how do you know?"

"Please, please, David!" she pleaded softly.

"All right, Jean! God! what a hash we've made of our lives."

"All my fault, David."

"Don't be greedy, Jean, and I'll not be generous. Half

mine, and half yours! Half-and-half, and ne'er a drop o' water!"

"Oh, David! My gallant, gallant David!"

She put her head on my shoulder, and mourned. And I put an arm quietly round her waist, and let her mourn.

She cried nicely, but not silently, after the manner of her race—and my race. There was a small, soft, minor lamentable *keen* of loss in her voice that was full of sorrow, and at the same time led to the soothing and surcease of sorrow. It was not long-drawn-out, and at the end she drew in a long quivering breath and felt for her bag.

I got out my handkerchief, turned to her and lifted her chin. Her eyes were closed, she was a small maid being petted, and my throat ached. I wiped her eyes and her nose, patted her cheeks dry, and gave her one small peck of a kiss on the round of her chin. Then I was on my feet, and had her on hers.

"Let us go home, piccaninny," I said, and firmly hooked her arm. So our afternoon that began in gaiety finished in a quiet mood. But there was one small and unnecessary explosion that showed the rebellion that was suppressed in us.

We crossed the golf-links too carelessly, cutting across fairways; and, as every schoolboy knows, a mere pedestrian has no rights on a fairway. A stentorian bellow of "fore" made us beware, and I ducked my head down to shield Jean's. And, next instant, a ball trickled by my feet and stopped. I turned. A big man—one of four—was back there, club and fist lifted. He should not have played that ball at all, for he was not eighty yards from us, and, moreover he must have topped it badly for it was thirty yards short of the green. As a boy I was able to throw a flat finger-stone one hundred and twenty yards. I picked up that ball, and threw it a straight eighty yards—say sixty anyway—and the big man had to get out from under.

I stood on wide-planted feet, hands away from sides, and waited. I just wanted a safety valve like this. Jean stood at my side, head forward, and her hair was actually bristling. The voice in her throat was as deep as a man's, and, maybe, it carried.

"Come on, you hound! Come along! and we'll see why you tick."

That girl and I had always made a team, right or wrong, and we were wrong now of course. The big man, however, would not abide the issue. He moved a deprecating hand, and turned back for his ball. Jean and I marched away, banners flying, from the stricken field.

Mother was waiting for us at the car. We got in and the self-starter throbbed.

"Hoy!" I said. "What about Molly Cray?"

"Molly's not coming," said Jean carelessly. "She is going to a dance—with someone."

"I don't like it," my mother said doubtfully. "He's a nice boy, but he's half Jew, and her Aunt Julie——"

"Let Julie lump it," said Jean heartlessly, "and get your son, David, to talk to Father Eujun."

"Who me?" I said.

"Yes, Davy! You are the big-talker from this on."

The wheels spurted sand, and away we went. And we were quiet in the quiet gloaming. Jean would not come to supper at Grianaan. She had things to do, and, my mother, seeing her mood, did not press her.

Well, she had said good-bye. She would not see me again —for a long time. Fair enough! I did not see her that night. I stayed at home. I talked to my mother. I had a drink and a talk with Tade Murphy in The Outside Room. I went to bed early. I heard Molly Cray come in, and heard the resonant, reprimanding murmur of Julie Brady's voice.

Shut up Julie! There's nothing separating these two nice young people but a little prejudice, mostly religious. Behold, what is between my love and me! There may be nothing to-morrow night, and to-morrow night I may be dead.

CHAPTER XVI

THE BLEATING OF THE KID

I

I am sick and tired of this blasted writing. Why ever did I start it? I thought, at the beginning, that it would be a leisurely sort of diary over months—or years, but things happened to quickly for me, and I have a bad habit of trying to finish what I start. That is about the most deplorable habit in the world, for it leads to dullness and futility, and the sameness of hell—or the heaven of the unco' guid. One should always leave a couple of strings dangling to be tugged at in idle times.

And, when I think of it, I need not write any more at all. The end must be obvious to anyone with a speck of grey matter above eyebrow. I could write it in one paragraph, and no one would be surprised. But conceit lifts a head.

From the moment I met him, Jerome Farley had faced me with a problem, and led me up to a climax, and challenged me to write *finis* to it. Well I will write *finis* to it, and if the end is anti-climax I cannot do anything about that. So I'll carry on for another couple of hours—and leave a few strings dangling. Here goes!

II

I am saying nothing about the long day of Monday, except that it was a long day, and that there was a good pelt of rain for the first time in weeks. But it cleared up nicely in the late afternoon. I kept away from my mother as much as I could all that day, for I did not want any strings being tugged. I stayed mostly in my Outside Room, and as time went on a strange remoteness came over me.

The sun was setting behind the long ridge sloping down to the Estuary when I decided to set out there and then for Beananaar. I did not go across country as I had—no, I had never intended to go across country. That was meant for a blind. I filled my pipe and lit it, dropped the loaded Webley into my skirt pocket, went round the gable-end, and strolled down the drive. If my mother was looking she would assume that I was only going for an evening ramble.

At the gate I turned to look up at the white house. The sunset glow had died out of the windows, and my mother was leaning out of one and waving to me. I waved back. It might be "the long farewell", but I was not feeling in the least sentimental. I walked on up the centre of the road.

The sough and babble of the river came up to me, a little louder after the rain. The sun was down and the light was still good, and the sky was again clear of clouds. The roofs of Kantwell glistened on the slope; the contours of the vale were etched clearly in the washed air, and the lighthouse on the estuary was already winking. The moon would not be rising for an hour yet.

At the fork of the roads I paused, but only for a second or two. The branch on the right led to Beananaar—and The Cottage, but I did not want Jean to have any part in to-night's work—if work there was to be. I did not want to see her at all. All desire, but one, was dead in me. I walked on up the main branch to a break in the fence that I knew, went through, and, in the shelter of the hedge that bounded the cottage field, angled across to the Beananaar road, and walked on slowly on the grass margin.

Some distance short of Beananaar I leant against a dry lump of rock built into the fence, knocked out my pipe, and filled it again. I was in no hurry, and smoked tranquilly. I listened for sounds of movement: a tell-tale rustle, the pad of a stealthy foot, anything. There was no sound. Evidently Tade Murphy had been taken off the job, probably Charley

Cashan was waiting for dark, and I never believed in that other prowler.

I was watching the shadows gathering in the folds of the slopes; I was watching the lightening of the sky in the south-east where the moon was hidden. My sense of time had come back to me. I saw the first faint glint of the planet Jupiter low down, I saw the orange-red arc of the moon. It was on ten o'clock, and my time had come. I felt as cool as—but is a cucumber cool at all I wonder? All right! I felt detached.

I knocked out my pipe and pocketed it, and walked slow-footed to the gateway of Beananaar. There was no gate. The old wooden gate had been decayed even in my time. Now, across the gap was a warped pole thigh-high that might or might not keep out straying beasts. I stood out on the road and looked along the ivied front of the long house. There was no splay of light from any window. There wouldn't be if William Daunt was away. Charley Cashan's room was around the end of the house.

And, then, in the half-light, I saw the bonnet of the station-wagon jutting out at that end of the house. What did that mean? Did it mean that Bill Sheedy had not yet come to take the car to the station? It might mean other things as well. I did not care. But where was Sheedy? I didn't care a damn. I would just carry on.

I straddled over the pole in the gateway, and moved silently along a drive that once had been gravel, but was now a spongy carpet of moss. I kept well out from the house wall I was paralleling, and watched the blind ivy-shaded windows as I passed. The front door was wide-open, but I expected that. I could just see the narrow empty hall inside, and the uncurtained arch at the back of it. Behind that arch I knew there was a passage running right and left with many doors opening off it. There was a faint glow in there coming from a light somewhere.

I listened, my mouth half-open to help my hearing. There was no sound, no stir. I took one look round, went quickly across on tip-toe, and took one silent stride into the hall. I halted there, waited for four-five seconds, and lifted up my voice.

"Charley! I am here. Show a leg!"

And at once Charley's cheerful bellow came from down the left wing of the passage.

"Right you be-e-e, Daveyoh! Come on in! The light is on."

I moved flat-footed to the arch, and put a cautious head through. First I looked to the right, and saw only emptiness. Then I looked left where Charley's voice had come from. At the end of the passage, and facing me, was an open door, and the room inside was lighted. I saw only the legs of a table. Yes, that was the room that Charley had bolted into last night.

I went down that passage without pausing. I went as quietly as I could, but old boards are never silent. They creaked. There were doors, but they were shut, and, momentarily, I wondered which room had held the precious bed. I stopped in front of the open door.

"Is Mr. Cashan at home?" I said.

"He is, begobs!" said Charley. But his voice was behind me, and there was a grate in it. And then I got it.

II

I was prepared for an attack. I was even prepared not to flinch. But man is not built that way. I saw the shadow move in a doorway half-behind me, and I instinctively ducked my head aside. The blow was almost a glancing one, but it knocked me flat on my face. And I stayed down. With all my will I stayed down. Let him hit me again if he wanted to. Let him kill me if he wanted to. I had come this far, and, now, I must play the game as it lay—as I lay.

I was dazed, but I was not out. I was like a boxer, who has taken a sharp clip, but can still listen to the count. I could curl over at any second and, possibly, take my assailant's legs from under him to a dog-fight on the floor. Instead I lay flat, completely out. But I was not too realistic. I might scrabble on the boards for instance, but that would invite a quieting and deadly blow. I had better say here that the thing that had laid me out was a heavy woollen sock, the foot of it packed with wet sand. Quite a moderate blow would stun a man; a heavy one would probably kill; and there would be very little mark.

I was not hit again. That was not in the game as arranged by the player, and I had staked my life on it. Charley's voice spoke above me and the grate was no longer there.

"Easy as pie!" he said happily.

There was a firm clutch at the back of my neck, and I was lifted and dragged forward into the room, my legs trailing helplessly behind. I opened a slit of eye and saw a scuffled boot. Then I was swung up and over, and dumped again like a lifeless sack; and I was sitting on the floor, my shoulders propped against a corner of the room. My head dropped on my breast, and I said to myself: *So far, so good. Now you are in it, Dave Daunt, and you stay in it with all you've got.*

The door banged. There was a scrape of wood on wood, as of a chair being pulled. No, it was too heavy for a chair. Charley's cheerful voice came from near the door.

"The stage is set, and now we shan't be long. Wake up when you're ready, Dave boy! It was only a friendly tap I gave you."

And it was about time I waked up, too. I shook a heavy head and groaned, and it was no fake groan either. I felt the back of my head, and winced, but the wince was mostly fake. I looked up and across at Charley Cashan.

"Blast you and your horseplay, you big ape!" I said, and drew a knee up, as if I were about to rise.

The grate was back in his voice. "Stay where you are, Dave Daunt. I've got a finger on the trigger."

He was standing with his back to the door, and a rough, home-made deal table was pulled in front of him. A short-barrel Webley was thrust forward in his right hand, and the muzzle of it was pointing directly and steadily at my midriff.

I slapped a hand on the outside of my skirt-pocket. My Webley was gone. I had not felt it being taken, so I must have been out for a second or two. *God is good!* I said to myself. *That's another trick turned for me.* No one would think so, with my gun in Charley Cashan's hand.

"Yes, Dave! It is your gun," he said, "and I'll use it if you make me."

"You can't, you fool!" I said. "The safety catch is on."

"Fool yourself!" said Charley with contempt. "A Webley has no safety catch, and, if you want to find out, just make one move."

I did not. I noticed, then, that the country lilt was no longer in his voice, and that he was not using many colloquialisms. I leant back in the corner and considered him. I had often thought that he had evolved a satisfactory philosophy for himself; I had often wondered how much was false in his posing; now, looking at his pallid face and pale eyes I knew that he had never been all sane, and that he was well beyond the edge of sanity at this moment. The game I had to play was a deadly one. He gestured aside with head and gun.

"I have no manners at all," he said. "Let me introduce ye!"

I turned head to look. I was not surprised, for already I had caught a glimpse out of the corner of an eye. In the corner at my right, my uncle, William Daunt, was sitting on the floor, just as I was. But his plight was very much worse than mine. His hands were behind his back, and I assumed that they were tied there. His ankles were tied, too, with a piece of old rope and, still worse, a faded-red bandana was tight over his mouth and chin. He mumbled at me desperately, so I knew that a mouthful of the bandana was gagging him. His bald dome was pink and sweating. His amber eyes were staring at me, wide and piteous. I knew by the twitching of his cheeks that he was trying to smile friendlily. And the eager nod-nod of his head had the soul of appeal in it. On me he depended utterly.

You will be all right, you poor old schemer, I said to myself, *but you are going to get one hell of a fright*. And aloud I said, "Sorry to meet you like this, Uncle William. You got home too early."

"I knew he would," said Charley with a little crow.

I kept my eyes on William Daunt. "And where is our henchman, Mr. William Sheedy?"

He shut his eyes for a moment, and there was a shiver in the desperate negative movement of his head.

"Bill will be along when he's wanted," said Charley, and sniggered. "But we're in no hurry at all, are we?"

I leant back in my corner, folded hands on my thighs, and looked about the room. It was not a big room, fourteen or fifteen feet square. There was no fireplace, but where the fireplace might be were piles of books and papers—against the wall and on dilapidated kitchen chairs. In the corner beyond was a jumble of old blankets on a straw palliasse. I could not see the window which was in the wall between my uncle's corner and mine, but, no doubt, it was closed and shuttered. Flowered paper was peeling damply off the walls; the ceiling showed a wide black patch where the roof had leaked, and plaster had fallen from a square yard of ceiling in the corner near the door. I could see the laths and the cavity of a break in them. The light was from a lamp on the wall, near the window: one of those kitchen lamps with a fluted tin reflector behind the globe. It gave quite a good, mellow light.

My eyes came back to Charley. His long, pallid sheep's face was slit with a satisfied grin, and his pale eyes glistened.

"Safe and snug as a bug in a rug, isn't it, Daveen?" he wheedled. "The two Daunts under one roof with mad Charley Cashan! The last of the Daunts! Isn't that a good title? And let the play that began nine years ago finish to-night! The scene is set. You had a good look at it, Dave. And did you notice my new lock on the door?"

I looked by the side of his shoulder. I looked again.

"You poor fool!" I said. "You put it on outside in."

"Bright fellow! So I did. The sort of thing poor-fool Charley would do. But mark you, wise man! If I go out, and pull that door shut after me, no one else can get out without the key that will be in my pocket. Are you beginning to see?"

"I see fine," I said mildly, but I was not seeing what Charley Cashan saw. I could feel my heart beating. *Let the play that began nine years ago finish to-night.* That is what he had said. That was why I was here. And Charley had given me a lead, a lead that I must get him to follow. I gathered all my resources close.

I threw my head back into the angle of the wall and laughed. I laughed too long and found something coming up into my throat. I stopped myself abruptly.

"You'll laugh th'other side of your mouth!" said Charley, sourly now.

"Dam' your eyes Charley!" I swore cheerfully. "You had me going for a minute. You are only rehearsing the climax of your new play to see if it gets across. It doesn't Charles. It stinks."

He could always be raised by deriding his plays, and I wanted to raise him now so that he might talk to the boasting point. I raised him nearly too much. He leant a hand on the table, and threw the gun forward. If he pulled trigger!—but he didn't.

"Blast you, Dave Daunt! I'll make it real for you."

"Rank melodrama, Charles!" I said, my eye on the gun.

"What do you know about melodrama, you clodhopper?" he flared contemptuously. "Melodrama is drama with songs in it. And by all the devils in hell! I'll make someone sing when I'm good and ready."

"Ready for what you big bombast?" I taunted.

He gestured aside with the gun and his voice lifted in triumph.

"I'll tell you. Ready to shoot that old fellow there right through the gizzard—in two more minutes if you vex me."

I looked at the old fellow. He must have been pretty thoroughly manhandled earlier in the evening, and now, he did not think that this was make-believe melodrama. He moved his head desperately, and his eyes implored.

"Don't you worry, Uncle William!" I comforted lightly. "There is no harm in old Charley. Sure the last man he killed was home before himself."

"Ho-ho-ho!" Charley was bitterly derisive. "Home before myself was he? Flat on his back, a bullet in his heart, and his eyes open, was he? Ho-ho-ho!"

This was getting close home, but I wanted more. I moved an unbelieving hand. "It was a dream you had, Charley. You are as gun-shy as a spoiled dog, and, anyway, you couldn't hit a hay-stack."

"Ah ha! Couldn't I?" He threw the gun and steadied it on me. He jerked it up shoulder high and brought it down in the marksman's throw. He whipped it up for his thigh, and it was dead on me from hip level. "A touch, and you're a goner, and you as brave as Hector!" He almost shouted jubilantly. "I know this Webley inside out. That's where I fooled ye all. In them old days this bit of a gun used be lying about care-less, and a handful of bullets in this box and that box, and it was no trouble at all to slip round the back of the hill and practise at a sitting blackbird. I'll show you what I can do in a matter o' minutes." He threw the gun forward at William Daunt. "Do you see the middle button of that waistcoat! I'll put a bullet one inch to the right of it. One inch! When I'm ready."

William Daunt squeaked and squirmed, and would have flung himself sideways if Charley hadn't recovered the gun.

"Stuff and nonsense, you old boast!" I pricked him. "You could have practised with Jean and me if you wanted to. Why didn't you?"

A note of cunning came into his voice: "Because I didn't want anyone to know; because I had a use for that gun, and the time was ripe to use it."

"Ay! a man on his back and his eyes open!" I said scathingly. "And then you woke up."

"What's that you say?" He nearly squealed.

"A nightmare you had, you old cheat, and you've come to believe it. But wait!" I spoke slowly and judiciously. "Let us be fair! Nine years ago! Was there any old tramp or drunk tinker missing at that time? N-o-o! The only man killed was Robin Daunt, and everyone knows I killed him, and got twelve years for it."

The speechless Charley found speech then. "Everyone knows! Everyone knows!" he shrilled derisively. "What did you know yourself? Dam' all! But what did you think? Do you hear me? What did you think?"

"I did not think at all."

"You did," he snapped. "You thought that Jean Harrington killed her husband."

"Fair enough!" I said evenly, and pricked him again. "If I did not kill him, Jean Harrington did, and you had nothing whatever to do with it. Nothing! Nothing! Nothing!"

"Wait now! wait, wait!——"

"I will not wait," I said fiercely, and thumped fist into palm. "Don't tell me you killed Robin Daunt! Robin was killed from in front, and you wouldn't dare face him. Whatever he was, he had guts, and you have none. He would have taken the gun away from you and lammed you over the head with it. And that's what I am going to do in your two minutes."

Charley's vanity was hurt beyond endurance. "By the gor!" he shouted. "I'll empty the six chambers into you if you don't listen to me."

"I've said all I wanted to say. Talk away!" I said half-impatiently.

"Dammit man! give me a chance." He leant forward on the table and tapped it with the butt of the gun. His voice appealed. "Give me my share of the credit, Dave Daunt. You'll have to, and be fair. Oh, yes! you were the great panjandrum, and I was that half-come Charley Cashan. But who did the work when the time came? Listen to me. I had my mind made up to kill Robin Daunt from the day he married Jean Harrington, the apple of my eye. And I was waiting for the right time and a chance to kill two birds with the one stone. Are you listenin'?"

"Yes, I am listening—just!"

"Listen on! I was here in this house that morning when you set out to rend him, and I saw my chance. I took the gun that you left behind, and I knew whereabouts to look when you didn't. I got in ahead of you, and faced him face to face—face to face, I'm telling you. 'Say your prayers dead man,' says I, and he laughed at me. 'Gi'e me that gun, Charley the fool,' says he. And Charley the fool gave it to him—a bullet through his heart. Man! he was tough. Dead on his feet he was reaching for the gun, and I had to shove him away, and he fell on his back. And on his back you found him. Am I right?"

I kept my voice cool. "I don't know. How do you prove it?"

"I'll prove it," he said patiently. "To the hilt I'll prove it, with the words out of your own mouth. Listen again! I knew where you were, and I knew you'd come to the sound of the shot. So I wiped and dropped the gun fast, and dodged down between two furze bushes on the edge of the trees. But Jean had heard too, and she came first. And she saw the gun—your gun—and she picked it up to make sure. And her voice was strangling. 'Oh God! Oh, David! My poor David! Why did you kill him?' That is what she said. And then, you came running, and there she was with the gun in her hand, and what did you think? It isn't what you thought. It is what you said. What did you say, Dave?"

"You tell me." I kept my voice quiet, and my body quiet too, for I wanted to launch myself at him.

"I'll tell you," he said agreeably. "You started making excuses for her. 'He had to die, Jean,' says you. 'He had to die. Didn't I tell you that? Didn't I set out to kill him?' And you took the gun from her, and gave her a good hard push to waken her up. And she ran wild away, her hands up to her ears, and the thought in her head was that you had killed her husband. And, then, along comes Bill Sheedy, and you wiping the gun. Was I there Dave Daunt, or did I dream it all?"

"You were there," I said heavily, "and you reaped your reward, but not yet the whirlwind. You'll reap that too."

IV

I did not know what was happening outside the door or window, but I knew that Jerome Farley would not be idle. Did he want me to carry on? The strain was telling on me. I was feeling sick, body and mind. But it might be necessary to play Charley some more—like a hooked salmon. No, not a salmon. A salmon is a game fish. A pike, then! Oh damn!

Charley was at his ease against the door, arms folded, and gun in the crook of an elbow. His long head was turned towards the cowering William Daunt, and he might act at any moment. I said:

"That was quite an act that first one, Charles."

"It came alive, didn't it?" The man had no bowels.

"Are you telling me?" I said, and went on casually, "The second act was not so good. You made a mistake right at the beginning."

"How do you know?" He straightened up and was interested.

"I know. I knew. You did not tell Jean Harrington I was home though you passed her door. You did not want her to know. Why? Because you hoped to get rid of me that first night. I kept an eye on you after that, Charles."

"Much good it will do you," he said with a growl.

"Not a lot," I agreed. "You are a dangerous man, Charles Cashan." I could see him preen. "Though you failed to kill me four times, you had the best plan of all up your sleeve. You laid a trap for me to-night, and I walked straight into it. How do you spring it, you murdering hound?"

He leant over the table and brought his gun to the ready. "That's right! Cut the cackle and get to the hosses! This is the third act, Dave Daunt. It will end in one of two ways, and you can take your choice." His voice slowed. "Do you hear? You—can—take—your choice."

"No!" I said. "I have an end of my own——"

"No, you have not!" He raised two fingers. "Two choices: You hang or you hide. Look! I always like to kill two birds with one stone. Kill William Daunt, and Beananaar is mine. Hang you, and I have Jean Harrington. Wait! I shoot old William. That's easy. Bill Sheedy is hiding in the byre back of the window there. When he hears the shot, he comes through that door at the gallop. And it was you shot William Daunt. How's that?"

"I hang," I said placatingly. "How do I hide?" The man was utterly mad to think he could pull this off. And yet!

And, there, he showed me another and saner side of his extraordinary character. He leant to me eagerly. "That's what I want, Dave. I'll let the old fellow go, if you'll promise to clear out." His voice was urgently persuasive. "Damn it Dave! You don't want to hang, and I don't want to hang you. You got your dose nine years ago. And—and—you know, I'm sort of fond of you. Next to Jean you are the only one I care for in all the world. But I'll not share her with you. I must have her all to myself."

"You poor madman!" I said sorrowfully, wearily. "Jean will never have you."

"I don't want her to marry me. I told you that already. I —I want her to look up to me, to make fun of me, even, but always to depend on me as she depended on me for nine long years. I tell you I'll not share her," he said desperately. "You'll clear out, Dave, and God love you! I'll take your word for it. You will disappear. You will never be heard of. It's that or hang. Well?"

But I only moved a thumb towards William Daunt.

"That man has you in his hands," I said. I did not look at the man, but I heard his squeak.

"Begobs! he hasn't," said Charley confidently. "'Tis I that will have him under my thumb. He'll get back to Grianaan, and I'll have Beananaar to myself." He thrust a head. "You'll do what I tell you, my loving stepfather, won't you?"

I looked at him then. He was looking eagerly at Charley, and he was nodding his head, and nodding-nodding his head, a guttural affirmation in his throat. William Daunt would hold his life whatever the cost.

I did not nod my head, and it was almost too heavy to shake. "No, Charles Cashan! I will have none of your endings. This will end my way." I saw his gun move. "Wait, you fool!" I said sternly. "Be warned in time. The game is played. You'll not hang, Charley, but there is a nice quiet place for you up in Dumdrum. Look! See that hole in the ceiling! There's a listener up there—with a recorder probably; there's a gimlet hole in the window frame, and another in the door jamb. It is all over—all over—and you'll just toss me that gun?" I reached a hand.

Charley laughed jeeringly. "Dave the Playboy trying to frighten me! But he can't fool me. I ask you one more time——"

"Go to hell your own way!" I said. "I'll take that gun now."

I rose in the corner, but I was rather slow, because my legs were queerly pithless. But, no matter how quick I might be I could not be quick enough for that madman. He threw the gun down and forward at William Daunt, and hell broke loose. There was a flash, and an explosion that sounded loud in that confined space. William Daunt grunted from the very diaphragm, fell over on his side, rolled on his face, and was still. His bound, short legs did not twitch once.

"Lethal, by the powers!" I said, and wondered. I tried to drive energy into my legs. I couldn't.

"And, there, the door-lock clicked. Charley moved aside without a glance behind, for he was watching me, gun poised, shoulder high.

"Come in, Bill!" he invited.

A man stepped in actively, lithely. But he was not Bill Sheedy. He was tall Joseph Yoseph, quick and sure. An arm darted, and a hand clamped on Cashan's gun-wrist. But Cashan was active too. He whirled and heaved backwards, and the table went over. I did not see the upward drive of Joseph's left that went with the heave. But I saw Charley's knees buckle, and I saw the gun coming in a parabola towards me. I caught it neatly, and thrust it into skirt pocket.

I was leaning in the angle of the wall. I had to lean. I was done and fordone. If I took a step forward I would have fallen on my face. But my work was finished, and let others carry on.

There was Tade Murphy now, and Charley Cashan would need to be strong as Samson. He was dragged to his feet, and held helplessly against the wall. He sagged. Again he was the pithless, supine Charley. But I knew better.

A massive figure was standing in the doorway, and a quiet voice spoke slowly.

"Take him away, boys! Whistle up the cars."

"Bill Sheedy is in the byre," I said, and I could hardly lift my voice.

"He is taken care of," said the quiet voice.

And it was all over. It was over as quick as that. In half a minute or less, Jerome Farley and I were alone in the room. But were we alone? William Daunt was prone and still in his corner; and, if he were dead, was it fright or a bullet that had killed him?

Jerome Farley was facing me now. His great face was impassive, but there was a coldness in his voice.

"So you let that madman kill William Daunt?"

"Did you get all you wanted?"

"You need not worry about that. Pity you spoiled it at the end. William Daunt——"

"Oh hell!" I said. "Go and see how dead he is."

"You callous young devil!" he said, and turned away.

He went round the fallen table, and looked down at the still figure. He would have to go on his knees now, and I could not see him do it. Sensation was back in my legs, and I shuffled round the table too.

"Let me do that for you!" I said, and dropped on my knees.

The old rope tying my uncle's forearms was loose with strain, and I whipped it off easily. But the bandana gag was tightly knotted at the back of his neck, and it took me a little time to pick it loose. Jerome Farley bent over me, put a hand on my shoulder, and for once his voice hurried.

"Quick, boy! He's stirring. He's not dead—yet."

"Fright sometimes kills," I said, seriously enough.

"Fright! There was a shot——"

"Sure. And it hit him right over the heart. I followed it with my eye."

"Blast you! you playboy. Turn him over! Gently now!"

I turned him over, not gently, and plucked the gag out of his mouth. His mouth shut, and opened wide again. He gasped at air. His eyes flickered open and shut and open again.

"God ha' mercy on me, a dying man!" His voice was strong for a man in extremis. "I want a priest—at once—now. A priest, I say!"

"A bishop at least," I said.

"I'm dying. The blood is pumping out of me—I feel it. Send for a doctor—but the priest first."

I looked at his striped waistcoat. There was no blood on it. I put a hand over his heart. It was far from fluttering into death. And then my palm pressed on something hard. It had penetrated a little way in a fold of the vest. I picked it out, and rose to my feet.

"There you are, Superintendent!" I said, and dropped the hard object into his palm.

He looked at it, and looked at me, and his face was no longer a passive mask.

"That bullet was not lethal, Superintendent Farley," I said.

Chapter XVII

DAVID AND JEANATHAN

I

On the fringe of hearing there had been the sound of motor cars out on the road and in the front yard. But now, and shatteringly, my attention leaped alive to a sudden clamour. Voices shouted, car-doors banged, feet thudded. And, then, voices and feet faded round the back of the house. I knew what had happened: Charley Cashan had made a break for liberty. And I was no longer pithless.

I leaped for the door. I made the arch in three jumps, collided with the upright, whirled round it, and burst out the front door. I saw headlights, and a figure or two, and I heard a view-halloo from the field behind the steadings. But I did not go that way. Charley Cashan in his own terrain was not catchable even in moonlight. But I knew what would be in his mad mind, and I knew where it would lead him.

I made for the road. A guard made a hesitating movement to stop me. I dodged him, and leaped through the gateway, where the pole was thrown aside. And then I ran. I had never run like that before, and I never will again. Head back and elbows up I spurned the road as in a hundred yards sprint, and kept spurting. I drove myself. And I had nearly half a mile to go.

The moon was well up now, but still orange-tinted. And as I ran I kept watching the left-hand hedge bulking darkly against the sky. I could not hear anything for the wind past my ears.

I did not slacken once. Luckily the trend was slightly

downhill, and that helped. But, at that, I was only just in time. I was still some distance short of Jean Harrington's cottage when Charley Cashan burst through the hedge opposite the gate. He took no notice of me thundering down the middle of the road. Concentrated on one thing only he probably did not see me. He did not pause to open the gate, but vaulted it, effortlessly as a cat—or a tiger.

I swerved in towards it, and threw myself over somehow, and, winded as I was, fell on my hands and knees. That delayed me for a second or two. Charley was already at the door. Would he burst it in? No. He knew better. He was tapping on the panel: *Tap, tap—tap, tap tap!* Our old signal, the signal that would bring Jean Harrington hurrying. There was a light in her sitting-room window, left of the door, and I heard a chair move. I filled my labouring lungs.

I was going to take him quietly, with one faint hope of pacifying him. "A word with you, Mr. Cashan!" I said agreeably.

He turned then, not hurriedly, almost leisurely. He was breathing heavily, but not exhaustedly. In the moonlight his face was dead white and his eyes white blazing. He thrust his long jaw at me.

"Go away, you traitor!" he scorned me. "Go away! I am taking Jean Harrington with me where I am going."

"Fair enough!" I said. "Let the three of us go off together, the same as always." Give me half-a-minute—or the minute between rounds—and I could hold him until help came. I did not get any half-minute.

The door opened behind him, and there was Jean Harrington on her own doorstep. The light in the hall behind her made spun red-gold of her hair. She shook her head, and there was regret in her voice.

"Sorry, boys! I'm not playing any more."

I shouted to drive my words home. "Look out, Jean! He's a killer."

I saw by the lift of his hands, the hunch of his shoulders, the crook of his knees that he was on the point of launching himself at her. I stopped that. I thrust a foot between his feet, and drove my shoulder against his. That should have sent him down sidewards. It did not. Charley Cashan was no longer thewless. He staggered two paces, gathered himself, and bounded forward. But I was between him and Jean now.

"Right, Daunt! You're for it."

I hit him twice: left to the mark and right to the chin. Was it only three nights ago that I gave him that double and put him down? But I was not spent then. And this was a different Charley Cashan. Hitting him was like hitting a wall, and my arms jarred. I stopped him indeed, but only for a moment. He leaped again, and I failed to time him. But I got close in, and tried a wrestler's trick: a grip on his wrist, a foot behind his, and a thrust of shoulder. He went down on his back, but he took me with him, and I gave him a hard knee in the pit of the stomach.

He yowled like a dog, and rolled me over. He rolled me with such force that, going with the roll, I rolled him over in turn. I spread my legs for purchase and yelled towards Jean.

"A killer! Help up the road."

I did not see her for some time after that. I was too busy trying to save my life. We rolled in and through a flowerbed, and on to grass. I knew that, given time, this madman would kill me with his bare hands. He had the madman's inhuman energy and imperviousness, and I was too spent already. But I did my damndest.

I held close in to him, I would not let him tear himself free, and with head and shoulders and arms guarded and warded the throat he was trying to reach. He was so eager and in such a hurry that he hampered himself. And, then, he rolled me over again, tore an arm free and up, and I saw his clawed fingers.

This is it, I said.

It was not. Something whitish flashed in the air, and there was a sound like the cracking of a stick. Charley Cashan yowled again, and his arm fell loosely close to my face. Out of one eye I saw Jean Harrington. She was standing over us, and the moonlight lit her fighting Highland face. She was poised forward, her arm lifted, the whitish weapon shining, and, with cool ferocity, she was picking a spot for the next blow.

"Scotland forever!" I panted. "We can lick him ourselves."

I am not at all clear about what happened next. I didn't hear the car. I didn't hear the gate. Feet were all round me. Charley Cashan's weight was wrenched off me. There was a thud that might be a blow. Tade Murphy's voice said: "Bracelets this time!" I must have passed out for a few seconds. And then, I remember, I could never, never again get enough air into my lungs. Someone was crowing like a cock on the intake. That was me.

Then I was being lifted easily by the armpits, and a firm arm went round my waist.

"Dammit!" I said. "I'm all right. I'm only winded. Where's Jean?"

"At your shoulder, Davy," said Jean.

"That's the place. Did you hit him again?"

"Twice!" said Jean.

"Fair enough!" I said. "Let me walk so."

"Walk into her parlour then," said Jerome Farley. He was holding me.

II

I found myself walking—half-lifted, half-pushed—in at the front door, along the short hall, and into Jean's sitting-room. Now I was lying on a couch, but I wouldn't stand for that. I pivoted my legs and sat up.

"Nothing wrong with me," I said petulantly. "I'm only getting my wind back. Give me time, I tell ye."

"All the time there is, boy," said the quiet voice of Jerome Farley.

I was dizzy for a moment. I put my head down between

my knees, and my shoulders lifted slowly as I inhaled; and I straightened up to inhale more deeply. I looked round me. I had known this room in the old days—a shabby old room. But now it was a woman's room: softly carpeted, bright prints and pastels on greyish walls, curtains and chintz, a cottage piano, and a business-like flat desk under the window. Jerome Farley was leaning against the desk, impassive and patient as Buddha—giving me all the time there was.

I looked at Jean. She had her back to the door. She was leaning against it as for support, and her face was not now the face of a woman fighting for her mate. There was perplexity in it, and doubt and anxiety and fear—and, maybe, some hope. I don't know. At that moment I could not help myself. I started to laugh.

"No, David, no!" She took a step forward, and her voice was a little distracted. "Pull yourself together! Mother of Heaven! Are we all mad?"

I stopped laughing. I pointed at her. "Behold, Super!" I said. "The housewife's blunt instrument!"

And so it was. In her good right hand she grasped a rolling pin—a white-wood rolling pin, such as comic artists have drawn a million times.

"She saved your life with it," said Jerome Farley.

Jean dropped the pin and kicked at it. She took a step towards the big man and her hands lifted. "But that's it, Jerome! Charley Cashan was death incarnate. He was killing David, and I wanted to kill him. I would kill him. I would! I would!"

Hysteria was threatening her now. Jerome Farley straightened from the desk.

"Stop that, Jean!" he commanded. "Everything is fine." He pointed at me. "Look at that man of yours! He is going to pass out again. Have you any whiskey?"

That pulled her together as it was meant, for I had no intention of passing out. She disappeared behind my back. I heard the clink of glass on glass, and the glug of liquid.

"Hold it—hold it!" said Jerome, hurriedly for once. "You'll asphyxiate him. Pour some back, and the rest down his neck. Yes, that's about right!"

Jean hurried round in front, and thrust a glass at me. It had a good three inches of golden liquid in it. I shook my head.

"Down with it, boy dear!" she coaxed. "Armagnac! it's quite harmless."

I looked up into her eyes, and she looked down into mine. She would be weeping in a minute. I felt for the glass, and tossed the contents straight down my gullet. It burned all the way down, and I choked for a moment. Jean thumped my back.

"Harmless!" I gasped. "Goramichty! The she-devil is trying to kill me too."

"Isn't he one pukka tough, Jerome?" she said, half-laughing, half-crying. She sat down at my side, caught my arm firmly in both hands, and regained control. "Won't anyone tell me anything?" she pleaded. "I can't stand any more."

Jerome Farley stepped forward. "Just a little patience, my dear, and you'll hear it all. The car is outside, and you two are coming down to Grianaan right now——"

"But something to go on with?" she pleaded.

He hesitated and nodded. "Oh very well!" He leant to her, his hands on his knees. He was like a squat toad. "First of all, my girl, David Daunt did not kill Robin Daunt."

"At the back of my mind I never really thought he did," said Jean simply. "It was something he said——"

"Just so! Something he said, making excuses for you. But you did not kill Robin either."

I felt her hands slacken and tighten. "Wait a moment!" she said quietly but dangerously. "Are you telling me that David Daunt thought I had killed my husband?"

"Blast it all——!" I blurted.

"Shut up, you!" said Jerome Farley. "Look here, woman!

You were standing over the dead man, a gun in your hand——"

"I know—I know!" She was completely reasonable. "I know my temper, and if I had a gun in my hand——! But——" She shook my arm fiercely and put her finger on the point I was afraid of——"but would I let David take the blame?" And then her mood changed, and she stared into my face. "Oh, David! my poor David! Nine terrible years, and you thinking——!"

"At the back of my mind I never really thought that," I said, and I spoke in her very own voice.

"Shut up you two!" Jerome Farley almost blared. He straightened up and thrust a small, tight fist at us. "You two pukka toughs! Isn't it enough for you to know that there is no blood on your hands, no blood between you. Not another word——"

"You are perfectly right, Jerome darling," said Jean humbly. "Please go on!"

"I thank whatever gods may be that I'll be finished with you two this night," he said warmly. "Very well then! Charles Cashan killed your husband. Silence, I say! You know it now, David, here, knew it three nights ago. I knew it years ago. His life, his character, his insane vanity so well hidden, his possessiveness too intense to be sane—the key was there. But I could prove nothing until David Daunt came home. Well, David Daunt came home, and to-night we proved our case. David Daunt did the proving at the risk——"

He stopped. He stared at me. He thrust his hand at me. "Give me that gun? I saw you."

I felt my skirt-pocket. The Webley, in spite of all our tumblings and rollings, was still there. I hauled it out, and handed it across.

He broke it, picked out a cartridge and smelled it. "Yes, this was fired." He picked out another—and looked at it doubtfully. "Seems all right!" He hefted it, put it to his ear and shook it, and looked at me interrogatively.

I nodded. "Only a scrap of cordite behind the bullet. It took me an hour."

"Your brain was working in ice, boy," he said quietly.

"No," I said. "All I knew was that that gun would not kill in anyone's hand."

Jean was on her feet, hands lifted. "But—but—what is all this about?" she demanded.

"Not another word now," said Jerome Farley firmly. "You will hear it all at Grianaan. Ellen Furlong is waiting. She knows something is up, and I sent Tade Murphy ahead to tell her all is right. I'll not keep her waiting one minute longer." He took a stride doorwards.

"Let us be going then," cried Jean. She whirled round and reached me a hand. "On your feet, lazy——" She stopped.

I did not move. I was feeling mighty queer about the middle. It was that sudden gulp of brandy. I swallowed saliva. *Lord! if I'm sick now I'll be ridiculous.* I sat up firmly, and swallowed again.

"Boy, you're ashen!" she said in a frightened voice.

"A minute," I said. "Nothing at all—that brandy—I'm not used to it—I'll be all right."

She actually plucked me off the couch, and Jerome Farley had the door open. I was out in the hall, and through another door. I tried to shut it against her, but she came straight through, an arm around me. She held my head. . . .

After a while she held my face down over a wash basin, and used a sponge vigorously.

"Dammit!" I grumbled. "Leave me my nose. It's the only nose I have."

She chuckled, and crooned half-crossly, like a mother.

"Dirty boy! No, not a scratch on you! but what a mess! Your white shirt in rags, and this sleeve hanging by a thread. There now! and here's the towel!"

I took the warm towel from her, and tried to scrub colour back into my face.

"You are not hurt anywhere?" she asked a little anxiously.

"I am," I said.

She was startled. "Where? Your——?"

"Everywhere," I said. "It's the thought of you going away."

She got my mood at once. "Och! That hurt is easily mended."

"Maybe it is," I said, and threw the towel in a corner. I put my finger on her wrist, and didn't lift my eyes. "All the same, Jean, I think you should go away—for a little while," I said humbly.

"Yes, David! I suppose I should," she agreed some despondently.

"Of course," I said judiciously. "I will go with you—if you let me."

She grasped my wrist firmly. "What do you mean, David?"

"Everything," I said. "And we could get Father Eujun to say a few words."

"Oh, that's all right, so long as I know!" she said, cheerfully now.

I gave a little tug and pretended to turn away.

"Very well so!" I said. "Let us off down and break the news to Ellen Furlong."

She swung me back with extraordinary vigour.

"Oh, you thug!" she stormed at me. "You great big stick-in-the-mud! You turnip-without-blood! You—you—darling playboy! Damn you! Wouldn't you think of giving me a kiss?"

"I knew I was forgetting something," I said.

Fair enough! And to hell with writing! And if there are a few strings dangling, let them dangle.

THE END